D1741527

LET THERE BE LOVE

LET THERE BE LOVE

Gwendoline Butler

This first world edition published in Great Britain 1997 by
SEVERN HOUSE PUBLISHERS LTD of
9–15 High Street, Sutton, Surrey SM1 1DF.
First published in the USA 1997 by
SEVERN HOUSE PUBLISHERS INC., of
595 Madison Avenue, New York, NY 10022.

British Library Cataloguing in Publication Data
Butler, Gwendoline
          Let there be love
          1. Title
          823.9'14 [F]

          ISBN 0-7278-5214-0

Typeset by Hewer Text Composition Services, Edinburgh.
Printed and bound in Great Britain by
Hartnolls Ltd, Bodmin, Cornwall.

Part One

Chapter One

We were the wild ones, the girls who sat at the back of the class, spouting our wicked words of wisdom, attracting the younger kids and giving them our hot gospel. Dodo, Val, and Charley.

I was born to Bohemia. So someone later said of me, by which she meant not a castle in Bohemia, but that she did not like me, or like my birth, and that I lived by my own rules.

Dorothea, usually called Dodo. Dodo who?

Yesterday, it being the last day in April, I went back to Fontenoy House.

As I walked through the gates I recognised for the first time that it was a beautiful house.

Built in about 1740 by a general who had fought in the continental wars of the time and survived the victory of Fontenoy, the house was a graceful red-brick house which had stood in the English countryside, gracing it and becoming a part of it.

When I had lived there as a child it had seemed uncompromising and bleak, but I knew now that I had never really seen it as it should have been seen. When we lived in it, it had lost its heart, become an institution, brutalised with odd temporary structures built onto it. In those days it had even lost its name, becoming the Sunshine Home. Orphans are the better for a bit of sunshine about them, even if it gets no further than the name.

After various scandals the Home had been closed. I believe the house then became a school. After the last war it was bought by a rich man who restored it to its original beauty and then died before he could live in it. For some years it had been empty. People said it had a ghost. For me, it had many.

Far away a church clock rang the hour. It was at this

point I remembered that I had another reason for coming to Fontenoy today.

I walked in the deserted grounds, huddled in my furs, because it was cold for April. I paused under an oak to look at the house. Then I suddenly felt a tightness in my throat. Some people say that taste brings back memories, a cake warm from the oven, or others say a sound is what does it, a waltz, church bells ringing. For me I think it is smell. I smelt violets.

I knelt down and poked in the earth, dragging aside the grass to uncover a bed of small sweet violets, heads down, and floating upwards from their bent heads that gentle, subtle smell of violets when the rain has been on them.

Memories, pictures, came rushing back.

In my bedroom where I can see it when I wake is a large oil painting. A conversation piece of a young woman dressed in the style of the years after the Great War. This is a quiet picture by an artist better known for strong, violent, shocking canvases. At the bottom are scrawled the initials: C. de S. A tiny violet is painted underneath, so small that you have to know it is there to see it. I knew this C. de. S. No jewels on the young woman in this portrait, I did not wear them. I knew I loved jewels but must earn them for myself and not be given them, knew I had love to offer but sometimes had none to love. Knew that I had come to wealth and self-knowledge a most painful way.

The young woman in the portrait had three friends who should have been there in the picture with her: the beauty who is Val, the plainish one who is me, and the tall one who is Charlotte.

I am Dorothea, mostly called Dodo.

We were the girls who sat in a row at the back of the class. We were wicked, evil. Dodo, Charley and Valentine.

The judgement came as no surprise to us. We felt that way, not exactly outcasts, but different. Born to be so.

No presents for us on our birthdays; we barely had birthdays, although at Christmas the local children were encouraged to give up one of their toys. Sensibly, they chose something broken or not quite complete like a jigsaw missing a bit of blue sky, or a

4

one-eyed doll. Half a cup of niceness, half a cup sour. We were used to this brew.

We came to the Ashridge Senior Girls School every day from the bleak building down the road, walking on the pavement and not treading in the gutters.

We were the Big Girls from the Sunshine Home for Female Orphans,

The sunshine, well advertised in testimonials for the Home, did not fall on us with much warmth, although we felt strongly female. Perhaps that was what made us evil. To be an orphan was bad enough, to be a female orphan was about the worst thing you could be. We were not all bastards, although it was assumed by outsiders that we probably were. Some of us knew our parents, others of us had no means of knowing anything about them at all.

No, we were not evil, we three, but the forces of life ran more strongly in us than in most, in spite of any discouragement from the authorities, giving us the hope that life would, in the end, deliver us a present wrapped up in tinsel.

Missing parents were what we all had in common in that place, but we three had a bit more as well. We were trouble and went on being trouble, even though, in time, we learnt to package ourselves into pretty, well-behaved girls. At least, Valentine and I did, yet of Charley, christened Charlotte (if anyone ever did christen her) but unwilling to be called by that name, I couldn't be sure. She was always different.

Our lives seemed to go in stages. The first stage when we lived at the Sunshine Home, followed by our time in Canada, then the amazing moment when life took a great turn and Val and I were taken up, like pieces of lost property that you have been searching for a long time and which turn out to be not quite what you expected, into the household of Honoria Madden.

Honoria meant to do her best by us, but our past was still alive and kicking inside us, and this made for difficulties. We had been shaped and measured up for something else before Honoria ever got her hands on us.

I saw this clearly the day when Val and I were eighteen. One of those days that start out so simply and end up putting a knife into you.

It was the 'circumstances of our birth' as Honoria used to rather snarkily say.

Seventeen years before, on a wild January night near the end of the old century, two young women – one an actress, the other a girl of some family, one married, one unmarried – had given birth, in the same charity ward in beds side by side, to two little girls.

This was how we usually started on the tale of the circumstances of our birth.

Valentine and I were the girls, the two young women our mothers.

I see my young mother setting out in her journey, I see Val's too; I see both of them. But which is my mother? Who is to say now?

A snowy January evening. Two journeys begun. Short journeys, soon to end, but long enough for the travellers, a lifelong journey.

One young woman started out, we know, from Margate in Kent, where she had been appearing in the theatre. The other young woman set out from London, her exact point of departure was never to be known. One of the girls may already have been in labour, but did not recognise it, the other, more wordly-wise, suspected it and hoped she would get to London in time.

Both would have accomplished their journeys but for the weather.

"Well, there you are, dear." In Margate, Mrs Sarah Thorne, Manager of the Margate Playhouse, addressed herself to a young lady standing in second lead's dressing room. "So you'd better be off. I'll leave you to get on with your packing."

She carried a tray of tea and a plate of biscuits. These she left silently on the table, not drawing attention to what was an act of kindness on her part.

"I'll be along to say ta-ta, dear."

"Thanks, Mrs T. You've been a brick." The girl – she was no more – had a pretty, light speaking voice. She looked flushed now, the perkiness she usually showed damped down, but her chestnut hair, still stylishly dressed, and her green eyes with faint traces of stage make-up on them, made her lovely to look at still.

Poor little bitch, thought Mrs Thorne, as she departed. I'll get Freddie to take her to the train. The kid swore she still had a month to go, but she wondered.

Alice Morton, balladist and actress, the "Girl with the voice of silver", looked round at such of her possessions as remained to be packed. The Italian mock pearls and the zircon ring had been pawned already at Alby Cohen's round the corner and small hope they would ever be seen again, but she still had her seal jacket with the matching pill box hat and muff. She was wearing them; a girl had to keep her end up.

Every so often, she paused and took a deep breath. She had seen enough births to know there was a way to go yet. Time to get to Lemas Street, South London, where Lotty would take her in and ask no questions. Lotty never let you down, she was a duck.

There would be questions to answer in the end, of course. A healthy full-term child had to come with some word of explanation. It would be a boy. She had inside her a perfect replica of Monty Menteith. Without the moustache.

The fact that Monty Menteith had loved her and left her was no secret in her world and Lotty would find out for herself soon enough. Everyone knew that Monty loved you and left you and she was a silly girl to get caught. He made the matter plain enough. "Girlie, there's nothing in it for you, but by God, I love you."

And so he had for the duration of the show, twice a night sometimes. That was probably what had done it. 'Standing up or sitting down or crossed leg up a wall,' as the saying went in the dressing room, 'but never twice nightly.'

Alice put the last of her possessions into the old black Gladstone bag and fastened the lock.

Then she sat down and poured a cup of tea. For the moment the baby was still. Perhaps, after all, this boisterous boy would not make his appearance just yet. She sipped the tea. The blessed old girl had laced it with whisky. She was one of the old school, one of the best in the theatre and good to the bottom of her soul.

The door of the dressing room was open, without appearing to have been opened, and without its usual tell-tale creak.

Alice put down her cup.

In the doorway a woman was standing whom she did not know; a dumpy figure in old-fashioned grey. She had a sweet smile, but otherwise no particular expression of benevolence.

"Hello. Looking for someone?" Even in her present state, Alice was a friendly girl. Getting no answer, she went on: "Is it Mrs Thorne you want? She's in her office. I'm just pushing off."

The teapot lid removed itself from the pot and bounced to the ground, remarkably not shattering itself as it did so. It made a noise, though.

Alice bent to retrieve it, replacing it delicately. She was naturally careful with objects, nor did she desire to harm Mrs Thorne's property. Apart from liking the old girl, she needed all the friends she could get.

"Sorry," she said, apologising to the silent visitor. "Interrupted you."

But the woman had already gone.

"That was quick. Hope I didn't offend her," Alice muttered to herself. With an air of philosophy she drained the teapot into her cup and drank.

Mrs Thorne put her head round the door. "How are you doing, dear? I've got Freddy coming to the door with a cab to get you to the station. On me."

Impulsively, Alice got up and kissed her cheek. "Thanks, you're one of the best." She bent down to pick up the Gladstone bag, and the action reminded her of the visitor. "Someone came round here looking for you. Lady in grey. Found you all right, did she?"

There was a pause.

"Asked for me? By name?"

"Never said a word. Just stood and stared and then buggered off."

"I don't know who she could be," said Mrs Thorne easily. "No one I know. But if it was important she'll look in again." Behind her back, her fingers made a cross. "I should forget her, love."

When Freddy – who was Mrs Thorne's assistant and much else besides – came back from the station, having deposited Alice and her bags on the train, she said to him. "How was she?"

"Managing."

"Fred, she's seen the woman in grey."

"You don't believe in all that."

"I do, Fred. I've never seen her myself. But others have. My late husband for one. And he was dead within the week. Fred, give me a nip of whisky."

Later, if Alice got to hear this story, and most stories get around in theatreland, she might have said her bad luck started then.

Mine as well. My luck and Alice's were for ever bound together.

We know that Alice got to Ashridge, that her journey was impeded by the weather and that at Ashridge she knew she could go no further.

"Well, this is it," she said to herself as she bundled into a cab obtained with difficulty, because it was raining heavily and the wind was up. She twisted on her finger the ring she had provided for herself. It would do. "Now you're for the high jump."

She was filled with a mixture of elation and fear. Exactly how she would feel when it was all over, she had no idea.

We know that she got herself to the lying-in ward of of the Free Hospital in Ashridge. This was a shabby building around which a turgid green river wound itself.

Here Alice went through several stages of self-discovery in which she was by turns, surprised, then frightened, and then very angry. Angry with Monty, and herself, and finally with the baby.

She wasn't sure she would ever get over the anger.

"Do try not make so much noise, Mrs Morton," whispered the midwife. If that's what you are. She had not been deceived by the ring. "We have a very ill young mother in the bed behind the screens."

With all that had been going on, Alice had barely noticed what was going on near at hand.

"If I can't shout, then I will sing," she announced.

"You won't have much time for that, dear."

"Only till this bloody boy arrives."

9

After a while, the midwife said: "It's a nice little girl."

"What? No moustache."

The nurse was alarmed. Was this fever? Madness? She had known mad mothers. Some before giving birth, some after. It could happen. In fact, most mothers were mad for a little while. "Lie still now, and be calm. I'll bring you a nice cup of tea."

But not to Alice's surprise, she did not reappear. Events behind the screen took precedence over Alice's cup of tea. She decided not to be ill herself. Or go mad. Or die. But survive and have a good life.

Meanwhile, she would wish well the girl in the next bed, who did not seem to be conscious which was her luck, and try to sleep, if that roaring wind would let her. For the child she had as yet no feelings whatever, except relief that it was no longer part of her.

Thus one of us, Val or me, came into the world.

The young woman in the next bed was more conscious than they gave her credit for. She was perfectly well aware that her child had been born, far too soon because of her fall down the railway stairs; that it was a daughter, and that she herself was in a bad way.

As she moved in and out of consciousness – always more with them than the people at the bedside realised, one foot in the present, another elsewhere – odd scraps of conversation took her with them like boats bobbing this way and that.

She knew she was here in hospital, and how it had all come about. She was not wandering, just a little disconnected to time.

If she had not been late for the train, if the weather had not been so bad, none of this would have happened.

No, it was the telegram.

Her landlady had come into the sitting room of her London lodgings with the telegram in her hand.

"For you, ma'am, I gave the boy a penny as it was raining so hard."

"Quite right, Mrs Todger," and she had taken the telegram, her hand steady. A soldier's wife had to be brave.

But what had she been obliged to be brave about? She could

not remember. A feeling of fear and anxiety connected with the army seized her.

A voice interrupted her. "Mrs Bruce?"

Not Bruce, it was Braose, an ancient, Anglo-Norman name of which James was so proud. But muttered as she might have muttered, then it could have sounded like Bruce. She must correct it.

She tried, but no words came.

But I was born Madden, she thought. Perhaps I could say that. Amy Madden.

"Don't worry, dear," said the voice soothingly. And then, above her head, "You see, doctor, we have nothing with her, no luggage, no bag. We think she must have left it all on the train. You can see for yourself she is a lady."

Dimly she remembered the journey, the hurry to get to Victoria to catch the train to see her soldier, husband, so falsely accused. Innocent, innocent, she muttered. I have an enemy and I know his face, but my mother will never believe me. Then the feeling that she was on the wrong train. Hurrying again.

Had she fallen? She remembered blood and pain.

One hour passed, and then two. She was vaguely aware of the passage of time, of daylight fading and lamps being lit. Voices came and went, talking sometimes to her, sometimes above her head. She thought she did answer.

Then time ceased to matter, disappeared. The day was done.

Alice stirred in her sleep. The wind was howling, and she heard sleet hitting the window panes. She sat up. She felt surprisingly light and well, better than she had felt for months.

There was a dim light on the table at the end of the ward where a nurse kept her station. Screens still shielded the bed next door, but all was quiet. Their two beds stood in a kind of alcove, somewhat removed from the rest of the room. At the foot of the woman's bed was a cradle; so the infant had arrived.

She took a look down at the end of her own bed. Yes, she had one, too. So that was where it was. Should she crawl to see its face? She was just about to do so, when the nurse, accompanied by another nurse, came up the ward and went behind the screen.

There was a muttered conversation and then they left, this time leaving a gap between the screens on Alice's side.

"You all right?" whispered Alice, into the dimness. "Glad it's over, eh? Last time for me, I can tell you. What did you get, a boy or a girl?"

There was no answer.

"Asleep, eh? Feeling cosy? Well, good luck and God bless."

By stretching out a hand she could almost touch the other woman. The beds were very close together; this was not the sort of ward where you got much privacy. And now she came to think of it, she didn't much care for the smell – carbolic, with an underlay of something nastier, as if generations of old and incontinent patients had nested there.

"An old workhouse, that's what this is," Alice said to herself. But she was comfortable and disposed herself again for sleep.

A screaming, roaring morning presently dragged her into full awakening. Then the wind dropped, but it still remained very dark with snow piled up against the windows. Every now and then, the snow fell away with a shushing sound, not pleasant in itself.

By degrees, by observation and by listening to what went on, she came to understand that the woman in the next bed was still bleeding more than she should and that it could not be controlled. There was death waiting by that bed.

Alice felt quiet and frightened. She lay rigidly in her bed, trying not to attract attention, as if death might come for her too.

There was a bustle and confusion beyond what she sensed was the normal in the ward, and it did not relate only to what went on in the next bed. They had other worries on their minds.

The wind had quietened, yes, but there were other noises. The hospital itself seemed to be creaking and moving. The ward was very cold, and getting colder. Surely it was colder than need be? All right, charity patients did not need to be pampered, but there was no need to freeze them to death. The babies were crying, and you couldn't blame them.

A nurse bounced up to her, the one with the big blonde face and the hard muscular body, and the smile that looked over and through you but never at you, and deposited a bundle on

12

her bed. It made a faint whining noise. "Here," she said. "Nurse her, will you?"

Alice looked. "I've fed her." Was it the same one? Some slight difference declared itself to her.

"It's the baby from the next bed." A nod towards the screens. "She can't do it, poor soul, and someone must. You might as well, your milk's come in."

Alice picked up the child and put it to her breast. She took a deep breath, surprised by the sudden rush of feeling for it. Love poured into her, warm specific love for this little creature. She had felt a preliminary breath of this for her own baby as it had fed, now the feeling came back in force and encompassed both of them. She lay back and let something that was both pain and joy sweep over her. No choice, she thought, it was happening to her.

And with the thought there came a kind of panic because she felt she was now being tied to both infants and would never be free again. A knot had been pulled.

Now there was one child on each side of her, swaddled in calico in wooden cribs and looking up at her with expressionless dark blue eyes.

She leaned over for a closer look at each. "I suppose I know which one is mine." She gave them a further study. Yes, she thought she could tell.

We know that after that the river flooded into the hospital, soon followed by a fire, during which there was considerable chaos, and that Alice took the opportunity to collect her clothes and hop it.

For a moment Alice hesitated, looking down at the cribs. She bent over each child, gently kissing a cheek.

"Goodbye kids, whichever one of you is mine." She touched one tiny hand. "You'll be better off without me, believe me it's the truth."

And she walked away, leaving behind her that question of our identities which was so to trouble Honoria Madden in due course, and disappeared in the confusion, not to be seen again.

This was how we told our romantic story (if it was romantic; to us it was the way things were), and how we put things together,

13

more or less accurately as we found our history out later. Some of it, especially the story of Alice, we discovered much much later, almost the last of all. There was always to be one final mystery for us.

Valentine and I were abandoned babies, one mother having picked up her skirts and run for it and the other dead, with her husband dangerously ill in a military prison and under sentence of death, in no position to search for a wife who had disappeared. We know he did try to find her, and his friends had searches made, but it was a long while before a private detective was employed.

And there was the complication that by then, our identities were not clear. Which of us belonged to which mother? In the fire that followed the flood and from which we were rescued, the Matron perished and the hospital records went with it.

As infants we did seem to bring bad luck with us. But bereft and lost, we were strikingly healthy babies and gave no cause for anxiety on that score. We were christened on St Valentine's Day, which was how Val got her name, and I was named after the curate's wife who was my godmother.

Three months before I arrived in the world she had lost her only child, a daughter, stillborn, who had never received a name. That name was given to me. And just a little of the love that would have been hers came my way.

Mrs Brent was on the governing committee of the Sunshine Home, the orphanage where we were brought up, and was one of those who pursued most ardently – fruitlessly but hopefully – the investigation into our identities. She was a charming woman, with money of her own, who dressed in the new art styles, advocated freedom for women, and thoroughly deserved that her husband should become, as he did, first the head of an Oxford college and then a bishop.

But there was a distance between us; class was class in those days.

The orphanage was a rough, strict, but kind enough place under the management of Miss Rachel Desmond, a cousin of Dorothy Brent. All the same, you had to be tough to survive. When a doctor had to be called in, then Dr Violet Ventura was summoned, an early example of what was called then a 'lady

14

doctor'. She had trained in Germany and Edinburgh and Miss Desmond was thought eccentric to use her, but Violet Ventura was yet another cousin. It was a small place with about fifty of us, from babies upwards, all female.

The older ones of us were required to help with the smaller. Nursery work, it was called. I hated nursery work. A hard little knot inside me got tighter and harder when I saw the babies in their cribs. I wanted to be cruel to them. Shake them if they cried. I never did so, of course, but I think what I felt must have been visible in my expression because the nursery nurse used to keep a sharp eye on me as I worked. "You have a hard little heart," she said to me once. And yet I was not as ruthless as Charley who had a peasant's practical toughness.

But something of the circumstances of my birth had seeded some terror of babies and childbirth inside me.

I used to lie in bed and think of that hard little heart inside me and see it as brown and dry as a nut. And I could never cry, never a tear.

Miss Desmond too had studied in Germany, and her regime was Prussian. Children must be ruled kindly but firmly, punished if necessary and not overfed. We wore brown serge dresses in winter and cotton in summer. Food was plain, and we bathed in cold water, and were purged once a week. A lot of store was set by purging, and even more by the cold baths for strengthening young limbs.

If in after days, Val sought luxury and comfort, who could blame her, after years of cold washes?

Everything was done according to rules, and at set times. On the hour we ate, on another hour we washed, on another did housework or gardened, wet or fine. All according to bells. We walked everywhere, never allowed to run, always in pairs, never alone. Bed before dark, up sometimes before dawn. Every day the same, exactly, and for ever. That was the worst of it, like an army.

But like all armies we had a secret life.

The bigger we got, the more a kind of lawlessness seemed to creep in, an anarchy beneath the apparent order. We were harshly ruled, but knew how to misbehave. We were not cruel to each other but we could be rough. I remember fights and bawdy talk.

15

Some names and some faces are still with me: Gladys, Nelly, who had red hair, Evie who squinted, Ada, niceness itself; and Margaret and Ethel and Mary who are now nothing but names. And Charley. Charley was not a bawdy talker, nor a flighter, but she could when angered spit out farmyard terms with explosive force.

At first we had nothing much to do with Charley, who had lived with her grandmother till the old lady died. That was not to say we did not notice her. Charley was very noticeable. A tall, broad-shouldered girl with a red-cheeked peasant face and a loud voice. Charley had broad strong hands which could do anything she asked of them. She had one advantage over us two in that she knew about both her parents. What she knew she did not like.

"You two can make up stories about who you are. Call yourself princesses. I can't. My mother was raped behind the cowshed, poor beast, and got me out of it. No, she didn't tell me, she died of me, but there was plenty ready to tell me."

"You didn't know who your father was?"

"He was an animal. She was thirteen years old, poor kid, and he dragged her legs apart and stuck his great . . ."

I put my hand over her mouth, and she bit me. That was Charley.

The next day, Val came in with a tiny bunch of violets hidden in her pocket. She let me see them, giving her secret smile.

"Where did you get them?"

She shrugged.

"You got them from the gypsies." There had been a small group of gypsies hanging about the gates, trying to sell pegs, and these bunches of violets.

"One of the gypsy boys gave them to me," admitted Val.

"And what did you give him?" asked Charley. "He'd want something, I'll be bound."

Val smiled and gave another little shrug.

"A kiss, I suppose. Or two."

Val continued to smile.

"If you'd got caught!" I exclaimed in horror. I was more than a bit of a prig.

"He looked sick to me, that boy," said Charley. "All flushed."

"That was my kiss," said the wicked Val.

However, he was sick and it was not her kiss that made him sick. We heard later that the gypsy camp had the scarletina infection, and in a short time, Val sickened.

Two days later, I took the disease. My throat was raw red and my head ached. We were sent off to the Fever Hospital on the edge of the town.

"I could die," I groaned.

"It would be a pleasure," moaned Val. We were in a small ward on our own with two empty beds in it.

Within a few days, however, we had an unexpected recruit. The door opened and a stretcher was carried in and we saw Charley lying on it. She had come to join us.

When the nurses had gone, she didn't seem at all ill.

"Couldn't let you two die on your own, could I?" She settled back on her pillows. "No, I came for the holiday."

"No holiday," groaned Val, leaning her aching head on her hand.

"But how did you do it?"

"Scratched my throat with a twig, and rubbed myself all over with a bunch of stinging nettles till I had a rash and made myself all sweaty by jumping up and down. They couldn't wait to get rid of me, Matron and Nurse couldn't, for fear they should catch it."

Perhaps it was a judgement on Charley that she caught the scarletina from us.

During this time Val discovered something that surprised her.

"Dodo, this hospital is built where the old lying-in hospital was. We were born here, you and I." Her voice was excited, and not happy.

"It's only the place, the hospital is different."

"I think it's a bad sign. I don't like it."

That night, she woke me, shaking me into opening my eyes. Charley slept on, heavily.

"Dodo, I'm frightened. There's a shadow at the end of the room. It's a woman."

I sat up. "I can't see anything."

"Yes, Dodo, she's there. In the corner, standing looking at us."

17

I put my arm round her; she was shivering.

"It's only the moonlight."

Val gave a kind of howl. "If you can't see it, then it means it's for me. She's come for me. I'm going to die."

I got out of bed, my legs felt wobbly, but I was much better. "Look, Val, I'll go to the end of the room and you will see there is nothing there but moonlight."

She held onto me. "No, no, you mustn't. Then she will join into you and you will be her and she will be you and you will die too."

She was hysterical, so I gathered her into my arms. We crawled into bed together and stayed there till the dawn lit the corner with pale sunlight and showed Val that no one stood there. I reflected that Val was more highly strung than I had guessed.

But it was Charley who was tossed into a roaring fever so that she was the most ill of us all, and nearly died. She made a very bad patient, groaning and complaining so much that Val and I wished she had never come, then for two days lying very quiet and still so that we feared for her life.

But it made us a group. After that, we were bound together.

By the time we were thirteen Valentine and I were above average in height, not having been stunted by our upbringing as some of the others seemed to have been. We both had deep blue eyes, but while my hair was dark brown, Valentine had a mop of blonde curls. She was a beauty.

Our size and our looks got us the position of acting as unpaid little servants to Mrs Brent and the Lady Matron, which we both resented, although it was thought a privilege. As a consequence of being so much with them, we spoke well and had missed the strong Berkshire accent we might otherwise have developed.

Charley had none of these assets but there was no doubt she was the strongest girl in the Home.

We were all three of us wild and intransigent at school. Because we were so regimented at the Home we burst out at school, where we were feared and respected by the village pupils as girls you left alone.

We were not surprised somehow when the three of us were singled out by Dr Violet. She told us that she was doing a study of 'talented children' and we three were her specimens. Only

Charley looked pleased; Val and I felt bashful. After that, we had regular weekly sessions with Dr Violet and took various potions and pills, usually tasting of fish oil, that she handed out to promote our physical and mental wellbeing.

She measured our heights and developing persons rather frequently, when we stripped and stood naked for inspection. There was some favouritism here, if you could call it that, for Val and Charley were selected most often. I was rather thin and meagre then which may have been a factor.

Once I heard Charley laugh after such a measuring. There was a kind of swagger in her voice. I never liked that sound when I heard it, feared it almost, respected it always. Charley in that mood was something ferocious. What had her father been? An animal, she had called him; he might have been, I thought, when I saw that side of her.

I was not measured that day. But that was the day I felt that Dr Violet had released something in Charley and Val, and possibly me too.

What that something was I did not give a name, but it began to colour my life and my night dreams. But from that time on, there was yet another bond between the three of us.

One day when we were doing our obligatory stint in the vegetable garden, (we all gardened as a matter of duty, whether we liked it or not), Charley drew a violet on each of us with a stick stuck in blackcurrant juice. She was already a marvellous draughtswoman, could draw anything and make it look real.

The scratch hurt, and a slight infection set in, but somehow the emblems stayed on our skin. Val's faded somewhat, but mine never did, embodied in a raised, red scar.

"We are the Violet Adventurers," Charley said with a laugh. "We are united. We must never forget."

We were happy in our relationship, Valentine and I, not like sisters, but close, loving friends. We were matter-of-fact now about our birth, although occasionally we had fantasies, such as imagining ourselves as lost heiresses or abandoned princesses. Charley did not come into these fantasies but I know now she had dreams of her own.

Although we were regimented and constricted, we were a roughish lot and most of the girls there had seen something of life. They were country girls with no illusions about the nature of men, women and animals. And Charley was their voice.

"Do you know what she told me?" Val, her eyes full of excitement and interest, lowered her voice and imparted a few facts about life. She made a shape with her hands. "Big, thick. And Charley has seen . . ." A thoughtful look came on her face. "Charley explained something else as well, but I'm not sure if she was right."

"What about?"

"Dr Violet." She shook her head. "I shan't say. It's a secret. You're so simple, Dodo."

No, I was not simple, or hard, as she sometimes thought too.

There was a little bag of love inside each of us; I see now, we needed someone or something to empty it upon, but my bag was tied up tighter than most and needed loosening.

I had a secret hiding place in the old stables at the back of the Home, a place used for the storage of firewood since no horses were kept. It was warm and quiet.

One day I became aware I had a companion. A small, bedraggled tabby cat had crept in out of the rain. The country people around were not famous for their kindness to animals. There was string around her neck and she was wet; it looked as though an attempt had been made to drown her.

The reason was clear, she was in kitten, her belly swollen. She was frightened of me, I saw the fear in her eyes, but she did not move away.

I looked at her, and my heart began to beat faster as I saw her tummy heave and a kitten covered in film appear. The mother nipped the cover off with her teeth.

I ran out of the stable and leant against the old door. Blackness came over me, I felt sweaty and then cold, and then hot again.

The sun fell on my face and warmed me. Steadied me. I knew what I was going to do.

I crept into the big kitchen and stole some milk and bread. It was not easy to steal in the Home, but you could do it, and we all did at times. I knew how to wait for the kitchen-maids to turn away. The big larder and pantries were not locked.

Supposed to be, according to the rules, but not all rules were kept.

I carried out a bowl of milk and crumbled the bread in it. There was some cold porridge left over from breakfast and I had that too.

When I returned to the stables the cat had delivered herself of four small objects. They were already suckling.

She looked desperate for food herself. I put the bowl where she could get it and went away. As I looked back, she was already lapping.

Over the next few days, I managed to hide away some of my own meals and smuggle them out to the cat. I told Val, and later Charley.

Val said at once she would help, and so she did, once or twice. But I found one day she had forgotten or not bothered and the little cat was winding itself around my legs and crying with hunger. It had got bolder with me now.

Charley on the other hand, after a first "Drown them all, I say", was regular in her help. She was adept at stealing and a good provider.

Inevitably our secret got out; nothing was ever secret for long in the Home. The edict went forth that mother and kittens should be put down. Animals were not allowed. They had enough with us.

We were all punished, but as ringleader, my punishment was the severest: I was condemned for what we called kitchen and nursery hard labour for an indefinite period. The nursery nurse threw up her hands in horror and said she didn't want me, but she got me all the same. Amidst storms of tears and protestations that I would hang myself (a village girl had hung herself lately so the idea was in all minds) if the cats were killed, I was handed over.

But the death sentence on the innocent was not carried out. The gardener said he didn't fancy the job and anyway the mother cat was keeping the rats down a treat, so she was reprieved. But the kittens? Mrs Brent, a cat lover, intervened.

"You wouldn't really hang yourself, Dorothea," she said with an amused smile. "It's harder to do than you might think and you wouldn't enjoy it."

But my threats had done something.

"I'll take the kittens. I can find them homes."

My tears did cease a little. "But their mother will miss them." Although I knew of mothers who did not.

"Dorothea, you know; as kittens get older, their mother does push them away." I thought I knew of mothers like that, and they did not wait for age, either. So cats were like that too?

Thus the kittens were spirited away, and I never heard of their fate, and although Charley said Mrs Brent had probably had them destroyed, still I thought she was not a liar.

So the kittens went and I took up my hard labour. I was strong, you know.

The nursery was crowded in those days: six small wailers were installed. Five girls, poor things, and one boy. (Boys were allowed in infancy, weeded out once they started to walk and sent I knew not where. The antipodes, probably.)

I hated the crying and tried to ignore it. But one day as I was carting the slop pails around preparatory to helping with the laundry, my eyes fell on one cot.

The occupant was not crying, but was cramming its fist into its mouth and sucking frantically. Over the fist, eyes stared at me. It was past tears, past crying.

"This one's hungry," I said.

"Oh let it wait," called back the nurse. Overworked, tetchy, she didn't want to hear from me.

"No! Now."

"Oh you're hoity toity, miss. Feed it yourself then," and she thrust a bottle into my hands.

I hesitated.

"Pick him up, girl, do, and get on with it."

Whether that kid lived on, or whether his line went on, I never knew, but he took the bottle like a Trojan. So strongly that as he sucked, the vibrations of his little body carried through into mine. I felt warm.

The hard little knot inside me which must be my heart, began to loosen.

Nurse came over to inspect us. "You'll make a good mother, after all," she said, giving reluctant praise where praise was due.

"When you came in here, not weaned, it was me that fed you. I'd had a wean myself who'd died so I was your wet nurse. I saved you. And when they took you away, because you were weaned and could take pap – so you must go to the big nursery – you clung to my finger and cried." I think there was moisture in her eyes. "Babies that are not bred to the breast generally die," she said.

She was a simple countrywoman, and by forgetting, I had hurt her.

Inside me my hard little heart began to grow and soften. I held out my hand towards her and she took it. But a change was coming, and it was my fault. I exploded the bomb as innocents very often do.

We knew things were on the move when Mrs Brent and Miss Desmond started to talk to us about our future. Everyone in the Orphanage had a 'future', and it descended upon us about the age of thirteen, when we were expected to go out into the world and support ourselves. For girls this usually meant domestic service or a carefully selected apprenticeship to a court dressmaker or a milliner. You had to be nimble with your fingers for that, and neither Valentine nor I qualified in that direction.

Our 'future' began to look more alarming, or exciting, according to how you felt about it, when a lady and a gentleman appeared from London and were closeted with the Lady Matron and several members of the managing committee for some hours.

That evening, Valentine and I were called into Miss Desmond's room. She was standing by the window, looking out. Spring was late that year, and the trees were still bare. There was a log fire crackling in the hearth, scenting the room. I can always remember the smell; to smell it now still summons up that sense of excitement and apprehension that I felt. Valentine strode forward, I followed behind.

"Girls," said Miss Desmond; her face was thoughtful. She sat down behind her desk, facing us. She did not ask us to sit. One did not sit in the Lady Matron's presence. "You must have been wondering about your future."

We said nothing, no answer was expected or even desired. She was a good lady, Miss Desmond, but freedom of choice was not on offer to us. The committee and the Lady Matron made the decisions.

Then she told us. A charitable organisation in London had links with a similar society in Canada which provided homes and jobs for girls like us. Our fares would be paid and we would be met in Toronto. Naturally, careful checks were made on the families and occupations we went into. Great care was taken, we could be sure of that. We were going to a wonderful and growing country. It was a marvellous opportunity, we were lucky girls.

I hope she thought so herself. I believe she did.

We had one day to think it over; if we refused there were several local households looking for kitchen-maids.

"It might be easier to run away in Canada," said Valentine, as we left.

"Are you thinking of running away?" I was surprised. And yet I knew that underneath our surface tranquillity, we both longed to escape from the scene we seemed destined for.

"I'm always thinking of running away."

"But you've never tried."

"I've never known anywhere to run to that I wanted to go. I might in Canada." Valentine smiled. She did not look much like a frontierswoman, but one could never tell. "Besides," she touched my hand. "There's you, Dodo."

Next day, Mrs Brent arrived in her pony and trap. She drove herself, but usually brought a young groom to hold the pony. John was a short, young man with bright hazel eyes; he was as sturdy as the cob he drove. We had hardly exchanged words, but I liked him, and thought of him as my friend. Once he had showed me a little brown field mouse in a box and then let it go free because I asked him. That was John, whom Mrs Brent called Johnnie.

She took me aside. "How would you like to be a school teacher? It might be better for you than going to Canada. I think I can get you into a training college for teachers."

I suppose I looked very young and innocent, for she added gently: "We would take our time and see you got a bit more general education first. But you are clever, Dorothea, and should use your brains."

"Where is the college?"

"In Canterbury. You would live there while you trained."

I told her that I would like to see the college, and she promised to take me there.

I went back to the kitchens where I was working that day; we all took our turns, helping with the duties, looking after the younger children. I was good with children. I thought I might enjoy teaching.

Within a few days, Mrs Brent came to take me to see the St Margaret's College for Teachers in Canterbury. She left the pony and trap behind with John at the Orphanage and we travelled by train.

I must have done well. On the way back, Mrs Brent said: "She called you exceptionally intelligent."

"It's because of Dr Violet's pills," I said happily. I was excited; I was being offered a doorway to escape from the world into which I seemed to have been born, and I wanted to walk through it. "It's all three of us, but she loves Charley best." Which I think was no more than the truth.

"What are you saying? What is that?"

It was my first intimation that Dr Violet's study of us had been a secret from her. Unwittingly, I had opened a Pandora's box of Victorian prudery.

Mrs Brent let me tell her everything but frowningly said nothing back. Not then.

I had to report to the Lady Warden; anyone who had been out had to show themselves on their return and be marked off in a register.

I ran in through the back, past the numerous outhouses (we never used the front door; only the committee and grand visitors did that), and down a passage. It was getting dark and this part of the house was never well lit at any time.

In an alcove at the end where brooms and pails were kept, I saw John and Valentine, bodies pressed together and it looked as though they were kissing. To put it fairly, if any kissing was going on, then Valentine was doing her share.

I stood staring for a moment, then silently retreated.

That evening, I came across Val in the washplace. She was standing there in her shift, running her hands over her body; she turned and looked at me. "There's a feeling inside you," she said conversationally. "It sort of grows. You kind of open out. Charley was quite right."

She threw off her shift and stood there, naked.

"You'd better put that on again," I said coldly. "Matron is coming."

Val just giggled.

The explosion came upon us the next day. We were summoned into Miss Desmond's presence, Val, Charley and I, to be questioned about our behaviour with Dr Violet. I did not really understand the force of the charge being laid, nor did Val, or not then, although she may have suspected. Charley, I believe, did understand. She blamed me, and turned on me in a fury, saying that she would never forgive me and would have her revenge. "You don't understand what you've done," she cried.

As I left Miss Desmond's room I saw Dr Violet, her face red with weeping, run through the hall in front of me. I had never seen an adult in such state. I hardly recognised her.

Charley was separated from us, and I soon understood that we three were all to be sent away. I had hopes of my teachers' training college. No one had said not.

That night, as I got into bed, I heard Valentine crying quietly into her pillow. After a while, I whispered: "Why are you crying?"

She did not answer.

"Is it because of Dr Violet?"

"No."

"John then?"

She sat up quickly. "Why John?"

"I saw you kissing. You love him, I suppose. And you will be leaving him behind."

"John, indeed. There will be plenty of people like him in Canada. No, it's you I am crying for, Dodo, you I will miss."

From my bed, I reached out a hand; she gripped it hard.

"I'm not going to be a teacher, Val. I shan't go to Canterbury. I thought I wanted to, but I know now what I really want. I'm coming with you, Val. I'm coming to Canada."

"Truly?"

"Truly."

26

In the dark, we held hands. I felt very protective of her, dear vulnerable Val.

Did I really want to go to the college in Canterbury? Or was I secretly frightened at the idea of my freedom, and glad to use Valentine as an excuse? I did not know then, and I do not know now, but at the time it felt like a sacrifice.

Charley we did not see. I did not learn until much later that Dr Violet killed herself, leaving the Violet Adventurers to their fate.

Val and I left the Sunshine Home together. It was the last day in April.

'Toronto, 14 May
Dear Mrs Brent,
I hope you will have got our letters sent by the ship's boat the night before we were allowed to land. We arrived in the quarantine harbour at 8 o'clock when it was too late for the custom house and medical officers to inspect us. The ship lay to, and only moved up to the wharf where we were to land at about 8 o'clock the next morning. We were greeted by . . .'

During all this time, Val and I had never talked of Charley, but I did not forget her. There had been no tears from me when we left the Sunshine Home although Val had wept freely. I had the horrid feeling that my heart was getting small and hard again. There was certainly a feeling in the middle of me, about where my heart must be, of something uncomfortable and miserable. When I had this feeling I held on to Val tightly. I thought about Charley. And there was a mystery about her departure and ours that puzzled me.

There was something that no one was telling me. Perhaps I was expected to know and didn't.

I laid down my pen. The journey had been an ordeal.

It had started with the cheerless trip to Liverpool by train with the rain falling incessantly. The bad weather seemed to continue all the time after. The ship looked tiny, too small to our worried eyes to cross the Atlantic, and it had just been overhauled so it still smelt horribly of paint and varnish. Valentine and I were crammed into a minute cabin with eight other female passengers, most of whom were sick constantly. I felt sick too, but kept on

27

my feet. Valentine seemed to enjoy the stormy weather and soon made friends with one of the stewards who accordingly smuggled us some food from the first-class dining room. Everyone up there was ill, more or less, he said, and no one would miss the hot soup and the little puddings.

Our companions in the confinement of the cabin groaned and complained as we ate our beef soup and castle puddings with jam. But I felt I was made to pay for it as I helped Mrs Dalziel, into whose charge we had been put, into her corsets every morning and out again at night. She insisted on being laced into them even though she lay moaning on her bunk all day. Miss Stacey, going out to be a cook-housekeeper to a farmer, and Mrs Restrick, a widow, going we knew not where for purposes we thought better not to ask, never bothered to get out of their dressing robes for the whole ten days of the journey. Pretty grubby they looked at the end of it, too.

But when we landed our travelling companions appeared in all their finery. Mrs Restrick had a fur boa around her neck, together with a good deal of gimcrack jewellery, while Miss Stacey was in a fierce plaid. Mrs Dalziel, laced up for the last time by me, sported a bright, garnished hat that would have done credit to a harvest festival. I swear I even saw a carrot among the apples on her head.

We two wore plain gaberdine skirts and jackets with little chip straw hats, but they had been chosen by Mrs Brent who had good taste, and we had trimmed the straws ourselves with ribbon. We looked pretty, and what is more, as Miss Desmond said, we looked 'suitable'.

'Suitable' meant neat and unobtrusive, and this was what girls in our position were expected to be. Only my scarlet ribbon and Valentine's sapphire blue bows hinted that there might be more to us than first appeared.

We waited on the wharfside. No one appeared for us. Mrs Restrick hung around for a little, then departed saying she "would be back". She never reappeared.

Not that we were alone. The wharf was crowded with any number of men and women, who were loafing around with apparently no other purpose than to watch the new arrivals.

All around us was activity, which gave me the sense of a thriving city beyond.

Then through the crowd I saw a lad threading his way. He came straight up to us.

"Valentine Abbey and Dorothea Adam?" We had been given these surnames, they were handed out on the alphabetical principle.

"Yes."

What a frown, I thought, what a fierce face with those black brows drawn across it. He dislikes us already, and I shall never like him.

He held out a hand.

"I am Joe of Jerningham's. Give me your bags. I have the buggy outside."

Chapter Two

Jerningham's was in Toronto, and we were in Jerningham's, and for some time Jerningham's was Toronto for us. After a bit we went around and got to know the city, but we saw it all through the eyes of two girls who lived in the store called Jerningham's. Above the shop. Who lived, worked and smelt Jerningham's. Joe had a room above the stables but ate with us. He had a little more independence than we had, and a great air of it anyway. He had been there two years. If he had a past history he seemed to have buried it, for he never spoke of it. If he had another name he never used it, always referring to himself as Joe of Jerningham's. Where he had come from he did not seem to know, but he gave the impression of knowing where he was going.

I think Joe fell in love with Val straight away, as soon as he met us off the ship. To tell the truth, Joe had an eye for the girls but not much time for them. Old man Jerningham saw to that.

It didn't take us long to find out that old Jerningham had an eye for the girls too, but he had Mrs Jerningham to keep him in order.

"Wow! Hands!" I heard Val say as she skipped out of the stockroom where she had been arranging boxes with Mr Jerningham. He emerged soon afterwards with a pained look and bruised fingers where Val had slammed a heavy box lid on his hand.

He was not a wicked man, but I thought Mrs Jerningham might be wicked. She was kind, equable, cold. Inside her was something untouchable.

It might, of course, have been great goodness, but judging by the harassed, unloved look worn by Mr Jerningham, it did not seem likely.

As we drove from the docks in the buggy (a low, open vehicle drawn by one horse, a good-looking chestnut), we stared around us at Toronto which was to be our home. We drove up from the waterside, through busy streets with plenty of traffic of all sorts: carts, carriages, a few automobiles and many pedestrians, all making their way intently forward as if oblivious of everyone and everything. All the hurrying people looked prosperous, and were well wrapped up. It was late afternoon and getting cold.

If you fell down on the street, I thought, no one would do anything except drive round you.

Toronto was a city, and the first we knew, for Val and I had seen no more of London than Liverpool Street Station and then only the drive through dingy streets to the Surrey Docks. Canterbury had been the only town we knew and we had seen precious little of that, so we could not but be excited.

Val gripped my hand. "I think I like it," she said. "Isn't it grand?"

Toronto was a city with large, handsome buildings laid out on the grid plan with the streets running at right angles to each other. We drove down one wide thoroughfare lined with shops and large houses.

"Yonge Street," said Joe, giving a wave with his whip. "Mighty fine street. All the streets divide here. East that way," another wave of the whip, "west that way. Remember that and you won't go wrong."

We were going west, he said.

Adelaide Street, Richmond Street. I saw the names painted on the walls as we drove along.

"That's King Street," he said, giving another flourish, and pointing out a boulevard lined with large shops, business premises and handsome three-storey houses. "Finest street in the city. You get the gentry there. The carriage trade."

Toronto was then a city of some three hundred thousand souls and growing all the time. You could feel the growth in the air. It was a great manufacturing and commercial city and the centre of a rich agricultural area. It was a city that had known wars. The Indians, the French, and now the English had laid hands upon it. Soon we were turning into Frederick Street.

"There's Jerningham's," said Joe. He had a note of pride in his voice. My territory, I belong here, he was saying.

Jerningham's was a smaller store than many of those which we had passed. It was a long, low, two-storied building but with two big plate glass windows on either side of a central door.

Joe drove us into a cobbled yard at the back. We had arrived.

There was smoke on the air, and a whiff of the north; although it was spring, it was chill. The Great Lakes were not far away, and the city lay between two rivers and the sea. You could smell it. I shivered, half thrilled with the prospect of my new life, half frightened.

Joe helped us down, Val first. "I'll give you a heave with your bags. You lodge up there." He pointed to two windows on the top floor. "Hurry along now and I'll have you up the back stairs quick before Mrs Jerningham sees you or she'll scurry you in the store before you can say Myrtle Mulberry." This was one of his favourite phrases and he used it as an exclamation, expletive and even prayer.

He took us up two flights of a narrow uncarpeted wooden staircase, threw open a door, planted our bags on the floor and bowed. "Supper's on the table at seven sharp, soon as the shop closes."

And he was gone.

We were in a long narrow room with two windows, uncurtained but with a blind. Two small beds stood in the middle of the room, already made up with sheets and blankets. A wardrobe stood against one wall and a narrow strip of carpet ran between the two beds.

"Electric light," said Val touching a switch, but no light came on. Later we found it was controlled by Mrs Jerningham in the interests of economy. She sat down on the bed nearest the door. "I'll have this one."

In its own way the room was comfortable and certainly clean. It was a touch spartan but we were used to that, and it was our own, not a dormitory to be shared with other girls. A mild sense of possession stirred inside me.

"You won't see a ghostly mist lurking in the corners of this room," I said.

"You never believed in that."

"You had a fever."

"Supposing I should say that on the boat I saw Dr Violet without a head? Would you believe me?"

"Did you?"

"I didn't say I did."

"Oh Val!"

She gave a little shake of her head. "I might have done. For all you know."

"I would have been the first person you came to. You always do."

"Oh do I? That's all you know. Think I tell you everything, do you, Dodo?"

What with fatigue, excitement and the apprehensions of being in a strange place where we must live and make our way, we were nearly quarrelling.

Val broke the tension. "Don't let's argue, Dodo, we need each other; we need to be friends."

"We're hungry, that's what it is." No meal since breakfast on the ship and then we had been too excited to eat much; I had been too busy as well, in helping Mrs Dalziel into her corsets.

"I wonder where the supper room is?" asked Val.

"We will find it." I spoke with a confidence I did not feel. We did not have watches, how should we have? Such luxuries were not to be found at the Sunshine Home. There was no clock in the room. I made a resolve that with my first earnings I would buy a clock. "I expect Joe will come back and show us."

Val nodded. "Mmm. He's nice isn't he? Smells a bit of the horse, though, not that I'm against that," she added dreamily. "I quite like it." I gave her a sharp look, remembering John and the gypsy boy back at the Home. "I expect he lives over the stables."

"He knows how to look after himself, I'd say." His eyebrows made a firm line across his face that suggested he had a temper if he wanted one.

In silence we unpacked, bestowing our small possessions neatly in two piles in the wardrobe. I hung my hat on a hook at the back, parting from it sadly; it was a good hat and improved

33

my appearance. I stroked it, with a pang of homesickness for England and things past.

Without looking at Val, I said: "Do you miss Charley?"

Val nodded. "Oh yes."

"Do you think about her?"

I thought about Charley all the time. Then I put into speech the mystery that had puzzled me. "We were separated from her. She was sent away on her own. I wonder why they didn't separate us? Why not part you and me?"

Slowly Val said: "It was on account of a bargain she made."

"What bargain?"

"She swore that if they promised not to part us then she would not tell to the world what she knew of Dr Violet."

I thought about this, trying to work out what to make of it. Nothing I liked. "How do you know?"

Val turned away. "Oh you are an innocent, Dodo. I found out for myself."

"You mean you listened at the door?"

She didn't deny it. I wouldn't have blamed her if she had; it was one of the ways of finding out things at the Sunshine Home. The other way was to curry favours with the maids and cooks and get them to tell us. That could be done too. No one was to blame if we were underhand, it was the only way we had of finding out what was going on. There is nothing in the world nastier than to sense that people know more about what is going to become of you than you do yourself. I can tell you that as a fact.

"Do you think we will ever see Charley again?"

Val shrugged. "Not likely, is it?" Then, distantly in the building somewhere, a bell. Briskly, firmly. And at the same moment, came a rap on the door and Joe's voice sounded.

"Are you decent now, girls? Can I come in?" He had the door open before we could answer, and perhaps he would not have minded if we had not been, as he put it, 'decent'. "You heard the supper bell? Come and get it!"

He clattered down the stairway ahead of us; at the bottom of the stairs he turned to wait.

Polite enough, I said to myself. Perhaps that frown you wear doesn't mean so much. He had a nice voice. Always Joe had one of those voices that could convey more expression than anyone else I ever knew. He was not tall, but still growing into his true height, muscular and strong, with a crest of curly dark hair and bright eyes.

He led us through a series of back passages, past what I saw were stockrooms and storage places, some smelling strongly of food like cheese and coffee and others dusty and quiet. They were all quiet. The whole place was quiet. It held a kind of hush as if no one ever raised their voices there or took violent action, but went on silently labouring at what they were doing. Yes, you smelt hard work there.

It was an old building. I learnt later that the Jerningham store was a long-established one (by Toronto standards where a generation counted), old-fashioned but very trusted and respectable. That was another thing you could smell in the dusty yet orderly back premises: respectability. It had started out as a grocery store, hence the cheese and coffee, but was now expanding into other fields.

Val and I were part of the expansion. There was only one other employee, and she was standing in the dining room waiting for us.

At least, I suppose she was waiting for us. She had an air of waiting.

"You're late." She had a brisk, strong voice. "The master and mistress are on their way." To us she held out a hand. "Kate Rouster, that's me. Glad to see you."

Val and I recited our names, but she had them pat and we never needed to mention them again; we were obviously of great interest to her. But we each got a vigorous handshake, delivered with all the force of a wiry, strong lady. Greying hair, spectacled, and tall and thin, but very neat, in a blue striped dress with a white collar and cuffs.

"No one's late here, you know," she went on. "Always to be on time. I get here before the bell. I advise you to do the same."

She was a little odd, I thought. Kind, but odd.

"We're not late, Katie," said Joe easily. "Rest yourself."

A fragrant smell of food made my mouth water. On the table

were three large covered dishes which smelt of meat and gravy and vegetables.

"I eat here, but I don't live in. Got a room on Poland Street. Now you know all there is to know about me." And she sat herself down at the table.

"What's your wages?"

We did not answer. We were to get twelve dollars a month and our food. Whether that was a lot or little we did not know.

"If you won't tell me, I shall find out sooner or later. And if you have more than me, I shall strike for it or change my place."

It was our introduction to labour relations in our new continent.

Joe laughed. "What you don't get in dollars, you take out in food, Kate."

A ball, a small rubber ball, rolled through the open door and into the room.

"Ah, here they come," said Kate.

In came a middle-aged couple, both sombrely attired in dark grey alpaca, Mrs Jerningham in a skirt with a stiff blouse and jacket and her husband in a similar jacket, and trousers. He had spectacles, (I discovered later that Jerningham's sold spectacles by the gross); she did not. They were both tall and thin.

No introductions here, no handshaking; they knew who we were, they were paying us.

"Sit down and get your meal," said Mr Jerningham. He started dishing up platefuls of stew. It smelt good and it tasted good; we were well fed at Jerningham's, worked hard but well nourished. And if I sometimes felt like a horse that must have its oats so it could pull the covered wagon, that was probably my fault and not that of Thomas and Mary Jerningham. Ma and Pa J. as we called them when they could not hear.

There were no children; they were childless.

When I got my chance, I whispered to Kate. "Why does she do that with the ball?"

"Ah, that's a secret she ain't let us into," drawled Kate.

But there was a reason, as I discovered later.

"What happens to the ball?"

"We pick it up," said Kate, bending down.

Next day we started work. Val and I were sent everywhere: we served at a counter in the shop; we checked goods in the stockrooms, and we ran errands for both our employers. They were hard-working themselves. This was Toronto, Canada, and there was a sort of democratic freedom in our relationships; we were not put upon, but were expected to work as they did.

Val and I were mainly employed in what might be called 'the ladies' counter', selling fabrics, and paper patterns to go with them. But there were also made-up dresses and skirts and blouses. Ladies' underwear too, like corsets and horsehair figure 'improvers'. Pads, really, itchy things, I thought, to make the bosoms bigger.

Joe worked everywhere, but he was mainly employed as a 'trimmer', dressing the windows for which he seemed to have a natural skill. There was a new plate glass window to the right of the front door which revealed Joe's displays. Mr Jerningham varied them according to the season. The week we arrived the window display was a great pyramid of tinned goods, mostly of fruit. As Joe said, tins did not grow rotten in the window and did not attract flies. There were always flies. I suppose it was the numerous horses.

Compared with the big, fashionable stores like Batons and Simpsons – large department stores on King Street – the place was nothing, but growing all the time.

So every day we worked hard, on our feet all the time, often running, serving customers, packing their purchases, learning the trade, prices and values, and even getting used to picking up that rolling ball (the purpose of which I still had not learnt, except to recognise it as an obsession), but afterwards we played. We had freedom, Val and I.

Outside was Toronto and the free air of this great continent blew through it. We were emancipated by it.

There was plenty of amusement to be found in Toronto. Parks with bands playing waltz tunes from Vienna and the new quickstep from New York (the US was a powerful and evocative neighbour here whose accent we were already picking up); several theatres, a circus and many dance-halls.

Joe took us to the circus. He took us both, with a proudly

proprietorial air, and wearing his best clothes of a smart dark blue suit, plain white shirt and a dazzling tie. A soft hat softened his tough young face and masked those eyebrows that met across his forehead so fiercely.

Joe loved that suit, I could tell by the way he had of smoothing down the jacket. I guessed it was his first new suit for a long time, perhaps ever; I guessed, because I behaved that way myself with the little skirt and jacket I had worn from England. It was still good, but it would not do for here, fashion was subtly different across the Atlantic, or I was beginning to be different. To be 'suitable' was no longer what I wanted.

The circus tent was crowded and noisy. You realised then that there was a mixed population in this city, with French-speaking people and Indians helping in the circus ring with the horses.

As Joe led us to our seats and put a programme in Val's hand I thought he did it with a bit of swagger, as of a man proud of the girl he has on his arm. He had offered us an arm each, but it was not possible to walk abreast in those crowds, so I soon dropped his arm.

I suppose this was the occasion when I first realised that Joe was in love with Val. I could not blame him, she was lovely. Tall now, with radiant fair hair and enormous blue eyes. Did she touch up just a little? I had a suspicion that the delicate blush on her cheek came from the chemist's shop round the corner. But it might not have been so; she was a healthy lass was Val and the pink might have been natural after all.

That night Val and I were followed by a man. People were free and easy of manner in Toronto so that we had got used to friendly and admiring glances and the occasional hopeful comment. Val always gave a discreet smile, not exactly welcoming but hardly a repelling smile either. If we were together she quite naturally appropriated any admiration for herself. I could have my share if I cared to take it; she wasn't greedy. Plenty more where that came from, her manner said.

And it was true: Val would never want for admirers. Lovers. I didn't use that word but it was what I meant.

So we had got used to being hailed in a friendly way, but this was quite different.

After the circus, excited by the thrill of the high-wire artists and the skill of the jugglers, we went round the animal cages at the back of the big tent. Joe said he knew one of the lion tamers, an Indian he'd met in his youth.

He was still young, very young, but Joe's early life was as yet a mystery to us; he let out little bits by degree, not exactly secretive, but holding his past to his chest in a private kind of way. He hadn't been born in Toronto, possibly not even in Canada; I had a private conviction on this score.

The man was standing beside me at the lioness's cage, looking me up and down. I edged away, glad to move over to where Joe and Val were talking to the Indian. An Indian chief, he said he was, a tall, unsmiling man.

After the lions we toured the cages of the seals and bears. It was all exciting to me. I had never seen a circus before. The Sunshine Home had not approved of 'entertainments', we should make our own, but I felt drawn to this strange world. I had a moment of fantasy that I would run away and join them. Be a circus girl and balance hoops around me in the ring and swing from a trapeze. Not a lion tamer, I thought, observing the lion's pale, baleful stare and big teeth, and not a clown. Girls couldn't be clowns, that was a man's job.

We strolled round the caged lions, bears, elephants and horses. I had discovered that once you had a heart inside you that was soft and not like a hard little ball, then it could be soft more often than you might think. You could not harden it as you might want – how convenient and comfortable life would be if you could.

I was soft about that baby howling in the pram by the lion's cage and probably thinking its mother had left it for ever and it was the lion's lunch; I was soft about the girl kissing her lover in the shade of the big tent; I was soft about that sad-looking lioness and I was even soft about that mouse as it darted in front of the elephant who would certainly step on it and crush it to death at any moment. But no, the elephant did not and carefully drew back his foot from the mouse. Elephants were soft too.

I found that thought a comfort, as if the world, the universe, might be on our side after all, and that dark pit into which I feared I would fall one day and Val with me might not have been meant for us.

Then I seemed to hear Charley's voice speaking to me: Presently some other animal will eat that mouse. We are all food for someone, in the end we all eat each other.

I stood back from myself and knew that Charley would have ended with a laugh, she always was a fighter. I missed her.

The man was there again, as we moved towards the elephants. Joe had gone off to the stall where they sold ice cream and hot spicy sausages and drinks, to see what we would like, when he accosted us.

"Stay near the elephants," Joe had said. The man, he was tall and thin and dressed in a bright check suit with a matching soft hat, drawn down over his forehead, was right behind us both as we talked to the elephants who seemed on the point of answering back but never quite got round to it. Then as we walked away, he managed to get between us, brushing against us both.

"Hello, girls, lost the little fella? You can do better than him." He put his arm round Val and hooked his other arm into mine. I could smell his breath and another sort of odour that I think was just man.

Val twirled herself smartly away, but I remained firmly hooked up. I could feel his muscles pressing into mine.

"I've had my eye on you little ladies all night. And I thought, I'd like to get to know them better, the two of 'em, and I dare say they'd like to know me. So what say we all three go and have a drink?"

A gleam came into Val's eyes. Oh no, Val, you couldn't, I thought. But she might. He had somehow got his arm around her again.

Then I saw Joe pushing his way through the crowd, carrying a glass of lemonade for us in each hand.

He stared, stopped, and then put the glasses on the ground, and took off his coat. Joe cared about that suit of his and wasn't going to risk it getting stained.

"Hello, little fellow," said our accoster.

Joe walked towards us. Joe was not tall yet, still growing into his adult size, but I had already observed that he had strong muscles, and when he liked, seemed able to puff himself up into someone twice his size. I believe some toads can do this when they are angry. He did that now as he strolled towards us.

"Let the ladies go."

The man dropped our arms and advanced towards Joe. Joe delivered a sharp punch below the belt, followed by a kick to the shin. The man collapsed, gasping.

Joe jerked his head towards us. "Come on." He bent down and picked up his coat and drinks, then he hurried after us. Before he left he kicked him in the stomach.

The speed, economy and efficient ruthlessness of his attack had amazed me.

"That was rough," I said when we were well away.

Joe knotted his brows in that dark way of his. "You don't do it for fun. No game." He added: "I had you two to look after."

"Thank you," I said. "And we are grateful, aren't we, Val? That man was a horror."

Val did not say anything, but she gave Joe one of those smiles she was practised in and put her hand gently on his. Joe went red, a blush started on his cheeks and spread down to his neck. He did not smile back but looked very serious and straightened his shoulders.

"Back now girls, home we go."

Until that evening, Joe had treated us both equally, but from then on it was Val.

When we got back, I said: "Did you notice anything strange about that man, Val?"

"No." She was indifferent, taking off her hat and letting her hair fall down to her shoulders with a toss of her head. "And you were wrong to act the way you did. It never does any harm to play a man along. You can always get rid of him when you want."

Can you? I thought. That way lies trouble.

"Do you ever think about Charley?" I don't know why I said it then; I had asked before and not got much of an answer, but somehow it popped out now. I would like to have had Charley's opinion about that man.

"I wish you hadn't asked that." Val turned away. "Stop fussing."

But there had been something odd about that man. He was a watcher, whether by trade or by inclination, or both, I sensed.

What trade?

A detective? He didn't look like a policeman, but he might be a Pinkerton man. Kate was always talking about the Pinkerton Detective Agency in whose offices she had once worked. But the money had not been good and hours even longer than in Jerningham's. She had picked up a wide range of information about the way men and women behaved in love, most of which she passed on to us as we gossiped in the back of the shop. When Val and I eventually married we would be well informed about the variety of sexual practices. In theory, anyway. At the time I believed that Katie's knowledge was theoretical too, but although no beauty she had an endless supply of boyfriends and never lacked for a new one. She seemed willing for anything.

Val said: "Joe asked me if I'd go out with him." She gave me a look. "On my own."

"And what did you say?"

She studied her face in the looking glass we had fixed to the wall. "I said I'd think about it."

"But you will?"

She shrugged. "He's not a bad-looking boy. And he knows his way about." Until someone better offers, I thought, while also thinking that Joe was a tougher customer than she might believe. Hadn't she drawn any conclusion from the show tonight?

"What do you think of Joe?"

I shrugged. "I don't know what to make of him."

"You don't like him, do you?"

"It's you that seems to matter."

Val laughed. "With me, liking doesn't count. There are other things."

I said: "I'm a bit frightened of him, I think." And you should be too, but I didn't utter this aloud.

"I told him you didn't like him." She was buffing her nails. Val had strong hands which she kept in good order although our work here had a manual element to it. "It's always best to be straight about that sort of thing."

"You're so clever, Val, that it shows."

"Now I've made you angry."

I turned away. Yes, I was angry. She should let me manage my own affairs, not tattle about me to Joe, saying things that were not true. She hated a rival did Val, even me. "Just you be careful," I said.

One day she came back after a dance-hall evening with Joe. Her face was flushed. She held out her right arm.

"Look."

Five bruises, fingerprinted across her arm.

"Joe did it." she stared at her arm. "Just because I was dancing with another boy."

"And?"

"Well, there was a little bit of 'And', I grant you, but nothing much." She gave a reminiscent smile. "Joe dragged me away ... he didn't mean to hurt, he's quite gentle really. Till he gets mad."

"I warned you."

"I don't mind," said Val, as she settled into bed. "I quite like a bit of anger in a man. I shall go out with Joe again."

But there was no "again". He didn't ask her, and a tentative approach from a puzzled Val, produced a turndown.

"I'm walking out with Kate," said Joe.

"Must be some other Kate," sniggered Kate, when the news was transmitted to her, "not me. Wish it was. I'd go out with Joe any day, he's a fine fellow."

Joe's work was invaluable to Jerningham's, even I could see that. As a 'trimmer', dressing the shop windows, he did it well.

Val hid her chagrin and went about as usual. But there were a lot of pretty girls in Toronto and a few fine feathers were necessary too. In short, there was competition. Val was tall, and golden-haired, and paid for dressing, but we did not earn much.

As the shop closed one day, I saw Val holding up a length of lovely silk. "Pretty, eh?"

"Pa Jerningham would skin you if he saw you doing that."

"Yes, with long loving touches up and down me."

Kate in the background made that noise of hers, peculiarly transatlantic, that we called her snigger. She knew all about Pa Jerningham.

My eyes met Val's. It was certainly wiser to meet with Mr Jerningham, if you had to, in the shop with customers around, or with his wife in the room. It seemed to me that I began to understand her ball rolling. Was it a kind of warning of her approach?

Val laughed and put the silk down. "No, I shall buy a length, I've found a rich boyfriend."

The rich boyfriend – he never had a name, and perhaps was never the same one twice, or not at first – certainly showed Val a good time. It was one way of dealing with life, as that first harsh North American winter revealed itself to us.

Snow, and snow upon snow. Even in the city roads became blocked with small drifts, although tracks were kept clear for traffic to move. The wind blew with Arctic force, rattling the windows and piling up white mounds against the glass. And it went on, week after week. It was all new to us, a delight and an amusement at first, then something to fight against.

Inside the shop we were warm enough; pipes trailed everywhere, fuelled by a great boiler in the basement. I was amazed how the city carried on with its business in spite of the snow; the main streets were kept swept and for the rest, people seemed to push their way through the snow all hatted and booted, used to such a climate.

Val managed to maintain her social life. She had acquired a long fur coat; a kind of rat, she said, but the fur had a rich sheen and she looked pretty in it. I noticed she took care the Jerningham's should not see it, nor Joe, if she could help it. It was her way of dealing with life.

But I took a different course. I had used one of the big city public libraries that enriched Toronto; they owed their beginnings to an open-minded city government as well as many private benefactors. On one visit I had seen a notice about evening classes. One in literature and history took my notice; I enrolled. The classes were held in the autumn and winter at the Common School in Muir Road. I could walk there. Run, if the shop closed late, with a hot biscuit in my hand. A woman came in every day to do the cooking, but she departed before supper time, leaving us to serve the meal. Kate Rouster usually did it; she liked her food and any contact with it. Mrs Jerningham took no part in the cooking or household cleaning. Mr Jerningham ran the shop and she stayed in the back, attending to the accounts and ordering the stock. I had begun to see her ball rolling as a sign of fear of some sort, as though she had to let something run before her as a warning of her coming. Or to hit something hiding in the shadows?

We were a class of about twenty and a mixed bunch: some Scottish immigrants, some Irish, some native Toronto, some of unidentifiable mixed race, Indian maybe, with more women than men. The course had started in the autumn; I had come in about halfway through, but I was made welcome. I sat myself next to a large lady, blonde, middle-aged and friendly. She gave me a nudge.

"Anny Bellews. Mrs."

"Dorothea Adam."

"I heard you enrol." Her eyes rested lovingly on the young man on the dais.

Our teacher was Andrew Esson, a graduate of the University of Toronto. He was tall and fair-haired, not good-looking but with a gentle, friendly face.

The class was taking English literature, a chronological survey, and had reached the Romantic poets: Wordsworth, Keats, Byron and Shelley. That first evening, Andrew (he soon became Andrew to me) was reading a sonnet by Keats.

Then the class read it aloud, a line each, on which we must comment. I did my line.

"He likes you," said Mrs Bellews as we handed in our books at the end of the lesson.

I shook my head. "I've only just come."

"He likes your English accent. Your face too, I guess."

"Hush, he'll hear you."

But I think he had already heard her because he flushed. But he was a polite young man. He shook my hand at the door. "We will see you next week, Miss Adam?" As we dispersed I noticed that most of the class paired off into neat couples. There were more ways than one, I thought, in this city, of meeting your pair. Val could take a lesson.

But we weren't a rich group, working people all; I would say our average income was about twenty dollars a week. On the other hand, we were bright. Or some of us were, and might very well be part of the population that would make it rich. They said they would, anyway. They were all lads that spoke of this upward struggle; the girls kept quiet. I thought that was a shame. A woman ought to be able to make it rich too.

Next lesson I took a full part; I was keen to show my willingness to learn. I found our teacher interesting. He was not handsome, but there was an eagerness and gentleness in his face that attracted me. A farm boy who had found his way into a world of learning; I liked him for that.

For the first time, I was attracted by a man's mind. I admired what he said and the way he said it. I can say without vanity that I was a good student.

All that winter the snow fell heavily. I thought that in England the whole country would have seized up, but here, except for a few days when the snow descended in white clouds, life went on as usual.

Val was out more and more. The snow did not deter her, especially as one of her admirers had an automobile which he used when the weather allowed. It had no cover but a kind of leather apron that fitted over himself and his passenger.

Joe did not care for this young man; I could tell from the way he stood, hands in his pocket, inspecting the pair of them as they set off one evening from the stable yard at the back of Jerningham's. He did not spit on the ground as they passed him, but I felt he would have done if he had been that sort of a fellow.

"She shouldn't trust that chap," he said.

"I don't suppose she does."

Joe looked surprised, but he hadn't learnt as much about Val as I had. Not all girls trusted all men, nor wanted to; moreover in Val's case, she liked a hint of danger, the feeling she might get her fingers burnt.

"He's a drinker."

I was off myself to my evening class.

"You can trust your chap," he said.

My turn to be surprised. "I haven't got a chap."

"The teacher. Andrew Esson."

Not my chap, I thought. Well, perhaps he might be one day. "How do you know about him?"

"I checked him out. I make it my business to, you two girls are a pair of innocents."

Not so innocent, I thought.

"You shouldn't have done that, Joe, it's not your business. And he isn't my chap."

He ignored that remark as not believable. "You can trust him because there isn't a lot of red blood in him."

"That's not kind, Joe."

"Have you had a look at his mother?"

"No. Have you?"

"She shops in Jerningham's. Or has done once or twice lately. Tall, thin lady with specs. She looks a second sister to Mrs Jerningham. You were in the shop."

"What do you mean, Joe?"

"As soon as she heard about you, she came to have a look at you. Doesn't that tell you something? It should, you know."

He held the door for me. "I always check when you're back," he said cryptically, "and with you it's well after when the class ends."

It was true, we did stay talking, Andrew and I.

I had made myself a heavy cloak of deep red wool with a hood. As I got my books together and walked out into the night, Andrew said:

"You look like Red Riding Hood."

"I hope there aren't any wolves." I looked apprehensively at the snow. "Or any bears."

He laughed. "It's not the wilderness out there any longer, you know, but good rich farming country."

Once he had lived out beyond Waterloo himself, his father a farmer, but he had come to settle with his mother in the city.

"The snow is sparkling on your hair like diamonds. You should have diamonds."

I didn't blush, the Sunshine Home fairly knocked blushes out of you, but I looked away and smiled. I was pleased, happy beyond anything I had dared to hope for.

As the winter wore on, we got closer. I was invited to tea with his mother, and I did know her face from the shop, as she knew mine, but we said nothing.

They lived in a small low-built house that must have been one of the oldest in Toronto. It was wedged between two much larger and more handsome structures, and sat there firmly, as if it had in mind to keep them apart.

Or perhaps that was something I felt coming towards me from his mother. Not that she was unfriendly. She was gentle and polite and poured tea into delicate cups with a steady hand. But she had a pale, reflective eye.

And she watched me. I was very conscious of her assessing gaze. Was I good enough for her son? Would I do?

At the end of my first visit she must have thought I would, because she kissed me on the cheek and said I must come again.

Not soon, or anything like that, but come.

"She likes you," said Andrew, as he walked me home. "I knew she would. She said what a pretty speaking voice you had."

I went several times to the house in Barley Street after that, to be shown pictures of Andrew as a child, and to be told that he had a great future before him. But, and then came a sigh, but he had his way to make in the world.

I knew what that meant: a way unimpeded by an early marriage to a poor girl. I didn't blame her, I felt the same way myself. But that spring in life that comes to you at a certain time, a certain age, drew me towards Andrew and him towards me.

And so, straight-faced, not saying anything, almost as if it was two other people doing it, we made our little excursions into physical intimacy: a hand held, a cuddle, a soft stroking of the skin.

The spring began, bringing with it a slow thaw. My happy spring.

Mrs Jerningham in her sombre straightness of dress and face remained something of a mystery. Here was a puzzle.

"Have you noticed," said Val idly one day as we arranged the new woollen dress lengths on the shelves, good Yorkshire and Scottish weaves mostly, with a token amount of US weaves, "that Mrs J. is out of a different drawer from old Jerningham?"

It had gradually become apparent to us that Mrs J. was not quite what she seemed, that she was of a different social class from Mr J. One picked up echoes in her speech of a different world. Remote, polite, not unkind, but withdrawn.

I nodded. "Yes. Trust you to notice," I said. Val had a keen eye for class distinctions and social nuances.

"It always pays to know that sort of the thing." She deposited a bale of thick Harris tweed on the shelf with a wallop. "We have our way to make in the world, Dodo, you old pet." She added: "Mrs J. sometimes sounds like Mrs Dorothea, and she was a top notcher if there ever was one."

It was true: Mrs J. had started out life in England and in a pretty upper-class set-up too; however, and by what means, she had ended up in Toronto with Pa Jerningham.

I was beginning to see a pattern in the ball rolling. She did not roll those balls all the time; a nuisance it would have been even for her. No, it was only when the day grew dark.

Was she frightened of the dark?

No, not quite the answer, I sensed. A puzzle at the heart of a mystery.

Val had not only grown in height in the last few months but she had grown in sophistication, with what here in Canada they called smartness. She was smart. Smart of tongue and smart of manner. Later on, she went to a good deal of trouble to lose this air.

Val had made herself a dress of bright emerald green silk, that same green silk I had caught her holding up against herself. She had bought it honestly over the counter, but allowing herself all commercial discounts. Even so . . .

"How could you afford it?"

"It was the end of the roll," said Val, wide-eyed. "A remnant practically. I allowed for that. I aim to trim a hat to go with it." Val had a much better ear than I had and had picked up the nuances of transatlantic speech easily. Probably the better for her. High-hatted Britishers were not welcome.

She looked beautiful and wanton.

"Are you," I swallowed, ". . . a virgin?"

"I don't think I ever was one, Dodo, not in the spirit."

"Yes, but Val . . . not in the spirit."

"In the flesh? Well, I guess so. Just about." And she giggled. "After all, I'm a practical person, Dodo, and girls like us only have one card to play and you can only play it the once."

The unbroken hymen, she was saying, is my wedding passport.

49

But meanwhile she liked to play. She was off that night to play. Her escort, a big bouncy young man called Rex, drove up in his Ford; she stepped in, waved, and was off.

I had work to do for my evening class: an essay on Wordsworth. I liked to shine for Andrew, so I settled down with a copy of the Prelude in front of me. I usually worked at the kitchen table, it was warm and quiet in that room. The Jerninghams were tucked away in their own quarters. I will say this for them: they were not intrusive employers, although you had to watch old man Jerningham.

Joe sat across the table and watched me for a bit. Then he gave a great yawn and went away. "Got to see to the horses." He was up in the morning early always; a yawn was allowed.

After some hours I gathered up my books and made for bed. I never waited for Val; she would not be in for hours, might not come in at all until the dawn. I knew that even if the Jerninghams didn't; she came in through a loose back window. No guesses for who told her about the window, and with a snigger: Kate.

And how did she know about it? I asked myself, and why did she need to use it?

Keep it oiled myself, she'd said. She said it as if she wanted me to know too.

I was on my way to the stairs when I heard the kitchen door bang. It was not locked until much later; Joe did it on his late round through the house. He carried a lot of responsibility lightly; the truth was that although old Jerningham never touched a drop of whisky during shop hours, he was drunk pretty solidly afterwards.

When we left the Sunshine Home, Mrs D. said; "Canada will be an education for you." She had no idea how educational Pa Jerningham was going to be.

The I heard Val come running, stumbling into the room.

"Val! Val, are you all right?"

She was crying, sobbing in little gasps, her face streaked with dirt and blood. The pretty green dress was torn.

"Val, what happened? What did he do?"

I thought it was pretty clear myself, but Val did not answer; she stayed supporting herself against the wall and breathing in gasps as if she couldn't talk.

50

"Accident," she murmured.

"You're hurt." There was a gash on her cheek which was bleeding; she kept dabbing at it with a scrap of handkerchief, bloody and dirty in itself. I drew her to a chair and made her sit down. "You're trembling, poor love."

"The car crashed, ran into a wall. Rex . . ." her voice died away.

"His fault, of course," I said angrily. "Clumsy oaf. Drunk, I suppose."

"He was drunk, but he wasn't driving. I was." The words fell into the room like hard little bullets.

"Oh God." I still dabbed away at her wound. She winced and tried to draw away; I stopped her. "Is he dead?"

"He might be. I ran off . . ." Her voice died away.

"Oh Val."

She was trembling and crying. She hung on to me as I tried to draw away.

"Don't leave me, Dodo."

I put her away from me gently. "I'm only going to get Mrs Jerningham's first-aid box."

"Don't tell her, don't let her come."

"I won't, Val." Not my intention, I thought. Better that neither of the Jerninghams knew anything of the episode. A lot of life in the shop was kept from them, this was just one more little item.

At the door, I turned back. "No one followed you here, did they?"

"No. No one saw. But I didn't look back. I ran."

We didn't want the police visiting. I hoped Rex was not dead, but I barely thought about him, in my confusion and anxiety about Val.

I closed the kitchen door and made my way upstairs. Few lamps were lit but I was used to the darkness on the stairs and landing. I knew Mrs Jerningham kept the box of medicines and bandages on a shelf in the room laid out as her bathroom. Beyond it, through a communication door lay the bedroom, but the Jerninghams were bound to be asleep.

I went to the bathroom door and pushed it open very quietly.

51

To my surprise light streamed through the open door to the bedroom.

I withdrew a step back into the darkness, wondering what to do.

Then I heard a noise, a gasp, a moan, followed by a loud cry. Mrs Jerningham's voice?

But I had never heard that note in it.

I crept forward.

I saw Kate first. She was on the bed, stripped naked, her head thrown back, astride Mrs Jerningham. It was Mrs Jerningham who cried out. As I looked they leapt and rolled together. Up and down, over and over.

I realised I was watching Kate and Mrs Jerningham in sexual congress.

Kate's head turned and she saw me. A flash of triumphant recognition came into her eyes, and she laughed, as she turned back to her victim.

But the victim cried out in exultation.

She didn't see me. Her eyes were closed.

I drew back into the bathroom, turning away from the active, moving bodies.

As Kate sank down upon Mrs Jerningham, I saw that there was another body in the bed, the sleeping, snoring, drunken form of Mr Jerningham. They were there in the bed with him and neither of them cared.

Somehow, this shocked me beyond anything else.

When I got back to Val, I found Joe there.

"You've been long enough."

He was dealing with Val's wound; he didn't look at me, so he didn't see the state I must be in.

"I was getting the box of medicines."

"I've got enough stuff here."

"Oh, that hurts," cried Val. "What is it?"

"I keep it for the horses," said Joe, working away.

I started to laugh. Val had been in a bad accident, she might have killed someone, and now she was being treated with a mixture for the horses, and I had seen the unmentionable.

One way and another we were both in shock, I suppose, but

I got Val to bed. As I tucked her in, she said: "Dodo, there's something else. I forgot with all this, but I meant to tell you . . . That man was there tonight."

"What man?"

"The one who followed us. The one you didn't like at the circus."

The one Joe hit. I remembered him, of course, but didn't feel like talking about him tonight.

"Don't you ever think about anything but men?" I said crossly.

Val ignored this. "And he had another man with him. They were both watching me."

"Oh come on, Val."

"I swear it, Dodo."

"You're very watchable, Val."

"But it wasn't because they liked me. I can always tell. No, they were watching. Just watching."

Having delivered herself of this, she turned over and went to sleep. I always envied this power of Val's to forget today and wait for tomorrow, but it was one I could not share.

The next day I went down to see Joe. He was tidying up the kitchen, putting away the bloodied towels and packing the disinfectants into his box of horse medicines. He was good with horses and people, was Joe.

"What's going to happen, Joe?"

"If I know Val, she'll get away with it."

I considered. It did seem likely that her swain might say nothing about her. People did protect Val; I did so myself.

"What about the Jerninghams?"

Joe gave me a long look. "Do you think they'll know anything about it?"

"No, I guess not."

"There you are then."

"What about Kate?"

A look full of knowledge passed between us. He's known all the time, I thought.

"Kate don't talk."

"No," I said thoughtfully.

"Saw something, did you?"

53

"Just tonight . . . while I was looking for the disinfectant to help Val."

"Shock you, did it? Seen it myself once or twice. They don't care, those two. Leastways, Kate don't, treats it as a joke, and I think Mrs J. kind of forgets. Wipes it out, you might say."

"But Mr Jerningham . . ." I said.

"Ah well," said Joe tolerantly. "Who knows what goes on between married people."

Joe was right of course. Val did get away with it and Kate said nothing. Val's lover was too frightened of his father to admit that he had her in the car or had even been meeting her. He took all the blame. You could call it the act of a gentleman or a coward, depending how you looked at it.

He and Val did not meet again. His father sent him to New York to study business there, and that was that. He neither wrote nor came to see her to say goodbye. Val cried a little but not too much. "My pride is hurt," she said honestly. "I would like him to have been heartbroken, or anyway pretend he was. But I've learnt something." She didn't say what, but Joe said it must be only to go for sons who had their own money and no fathers and from what I knew later of Val this may have been so.

I worked alone in the shop with Kate the next day while Val limped around in the back premises, hiding herself. It was a normal kind of day. But I did fancy I saw the shadow of that triumphant smile in the depths of Kate's eyes.

That is, the day was normal until closing time, when a man came into the shop. Not many male customers came into Jerninghams, although sometimes a husband came with his wife, but such men seemed ill at ease even then, when so chaperoned, and usually strolled outside, saying they would get a smoke.

This man, a tall, lean, black-suited fellow with narrow gold spectacles on his nose came in and stayed in. I was serving a customer who was being pernickety about a length of black braid. You and I may think braid is braid and black is black, but not so with her. I had to get out all the varieties of braid we had, silk, silk and cotton, silk and wool, pure wool, this width and that width, even search for shades of black and still she was not satisfied. She left without buying an inch.

I had thought Kate might have served him, but she was lounging at the back of the shop exchanging jokes with Joe. As I glared at her, she told me in a sibilant whisper that she had tried to serve him but he was 'waiting for me'.

So I went over. "Can I help you, sir?"

It was the right thing to say and I had learnt to say it, but what I really wanted to say was "You are a queer one, sir."

He sat down on the chair and asked to see some violet ribbon. Why violet, I thought, but I got the roll. "Silk, sir? We have but this one in silk, there's not much call for it this season." This was not true at all, I was just talking for the sake of talking.

"Violet's a pretty colour, isn't it?" He was fingering the silk. "And a pretty name."

The name meant Dr Violet to me, so I both loved it and feared it. I had been a Violet Adventurer, but that was in the days of Charley and where was she now?

"I'm purchasing this for my daughter." He looked up at me. Although I wasn't disposed to like him, he had a kind voice, and an honest one. I believed in the daughter. "Will she like this, do you think?"

"It depends what she wants it for." It was a dark, deep violet; I hoped she wasn't in mourning.

"I think she might get the gown to go with the ribbon," he said thoughtfully. "I will take six yards."

That was quite a big order of ribbon and took some measuring out; he watched me while I did it. I kept my eyes down but my hands trembled a little; I wondered what was coming.

"Miss Dorothea, isn't it?" he enquired.

"Yes, how do you know my name?"

"Oh, I heard you called so by one of your fellow workers." And he looked towards Kate. But I did not believe she had named me. Or had any reason to do so, except that for the right sum of money Kate would have called me the Pope himself. And for Protestant Kate, he was very nearly the Antichrist himself.

"Well, Miss Dorothea, I'll take that ribbon, I believe, if you will just wrap it up for me."

I did so silently, not wanting to prolong the matter. But he still sat there, solidly, quietly in the chair.

"Not been in this country long, Miss Dorothea?"

"Not so very long." He hadn't been there long himself, I thought; he did not speak like a Canadian.

"A fine country."

I did not answer, just nodded and smiled. Somehow I did not want to talk to him; he was too curious, prodding at me, as if there was something about me he wanted to find out.

I watched him leave the shop; he walked a little distance, then turned round to look back.

I drew away from the door. He looked kinder than that other man – he who had first accosted me – but I liked him less. I began not to believe in his daughter. Or if she existed she probably had a bad time with him. He looked like a man who would give a woman, a girl, a bad time. Sleek and sick, I thought.

Or did I think that afterwards when I knew more? Oh much more. About him and his master. For he had a master; a paymaster.

I thought this man had gone, but when we closed up the shop for the night I saw him standing there on the street corner.

Joe drew together the heavy shutters. "Is that man bothering you? I'll teach him the way to go home."

"He's gone now."

"He's been hanging about."

"Has he?" I was surprised.

"Seen him."

Joe was watchful and alert, I knew that already, and ever pugnacious.

"Don't walk down any dark streets."

"I won't. Thank you, Joe."

He grunted; he didn't like to be thanked, and got on with the job.

I went to the shop door and took a discreet look: the man who had bought the ribbon was in a doorway talking to a dark figure. This man moved his head, the light fell on his face, and I recognised the man from the circus. He saw me, stared at me, while the other man looked away. I drew back into the shelter of the shop, closing the door behind. My hand trembled a little, but I controlled it.

I didn't like the two men. I called them Eyes, he with the spectacles, and No Eyes. When they were together one of them would look at you and the other would not. You know how it is with some people. The one who had come into the shop that night was Eyes. Now I liked him even less than the other.

But it was No Eyes who caught me. And it was not night, nor down any dark street. Terror in daylight is worse than in the dark. You can see everything that is happening to you, feel it the more sharply, dread the consequences all the more.

There was an alley at the back of the store where the rubbish was deposited in bins. We took turns, although to be fair Joe usually did the task, but that night he was out on a delivery and there was so little to move that I did it myself. Val got out of it when she could, which was mostly; she said could not stand the smell of the bins.

It was raining now. I put my head down as I ran to the bin, and he had me round the neck and waist, dragging me backwards before I could scream.

He must have been waiting and watching at the back, perhaps for days.

I did call out, but he had a rag ready which he thrust in my mouth. Gagging and choking, I was pulled into a covered cart. He got in with me and the driver started up.

"Don't worry, dear," said a mocking voice in my ear. "I told him you were my beloved wife who had run away from your lawful husband and bed . . . Don't try and cry out; he's deaf, and drunk anyway. Only the horse would hear and he doesn't care. Seen it all before, I dare say."

There was a dreadful snigger in his voice. I tried to kick and struggle, but a sickly sweet cloth was pressed against my face, and I sank back into a spinning darkness.

My head was throbbing, and I felt sick. I retched and opened my eyes. I was lying on an unmade bed with the dirty sheets covering my legs. I looked down at myself. I was naked.

In the corner of the room, sitting astride a chair, was No Eyes, my abductor.

"Well, you won't run away, will you?" he said. He was smoking a cigarette and sipping at a drink.

I drew the sheet up over me. I felt ill.

"Where are my clothes?"

He shrugged. "You got them in a fine mess, you did, sick and worse all over them. The kind landlady here'as taken them away to wash – or burn, as seemed best. I left it to her."

Again he gave that snigger that I remembered.

I stared at him, trying, to think, to settle my mind.

"The landlady . . ." I began.

"Oh don't worry yourself. She thinks you're my poor drunken wife and what a good husband I am to bring you back in the state you were in."

He came over and sat on the bed.

"And your husband I will be. You can marry me. Then I shall be your legally married husband."

"No. Never, never!"

"Or you can have what you might not like as much. It's all one to me. I will have you one way or another." He took his jacket off. "It's in the contract."

The room was darkened by drawn curtains, but they were of thin, cheap material and I could see light through them. Not daylight, but the yellow glow a street lamp.

So we were not in the country, but still in the city. Probably I had not been unconscious for very long. I tried to listen; I could hear the sound of traffic, wheels rattling over cobblestones.

Not a smart, macadamized road then, but it wouldn't be, a house in side street; yet a street where people came and went.

I was not alone in the world with this man. Out there were ordinary people.

This was a nightmare, and I didn't know why I was in it. What did he mean by 'contract'? But you don't have to stay in a nightmare, and I did not intend to do so.

There was a knock on the door. He scowled, but went over and opened it.

I could hear the mutter of voices. A woman. The landlady, I supposed. I could get up and try to talk to her. Another woman. She might help me.

But then No Eye, went through the door and banged it behind him. I heard the key turn.

For the time being; I was alone. I got up at once, draped the sheet round me and looked out of the window. I could see down to the street below but I was three stories up, too far to jump. I could scream though, someone below would hear. I shook the window, but it was jammed and would not open.

I could pick up his voice outside; I would not be alone long. I looked round the room. No exit, nowhere to hide. There was a cupboard which I opened. Inside I could see my dress and boots. So he had been lying.

On a table by the door was a bottle of whisky and a glass. I filled the glass. Let him be drunk; the more drunk and stupid the better.

The door handle started to turn. I grabbed my dress and put it under the pillow. It smelt clean and fresh and that gave me courage. I slid under the bed clothes and drew the sheet up over my head.

I could hear him stumbling around the room; he hit something hard and swore. There was a clink of a glass; he was drinking the whisky.

My head ached, my mouth was dry; I still felt sick, but I was one of the wild girls from the Sunshine Home. We knew a thing or two.

Thank God for Charley. Her mother having been raped, she had made it her duty to set about learning techniques of self protection which she had passed on to us.

Besides, I hated this man. It would be a pleasure.

He was a large man, large everywhere. I could see the hairs on his body, smell the sweat and the whisky.

He pulled at the sheet and got onto the bed. "Come on now."

I was not experienced, except perhaps in words and gossip, but a kind of animal instinct informed me; I knew at that moment he did not really want me.

There was no passion, no earnest overpowering desire. It just was not there. He had no strong feelings about me, one way or another. It may be that he did not even like women.

I did not understand.

"I shall scream," I said. "Don't be a fool."

You have to give even a fool a chance, although this was not what Charley advised.

I looked at him and laughed. It cost something that laugh, I was never going to be the same girl again. "Anyway, you can't. You're not ready. You need help."

And I sat up, crouching. Then I moved forward, down the bed. His eyes rolled upwards. "Well, you little slut . . ."

I leant forward. I don't know what he thought I was going to do. Well, yes, I do.

I opened my mouth and bit. Hard.

He screamed. As he rolled over, thrashing in the bed in pain and agony, I trusted, I grabbed my clothes.

Teeth and nails, Charley had said, and low cunning. Be an animal. I had been an animal. I was out of the room, with the door behind me, and locked, before he had stopped shouting.

I stood at the head of the stairs and took a deep breath. He was roaring inside the room, and the sound of voices could be heard from below.

Chapter Three

I stood with my back against the door of Jerningham's and took a deep breath. I was here. I was safe.

The back door of Jerningham's was strong and heavy; I had turned the key. I guessed Joe, not knowing where I was, had deliberately left it unlocked for me. He must be wondering where I was. Val too, for that matter, although her interest was a bit more unpredictable.

But I didn't care. Bliss to be alone. I wanted to be solitary to wash and become myself again.

I stood still and listened. The house was quiet and dark. No one was about; I could creep through, up the back stairs and to bed. In the distance a clock chimed eleven times. I had been gone about four hours. It felt like a lifetime.

No, not quite alone. There was a light and the sound of footsteps. Joe, I thought, he would come to look, check if I was all right.

But the footsteps shuffled. Stopped and then started again. Came closer.

It was Mr Jerningham himself. No sign of her. No rolling ball, no stern-faced figure.

He stood at the bottom of the stairs and looked at me. He was wearing a loose dressing-gown with a towel hanging over his arm, his feet were bare. He had obviously just taken a bath.

"What are you doing?"

I fumbled for what to say. Some instinct told me not to tell the truth. "I've been . . . out."

"I can see that. And you are late back. After hours, miss. I should punish you for that."

I didn't take that too seriously.

He took a step forward, and got a closer look at me.

61

"What are you wearing? What is that you have on?"

I had grabbed a dark woollen cloak from a peg in the hall as I fled from that house in Panmere Street. "I had an accident. So I borrowed a robe."

He looked down at my feet which were bare, like his.

"I fell into some water."

It was a lame excuse which I did not expect to be accepted without question. But he said nothing. Only studied me. Although he was looking at me, he seemed to be looking through me and beyond me. But he had heard what I said.

"Water? You got wet through. You need a drink. Come with me."

He turned round and led me into the sitting room, the private room where we had no admittance. I followed, docile and exhausted. He was my employer after all. He had authority of a sort. The room was dimly lit by one shaded lamp in the corner, but there was a fire.

On the table was a whisky bottle.

Well, we all knew by then that the Jerninghams drank. Both of them. Separately and together.

He poured a draught into a tumbler and handed it to me. "Drink up." He took another for himself.

"I don't think I want . . ."

He pushed the glass at me, so I took a sip. As he did so, his robe fell open, and I saw he was naked underneath.

It came to me then that Mr Jerningham was very drunk indeed and not himself.

He put his hand on the cloak that covered me. "Where did you get this terrible garment?" Close to, his eyes were large and troubled. I could smell his breath, whisky laden.

"Panmere Street . . . the house there."

"Panmere Street? And where's that?"

"Back of Viaduct Street . . . I knew it when I saw it."

"That's a strange thing to say."

I knew how it sounded; the whisky was muddling me and yet it was the truth. As I had come out of that house, I had recognised the street.

His hand moved across the cloak, then down it, tracing my body underneath.

"Oh, Mr Jerningham . . ."

When you have been through what I had been through, you come to a point when there is nothing left inside to fight with. You are empty, clean out of energy. You become passive, subdued . . .

I knew what he was about and was powerless to resist. I had used up all the resistance I had, my strength was draining away. Safe? I had thought myself safe, but instead here I was pushing Mr Jerningham off me.

He was heavy, soft and heavy and hot.

Somehow I had got thrust down across the table and he was lying on me. I tried to shove him off.

His face was almost on mine. I could smell the whisky again, smell the soap he had washed with, see that he had shaved, his skin fine and smooth, but darkly mottled.

There were tears in his eyes; he was crying.

He was pushing himself against me, into me, and tears were rolling down his face . . .

That other man, No Eyes, had not wanted me but had meant to take me. Mr Jerningham did want me, most urgently as he kept muttering, but wished he could stop.

Damn you, Mr Jerningham.

Then suddenly, he was screaming with pain and being dragged off me.

"Joe!"

Joe's face was hardly recognisable, he was so red and angry, his brows meeting across his forehead. He had Mr Jerningham by the hair and the throat. Jerningham staggered backwards and Joe hit him on the chin, a hard, full punch, which toppled him to the floor, unconscious.

Joe prepared to do it again. I gripped his arm.

"No, Joe, you'll kill him."

"Not he," said Joe with contempt. "He'll live. Old swine. I was asleep or I'd have been down here before. I was waiting on the upper landing to see you got in safe but I dropped off."

He looked at me, taking in my appearance. He put his arm round my shoulders and looked into my face. "The look of you! What did he do, the old devil?"

I hesitated. "Not so very much. You came in . . . before . . ."

"All right, don't go on." His voice was soft. "There's a lot to say, isn't there?"

"I'll tell you in the morning, now all I want is to have a wash and go to bed."

"You need a bath."

"No, not a bath." I shuddered, thinking of Mr Jerningham. "I'll make do with a wash."

From the floor came a groan.

"What shall we do with him?"

"Leave him. Come on, up the stairs with you or we shall have the old lady coming down."

I was suddenly desperately tired as we went up the staircase. I could see where Joe had sat, waiting for me, a newspaper and a mug of beer littering the floor.

"Where's Val?"

"Asleep," he said.

I kissed his cheek. "Thanks, Joe, we'll talk in the morning."

Val was asleep. Washed and clean, I slid into bed, and as I did so, she stirred.

"Where have you been?" she asked dreamily.

"Tell you in the morning."

I seemed to be saying that to everyone.

The next day, to my surprise, there was no sight of Mr Jerningham; he did not appear and nothing was said. I took my place in the shop, undecided what to do.

I couldn't stay in this house; I would tell Andrew Esson and he would take me out of it. He would suggest we get married straight away and I would agree.

But Joe and I talked, and Val listened. I saw the anger in Joe's face. Val gripped my hand. "Darling, dearest," she said. "In one night, all of that, you poor thing."

Joe said: "You must go to the police."

"No." I shook my head. "I'm not going to do that. I don't know that they'd believe me, and in the end, I hurt him more than he hurt me. Physically anyway. It was degrading and horrible and of course, in its way, the cause for what came after with poor drunken old Jerningham."

"All the same, I think you should . . . I've a friend in the police, a good guy. I'll talk to him."

"That man – No Eyes, that one. He was so strange . . ."

"I could kill him."

"That man," I went on. "He didn't want me, I could tell." Scraps of things he had said came back into my mind. "He said this would be as good as wedding me, and better than killing me. He didn't care one way or another. I don't understand, Joe."

"Killing you?" said Val, "No one would kill you." She put her arms round me.

"He wanted to do that thing, and yet he did not want to do that thing. I can't explain it but I knew." I stared at Joe, who shook his head. He must have thought I was imagining that part, but I knew I was not.

There was no need to avoid Mr Jerningham because he did not appear in the shop that day. Mrs Jerningham was seen at the end of the corridor, but she turned away.

Val and I would be better out of this place, and soon. I longed to tell my love and get us both rescued.

At the end of the day, lo and behold, Mr Jerningham, wearing his overcoat and top hat, slid into the shop through the front plate glass doors as if he was a customer. Without saying anything and without meeting my eyes, he placed a small, brown paper packet on the counter in front of me.

Val peered over my shoulder. "Open it."

I pushed the packet away. "I don't want to touch it."

"I will then." She was already tearing at the wrapping. "Anyway, you have touched it . . . Old Jerningham had a great blue bruise on his chin," she said gleefully.

Inside the wrapping was a brown leather box; Val opened it. Inside was a beautiful gold watch. She drew in her breath. "My goodness."

"I could throw it at him." I reached out. "No, I'll put it in the furnace and let him smell it burning."

"Don't be a fool." Val's hand went out for the watch. "It's beautiful, heavy too. Who'd have thought the old man has such taste. Or was generous."

"Generous? He's a horror."

"All the more reason to keep the watch."

"Give it to me." I stood up. "I'm going to burn it now."

Val shrugged. "Have it your own way." She was packing up the watch. "Here you are. Ask Joe and he will think you mad."

"No, he won't."

I went down the backstairs to the lower basement where the big furnace roared away. I lifted up the heavy iron lid and threw the package in. Then I stood there watching it burn.

The fire roared but there was no warmth here for me. We must leave this horrible and frozen house.

This house in which no one said the things that had to be said.

Next day the classes began again, the day I had been waiting for, when my life could start over, and I should see Andrew. I had had several letters from him in the vacation, welcome letters but not saying much. He was not a man to put his heart into what he wrote.

Once I had told him, purged myself of the hard stone of the story, then I would be free. I knew it. He would take the burden on his shoulders for me. That was what love was.

The class was crowded, everyone had turned up after the break, lots of familiar faces, all pleased to see me.

We were doing a long poem by William Wordsworth. I longed for the session to end, but it seemed to go on for ever.

But eventually it was over. "You'll come back and have a meal with mother? Then I will see you home."

It was just within walking distance, there and back. I wanted to hold back but I found myself pouring my story in great gulps. I needed absolution and I needed it quickly.

My love's pace slowed. His arm dropped away from mine.

"You mean, he actually . . . that he . . ." He did not go on; could not find the words, I suppose.

Hastily, I reassured him.

"Not everything. Not all that could happen, just a beginning." Did he know what I meant, did he understand me?

Suddenly I realised that he had not had the benefit of an education at the Sunshine Home. But he must be aware . . . I said nothing else for a bit, waiting for him to speak.

He did not.

"I am so glad," he said, in a dull voice. Where was the outpouring of love that I was looking for?

He took my arm again and began to urge me to walk faster. "We must talk."

Of course, I thought, we must.

His mother was waiting for us at the window, looking out through the lace curtains, as she so often was. She never came to the door, but waited for us, upright and calm in her living room. In the middle of a square of carpet the tea table was laid. Her parents had been Scots, from Aberdeen; tea was taken seriously here.

The table was set with fine china and old silver, which I now believe must have come from Scotland and been antique and valuable. Not that there was much money in this house, the Essons were not rich, but things were cared for; they valued their possessions.

"I'll just take my books upstairs." He looked at his mother.

"I'll go and infuse the tea," she said.

I offered to help, but my help was refused, so I sat there waiting.

The room was cold, the fire being low and sparse, but the brass fireguard sparkled with polish. Over the fireplace was an oil painting of a sober-faced man. Andrew's dead father, I supposed. It was a gentle face, but stern. Not much joking there, I thought.

I waited, but his mother came in first.

Andrew never came back. He, I never saw again.

Not in the flesh; in my dreams, he walked for a long while.

"This is a bad thing that happened to you, Miss Dorothea," she said. She spoke kindly, gently. "But you understand that there can be no more friendship between you and my son."

Friendship, I thought, was it only friendship?

"His position must be protected above all else. His wife must be . . ." For the first time that inflexible voice faltered. "His wife must not have known another man."

Known in the biblical sense, she meant. Not have had a criminal conversation with one, as the London police would have said.

"But I wasn't . . . it didn't . . ." I tried to speak. I couldn't.

"It must seem hard, but I am doing what a mother must do." She bowed her head, as if expecting my assent. "You will see that yourself when you think about it."

Then she rang the little silver bell that called the one servant they kept.

"I will send for a cab and you shall go home in it."

"I want to see Andrew." I rang to the door and began to call him.

"He won't come, my dear, I have sent him away. It is best."

"And he went?" said Val, incredulous, when I told her later.

"I don't know. I never saw him. He never came. I ran away. I didn't wait for that bloody cab."

I could still remember the look on Mrs Esson's face as I had sworn. If I ever have a son, I had said, I hope I love him less and charity more.

"I don't believe she told the truth," said Val. "I expect he was still there, Not knowing."

"No." I shook my head. "I think he did. He could have come after me. It's over."

A frozen, silent house and shop.

Of all people, it was Mrs Jerningham who spoke to me of the real things and began the healing.

I did not know what to make of her then, and all these years after I still do not know, but I believe she was honest, and what she said blew my mind wide open. There was a world with views and beliefs that I knew nothing of.

She stood before me, tall and spare and dark, that eternal ball twisting in her hands.

"Come into my sitting room, if you please, Miss Dorothea."

I looked at her warily. My trust in the Jerninghams was not great.

"Don't be afraid."

I took one step towards their living room, I suppose I had been into it once or twice before that other time.

"No, not that room. My own private sanctum."

Into that room I had never been.

She strode before me, head up. I had to remember that she did not know I had seen her and Kate together.

It was a small room and dark, with the darkness that seemed to go with the Jerninghams, but the furniture was good.

She turned and faced me.

"You have been and still are unhappy. You have been and still are being badly treated."

I said nothing.

"You think I did not know? Have not a heart inside me to notice?"

It had not been immediately obvious, I thought.

"I know what there is to know; I have made it my business to know. We are both women in a men's world."

Suddenly, she sat down at the table, always upright, always rigid, hands still tight around that ball.

"This is not easy. You are not helping me."

I found my voice at last. "I'm not trying to be helpful."

She had left the door to her room open, and in the looking glass above the fire (which was dull, not even fires leapt with flames in the Jerningham house) I saw a reflection of Mr Jerningham passing down the corridor; he did not acknowledge us.

She saw him too, but her expression did not change.

"You are staring at me. Please, sit down, on that chair there if you will, and do not stare." She was polite; I had already noticed that in her weird way, Mrs Jerningham was both well-mannered and well-educated. She was a lady, while Mr Jerningham was most emphatically, not a gentleman.

"I saw you and Kate," I said suddenly and loudly, no one more surprised than me. "I saw you and Kate together."

"I know that. Kate told me. Kate saw you."

Kate would, I thought. And she probably laughed.

"You were shocked."

I chose my words carefully. "It was unexpected." After our experiences at the Sunshine Home, I was neither surprised nor shocked.

"I am not as other women."

No, I thought, but not as unusual as you seem to think.

She raised her head proudly. "I am of a different sort. I am an Urning."

69

She spoke in a precise, ladylike voice, but if she had said she was an ancient Roman, I would have understood it as much.

"Mr Jerningham knows, has always known, married me knowing it; but it is hard on him, that is what you must understand."

She is asking me to excuse him, I thought, excuse and forgive. I was angry and stood up.

"Please." She took hold of my hand. "I am one of those on whom the light of Uranus has shone, we are not earth people."

For the first time, I saw a soft, gentle, pleading look in those eyes, which had seemed so opaque and blind. There was love there.

Not love for me, she had Kate for that, perhaps really loved that fierce wild lady, but a generalised love.

They must be nice people these Urnings, I thought.

An Urning; the first time I had heard that term. For Eleanor Jerningham there was a history to it.

"Did you always know it?" I asked.

No, she had not always known it. She had had a teacher, a man called Edward Carpenter, and this teacher had told her. He had recognised her for what she was.

Nelly Probart had been born into a comfortably-off, upper-class family. She been educated at a well-known college for girls in London, and afterwards, because she was of a scholarly turn of mind, she took classes with a series of tutors.

It was one of these tutors who introduced her to the Urnings; he was one himself. Well, he was everything, he was a man whose sexual activities ranged wide and free.

The term Urning did not mean that they had come from Uranus or some such place (he had come from Peckham and she had been born in Kensington), but that their sensibilities were different. On them the light of Uranus had shone.

There were many Urnings, he told her. He introduced her to a few.

It seemed that there was more than one way for young females to meet with injustice and oppression, and while I had been encountering one way, she in her time, had met with another. If you were rich or poor it did not matter.

Nelly Probart's father was a man who ruled his family. Behind the comfortable façade of the house in Kensington were cruelty and intolerance. In the heart of this Victorian family there was worse.

Nelly Jerningham did not do more than lower her eyes and hint, but she said enough to let me know how and why she feared her father.

With a shudder, she said it explained her ball rolling, "Because I never knew what was behind an open door. A silly habit I should now get rid of, but it is built into me. He might be there, ready to spring out at me."

Throwing herself into her studies, accepting the doctrine of those different souls who were Urnings, she had tried to shape her own life. There had been a lover, a predecessor of Katie.

She had tried to keep it secret, but one of her siblings had given her away. Her father, his respectability assaulted, had offered her a choice: "Give up these ways and marry the man I choose for you or I will see that you are put in an asylum; you are clearly mad."

Unbelievably, she had been put away.

"My life there was hard," she said. "Locked in, alone, fed on pap. It was to reduce the madness – the doctors, too, thought I was mad. It was their profession to find me mad."

She was two months in the asylum before she agreed to his terms. Marriage it should be, only then did she find that Mr Jerningham was her chosen spouse, who was waiting to take her back to Canada.

For him, there was the money that came with her, allowing the expansion of the shop that I had observed for myself, for him, too, there was a marriage that would never be more than fiction.

"I refused sexual union, and he knew I would refuse; it is part of the contract . . . but he finds it hard, harder than he thought. And so he drinks, and . . ." she shrugged.

I gathered I was not the first episode of that kind, but perhaps the first so near home and so likely to cause trouble.

"I hated him at first, but I have come to pity him. "I wondered what her pity was like. Pretty iron stuff, I concluded.

"Why have told me all this?"

71

"Because I think you might be one of us." And she stretched out a hand and took my own.

Either Mr Jerningham or Mrs Eleanor, I thought, I would certainly have to leave this house.

I withdrew my hand. "No."

She said thoughtfully: "Kate would do what she could." I gave her a startled look. "But unluckily he does not take to her . . . However, it may come to that in the end."

Not so unlike her father, I thought.

When I got back to our room I counted my money; I had some savings. I would have to leave, and I debated what to say to Val. I thought she might come with me, but I wasn't counting on it. She had been very bright-eyed and merry lately, and in my experience of her this meant masculine attentions coming from somewhere.

And then there was Joe. Jerningham's represented his only home, it wouldn't be fair to ask him to leave it. On the other hand, although Mr Jerningham had been quiet about the blow Joe had given him, it was only to be expected he would exact a price sooner or later.

I was adding up what I had to my name when Val came back. "What are you doing?" She looked excited, remarkably pretty.

"Working out what I have, I'm thinking of making a move."

"Are you?" She wasn't attending, but taking off her hat and staring at her face in the looking glass. "I tell you, Dodo, I have met such a nice man . . ."

I put my money away and started to undress. Val turned away; she had the slightest little bit of prudishness about her. "Have you ever heard of the Urnings?"

"No, never." She was still thinking about her new man. "Sounds as if they come from Asia or somewhere like that."

"No, I believe the planet Uranus shines on them."

"Shouldn't like to meet one in the dark . . . If they exist, that is."

"They exist all right."

But she wasn't listening; Val's mind was elsewhere. "He is everything a man ought to be."

"He's rich, I suppose."

She heard that. "What a rotten thought."

"I have lots of rotten thoughts."

She heard that too. "This isn't like you, Dodo; I'm the wicked one, you're the good one." Then she remembered something else she had heard. "Going, Val? Where will you go?"

"I don't know yet. I'll ask Joe, he knows a lot of people, he'll suggest a place. I'll get a room somewhere. Then I'll get a job in a shop, I know how to sell, that's something I've learnt. I'm good at it, I think."

"The Jerninghams won't be pleased."

"To hell with the Jerninghams."

"Yes," said Val thoughtfully. "It might come to that with them." She met my eyes and we both laughed. Not much mirth, but we laughed.

"Will you come?"

She went to the window and adjusted the curtain. For a moment she stood there looking out. "Yes, I might. Let's talk about it in the morning."

A little bit later, she said quietly: "Maybe you are right to move on, Dodo. I saw that man . . . you know the one, I mean – No Eyes. I saw him hanging around tonight. No, it's all right, Dodo, dear . . . He's gone now. Still, we ought to talk to Joe."

But we did not have to talk to Joe, life overtook us. In the night, I awoke, coughing.

I sat up. There was smoke coming under the door and up through cracks in the floor.

Fire.

"Val!" She was sleeping deeply, so I shook her by the shoulder. "Wake up, Val."

She was so difficult to arouse that I wondered if she had been drinking the night before. I had just begun to notice that she liked to drink. Gin, whisky or wine, she liked them all.

I started to drag her out of the bed. Then she did open her eyes and said, indignantly: "What are you doing, Dodo?"

I didn't bother to answer, but dragged a coat over my nightclothes and threw her coat to her. "Come on, and put on shoes."

She was awake now and had smelt the fire too. "Dodo," she

73

was saying in a frightened voice as she scrambled herself out of bed.

I opened the door and crack, then closed it quickly.

Outside was heat and light, a red, glowing light. Outside was noise – the crackle and hiss as the fire spoke through the house.

"We can't go that way. I think the stairs are alight."

Val gave a little scream and clung to me. For a moment we stood together. Then Val rallied. Val was brave, I would never deny that. Physical courage she has always had.

She went to the window and looked out. "No chance, we are too high up."

She took a towel and threw the jug of water from the washstand all over it. "Put that over your head, and we'll try."

"What about you?" I couldn't see her through the towel.

"Same for me, I've got one too." Her voice was muffled. "Lift it up a bit, Dodo, you need to see a bit. But don't breathe too deeply."

No chance of that, the smoke outside the door was joking.

No, not joking. Choking.

I was already confused, dizzy.

Val supported me with her arm. "Steady, Dodo."

Her voice sounded far away. I tried not to breathe in any more smoke.

Together we advanced to the top of the staircase and looked down. Smoke was billowing up, but we could see to the bend and the treads were not burning.

"Let's go down." Val continued to keep her arm round me, holding me against her. Together we went down the dozen steps. The wood was hot beneath our feet; it was hard to walk with that burning coming through our slippers to our soles and toes. I could smell the singeing leather on my slippers.

One step down, then another, and then a third. Then suddenly we ran into a wall of heat.

We cowered against it, breath was hard to come and scorching hot as it seared our throats and lungs. No breath. A dizziness and then a blackness.

I was falling, and Val? Where was Val?

Then I was being half carried, half dragged down the stairs.

74

I knew who it was, it was Joe. I knew him by the feel of his arm, by the roughness of his thick jerkin, by the clean, sharp smell of the sawdust, and animals among whom he worked.

"Val?" I gasped out. But she was there, he had his other arm round her, and then I was dumped on the cold, wet surface of the yard outside with Val leaning against me and the fire engine's bells ringing as the horses galloped in.

"Joe?" He wasn't there.

A hoarse voice behind me – it was Kate Rouster's – said: "It's the guvnor, he ain't out, and the missus, we don't see 'em. Joe's gone to find 'em."

Joe. I sank down onto the hard, damp stones. Don't let him die. Darling, darling Joe. I had felt his strength, his warmth, his love.

Joe did not die, nor, for that matter did the Jerninghams. They all struggled out together, smoke-stained and dishevelled. The Jerninghams had been found huddled on the backstairs, fairly paralytic with fear and drink. They'd live.

We were all of us housed next door with a kind old neighbour while we worked to get the shop and house in use again. The shop itself was not badly burned, although all the stock was useless, but the living quarters had suffered great damage – it looked as though the fire had shot up the stairs. The Fire Chief said in his view it had been started deliberately, with kerosene, and did we have any enemies?

I thought of the man that Val had seen hanging around.

But the sense I had had of life breaking up was real enough. Within a few days two men appeared. One was Eyes, the buyer of the ribbons, and the other, a well-dressed man who came with him and to whom Mr Jerningham was most humble.

It was a surprise to him that it was Val and me that they came to see.

Eyes introduced himself; he was William Vernon from London, a detective who had been entrusted with a search which was now over. The other man was Frank Connor, an eminent Toronto lawyer, who would prove his credentials.

It seemed that there was a wealthy lady in London who had decided, after a long search and on the basis of the work of

William Vernon, that one of us was her lost grandchild. One of us two it must be, but since it could not be decided which of us, we were both to go to London and live with her. Then she would make up her mind.

Vernon was pleased with himself. It had been a long search, he said, at one time deemed hopeless, but pushed to success with the help of a former nurse at the Sunshine Home who remembered us being born.

And so we were to go to London, one of us to be an heiress, both of us to be educated. Finished, that was the word.

Thus Honoria Madden came into our lives.

Events whirled about us; we were to be moved and we seemed to have no choice.

Val was delighted, the Jerninghams stunned but obedient to the change of events, anxious to oblige Mr Frank Connor, and somewhat nervous in their dealings with William Vernon from London.

No one questioned our good fortune, we were lucky girls and ought to be grateful. Passages were booked and our trunks packed.

But I could not feel so happy. The attack on me, the fire, these were planned events, I had the feeling that the man who had committed these crimes had been paid to do so. To attack me, to discredit me, to burn me, to kill me.

Was this imagination? No. I could have questioned Mr Vernon. He had been seen speaking to No Eyes, but somehow I knew he would turn me aside with a bland answer. One meets with strange people on a mission of this sort, Miss Dorothea, he would say.

There was someone, in the background, arranging events. Someone who did not like me. But this person had no face.

Who was my enemy?

And what would become of Joe?

Darling, darling Joe, I had felt his strength, his warmth, his love.

Part Two

Chapter Four

January 1915; the Great War had just started, and it had not been over by Christmas as predicted. It was a wet month with floods in the Thames valley and mud on the battlefields.

We were all being gallant and patriotic. Val and I who were barely grown up by the standards of the society we were living in, but who were in fact, full of our own secret knowledge; we had been living in London in the care of Honoria Madden for almost three years, having been rescued from our sojourn in Canada by her efforts. I call her my guardian, but our relationship has changed more than once and she has been both more than that and less than that to me. She was a good woman, but she had a dark side to her.

We were walking round a picture gallery in one of the narrow streets off Piccadilly. Honoria liked to see the latest paintings and sculptures and perhaps buy a picture, the proceeds going to a war charity.

Outside it was raining hard. Through the glass door I could see the shining pavements, the umbrellas of the pedestrians and the patient stance of coachmen and horses as they waited with the carriages lining the kerb. There were still carriages about but smart people were going in for Daimlers or Rolls Royces. The King had several. So had two of the princes and most duchesses. The young ones anyway, like Shelagh Westminster – and the very rich old ones like Evvie Avon, who had everything including a face lift and a young lover. Within the shop it was like being in a scented jewelled box with the steady glow from the illuminated pictures on the walls. A big bowl of potpourri rested on a marble plinth by an open fire.

With Honoria was Jameson Forsyth, her lawyer and adviser. He was always in and out, a tall, burly man who had once been handsome, still was if you liked that sort, with a bush of grey hair and cold eyes. Cold to me, anyway. I always felt his censure. Why he should dislike me, I did not know, but I felt he did.

Honoria never took a decision without his advice. He was going round the pictures, eyeglass to his left eye, his small, red mouth pursed up in disapproval. He didn't care for what he called 'modern art'. What he liked was a straightforward landscape or portrait you could recognise, and there were not many of those in this exhibition. In fact, I wondered why Honoria had come to it, but the gallery owner was a fashionable woman with patronage of royalty. One might meet the Prince of Wales.

On an easel was a small picture, a summer scene by the river, with a nude girl sitting on the grass. A man wearing a straw boater stood watching her. It was a strong, sensuous picture. Powerful, crude in a way, but you had to look at it. There was no signature, but in one corner was a small violet.

Not a gentle, shrinking violet, but a wildly curling violet that looked as though it might soon spring into violent life as something animal. I thought I knew that violet.

I stared at it as Honoria came over.

"Who painted this?" She raised her lorgnette.

"I don't know."

A lie; I thought I did, I recognised the violet. On my arm was a violet like it. Valentine had a such a mark, but on her shoulder. I hadn't seen it lately, it was more faded than mine, her skin, in spite of her pinkness and lushness being tougher.

"I find it indecent," pronounced Honoria.

I kept a straight face. Even then I knew more crude words and so-called obscenities than Honoria had ever heard. She didn't really know what the word meant. Forget it, Honoria, I wanted to say. Leave that side of things to me.

Suddenly I have a vivid picture of the three of us that January afternoon when the newsboys were crying in the streets about the war. The Americans were making peace noises and the Germans were behaving badly to civilians. I see Honoria, Mrs Madden, small, plump, white-haired but every inch the dignified matron, and Valentine with her tall, graceful figure, pale golden hair which she had just bobbed, and big blue eyes. The young Prince of Wales had already noticed her eyes. I see myself reflected in a glass on the wall, not as tall as Valentine, with eyes as blue, but pale skinned, and with wildly curling black hair, I was a kind of gypsy besides Val. Skirts were ankle length, with tight little fur collars and matching toques. And floating from Val's hair comes the scent of violets. But I might be imagining that smell.

Honoria moved away to view another picture, this time a safe scene of Surrey woodland. This she considered buying. Her taste, within its limits, was good.

Honoria no longer went out into society, occupying herself with looking after her property, in which she retained a passionate interest. She was at that time examining the two of us to see which should be elected her grandchild. An unusual competition, but there was a reason for it. Money and inheritance came into it too.

I drew Valentine over to the picture on the easel and pointed to the violet.

"Well, my goodness." She stared. "Charley."

"Yes, of course it's Charley. She would use that as her symbol."

"But what a picture."

"Honoria thinks it's indecent."

"More than she knows." Val gripped my hand and pointed to one corner of the picture. She was laughing. "Not only the violet, look there."

In the heart of a flower, something large, pink, fleshy, erect.

"It's part of the flower," I said.

"No, it's not. Look again. Isn't she naughty?" Val grinned. "I heard she was in London. We all get here in the end, don't we?"

"How did you hear?" I gripped her arm.

Val gave one of those annoying little shrugs she had learnt lately. Chic, she called it, which was different from Canadian 'smart'. "Now I wonder how? I must think."

From the window of the gallery I saw two figures by the door. A private soldier, not tall but sturdy, was engaged in an argument with an officer. Voices were being raised. The man seemed to be trying to come into the gallery. The officer was blocking his way.

But the private was holding his ground. Not taking violent

action but doggedly holding on to where he was. There was a certain defiance in his stance.

I watched, puzzled and interested.

A pair of soldiers came marching down Bond Street; they looked like policemen of some military sort. They were beginning to be seen on the streets of London on the lookout for offenders and deserters, although it was unusual to find them in Bond Street. The officer hailed them. Before my eyes, the private was grabbed, there was a scuffle, then he was thrown into a vehicle that was following up behind.

It was a nasty little scene with a hint of brutality. The British army was a terrible machine to come into conflict with.

A private confronting an officer wasn't a sight one saw often in the streets of wartime London. Private soldiers knew their place here. This one did not.

A stranger, but there was something familiar about him. I wished I could have seen his face.

The officer strode into the gallery and I could hear his voice. Him, I did know.

"Chap wanted to come in here. Can't have that. Damned impertinence. Well, he's for it now." There was satisfaction in the loud aristocratic voice. We could hear every word.

"That's Johnny Lyonnesse." I looked at him, tall, well built, with ruddy cheeks and strong blue eyes. "He was rotten to that soldier."

"He's an arrogant beast," said Val.

"But you find him attractive." I knew she did. And for the reason she always was attracted to men like him: because he represented a challenge.

She did not answer directly. "He'll make a good soldier. Violence is bursting out all over him, he can't wait to kill."

"I wonder who the soldier was?"

"How should I know?"

"And why he wanted to come in here."

"Did he want to? Perhaps he's interested in pictures. Like Johnny." She let her gaze rest ironically on Lord Lyonnesse. She knew that it was her Johnny was interested in.

"Did he remind you of anyone?"

She didn't answer.

82

"Joe Jerningham?" I said.

"Just because you've seen a picture of Charley you think bits of the past are getting up and walking all round you. Ghosts."

But ghosts did walk in this city of London. It was that kind of city, and that sort of time, January 1915.

Val turned towards Johnny who was already advancing confidently towards her. Johnny was already home from the trenches, wounded, he was brave enough. His bold blue eyes met mine with a hard stare.

"You'll get more than you bargain for there, young lady," I thought, vindictively, stories about Johnny being current in London society. But then, so might Johnny get more than he suspected from Val. Val was no ordinary young lady. And neither was I. The Sunshine Home, its training nicely covered up by a gloss put on us by Honoria, had left its mark underneath. Not to mention our life across the Atlantic.

"Ready to cheer a wounded soldier?" he was saying.

Joe, Joe Jerningham, I knew he called himself that now. Was it possible that he was here in London?

Honoria followed me to the door. Naturally, she'd heard. She never missed anything.

She knew who I meant. She knew all about Joe and his part in my life and meant to keep us firmly apart.

Joe had decided to stay in Toronto, he had wished us luck and bidden us both a terse farewell. I would never forget our parting. I had written and he had answered with short letters containing not very much about Jerningham's and barely anything about himself. I got the impression that the Jerninghams depended on him more and more; the store had been rebuilt and seemed to flourish. If it did, then it would be due to Joe.

Honoria held my arm tightly and stopped me trying to run down Duke Street. "Stop it, he is not the man for you."

Then she said the thing about me being born to Bohemia. And what she meant by Bohemia was poverty, cheap clothes and loose living. On account of my mother being a music-hall artiste. She was a good woman, but that was the black side of her coming out.

I knew then that she had made up her mind which of us was to be acknowledged granddaughter and heiress: Val, our beauty.

We drove home to Swires Square in silence.

We had a longish drive back from the West End to the City, where Honoria still chose to live in old-fashioned state, for the traffic was heavy.

Johnny and Val had quietly arranged to meet at a tea-dance.

"He won't marry you, you know," I whispered to Val. as we stepped into the carriage.

"I don't want him to. I'm holding out for an earl. Of course, there is the Prince of Wales, but he likes such pinky little women." Val was large and gorgeous.

When we got back to the rambling old house, Honoria was out of the carriage first, but I was striding after her, ready to question the man who sat in a great leather chair at the door in the hall ready to answer a pull at the bell. He was a surly, fat fellow.

But the old steward Forgan was in the hall, and he could never keep anything in.

"A young person was here, miss. A colonial, I would say, from his way of speaking. But since I had no instructions to admit him, he went away."

No snob like a really first-class servant used to good service, I thought.

"He seemed a very decent young man," said Forgan, anxious to oblige both me and his employer as was his usual way. More downstairs and servants hall, than upstairs and fit for the drawing room, be meant. And it was so untrue and unfair of Joe Jerningham.

If it was Joe, he must have come here looking for me, and somehow discovered where we were shopping. I knew Joe, a young man of infinite capacity for finding out what he wanted.

But he had been turned away twice. That might do for Joe Jerningham. He would not be snubbed twice.

"Damn," I said, "damn, damn and damn."

Honoria gave a tolerant sigh. "In the circumstances of your birth," she began. A man servant took her furs.

Honoria lived quietly, but it would never have occurred to her that she could get on without a manservant in livery. The war was going to change all that.

84

She was lavishly generous with money, not free from old-fashioned prejudice, but more often in favour of people than otherwise; once taken to you, she was loyal for ever. The best and kindest of women. If she had a hobby, and she had many, it was the study of hypnotism. She tried it out on us two girls. Valentine allowed herself to be hypnotised (pretended, I think), but I refused, a dark shudder rose inside me at the very thought, and when Honoria insisted I try, I fainted. That frightened Mrs Madden, and yet I saw it interested her too. If she had a darker side, and she had, this interest in hypnotism was the door to it.

Val laughed.

"It's no good," she said. "We shall never be like other people. It's not to be expected. It's those circumstances."

Not to mention the matter of the violet tattoos.

After we had dressed for dinner that night and we were waiting for Honoria to come down, Val said: "Do you ever think of Toronto? You never talk of it."

"No." I was surprised. "Only of Joe. I think of Joe, of course. It seems all him. I don't remember much else." This was true, a kind of blankness had descended on all I knew of Toronto.

Val looked troubled. "Dodo, I think that's dangerous."

"What do you mean?"

"When you have a thorn in your finger, then you dig it out. Otherwise it festers." She went to the big looking glass on the wall to touch up her hair, and without looking at me, said: "Do you think hypnotism would help? Mrs Gilmour is very kind, she cured my rash."

"You never had a rash, you were pretending," I said. "I know it and you know it. And I don't need help."

"If you say so, Dodo . . . and I did have a kind of a rash."

But the truth was that under pressure from Honoria, who could be very persistent, I had allowed Maria Gilmour to sit on the sofa and wave her amber pendant at me.

"Close your eyes."

Obediently, I had closed my eyes as she spoke softly to me. But at once a great, red, soft face pressed itself down upon me. I put my hand up to the face and felt flesh, clinging and hot. It was then I fainted.

Even now the memory made me feel sick, and Val saw something in my face. She took my hand and pressed it gently. "If I should go away; marry and leave – you will look after yourself, Dodo?"

I was still thinking of Joe when Honoria came into the room, soon followed by her dinner guests.

Mrs Gilmour, who besides being Honoria's expert on hypnotism (and much else besides) was the widow of famous lawyer and was there that night. Other guests were Jameson Forsyth, and Sir Edward Coke, trustees of Mrs Madden's estate.

Sir Edward was a barrister. It was he who had told us that the Sunshine Home no longer existed. Honoria did not encourage talk of the place but she could not stop this information.

"Mrs Madden asked me to investigate. It closed not long after you two left. Some funds that they depended on dried up and they were forced to shut."

"Mrs Adam? Dorothy Adam, what became of her?" The curate's wife whom I was named after.

"I believe her husband has become a bishop. Bishop Berkley, I understand."

"She was my friend . . . and Dr Violet?"

He looked at me curiously. "She died."

"Oh . . . of what?" Intuition made me ask.

"I heard it was suicide." He held up a hand. "No, I don't know the details."

I marked him down as someone helpful and kind, of whom I could ask questions.

At dinner that night he sat next to me. I had thought he was a bachelor, but no, he had married young and his wife had died in childbirth with their first child.

I let him sup his soup before I said: "Today in the Preston Gallery I saw a picture that I think was by someone I knew at the Home."

"Ah," he glanced at Honoria.

I lowered my voice. "I'd like to find her, but I don't know how to go about it."

"I might be able to help." He sipped his wine as he listened. I gave an edited version of the picture. He could find out for himself.

"Leave it to me. I'll let you know what I find."

As he left that night, he pressed my hand and smiled. "Will you be at Lady Willoughby's dance this week?"

I nodded.

"So shall I. Will you save me a dance?"

Two days later a note was delivered. 'The artist C. Rex (which I take to be an assumed or working name).' You're right there, I thought. "The artist is based in Paris. The gallery has no direct address but works through the artist's agent, also in Paris."

An address was enclosed: P. Gallant, Rue Montagne, Paris.

Something for the future, and I put the address away. But I wrote a short letter.

No answer came.

At the dance in Belgrave Square, Val was at once whirled into a tango with an admirer. Most of the men were in uniform of one sort or another. Johnny Lyonnesse danced with her three times, but the two young Princes, Wales and Albert, arrived with a party soon afterwards and Val was drawn into their group.

I had my own partners, including Sir Edward who led me into supper. It was the season when so many of the women were wearing heliotrope scent; the room was heavy with it.

After supper, Edward said: "I must leave now. I have some papers to look at." He was an MP as well as a leading barrister. "Will you let me give you lunch?"

Val whisked past on a princely arm and winked at me.

"Yes," I said.

He kissed my hand. As he did so, a shudder rose inside me. Edward looked at me, his eyes concerned, but he said nothing.

"I'm sorry. There's a draught, I think."

"Of course."

There was no draught, the room was stuffy if anything.

We met for lunch several times after that. Honoria made no objections, she promoted it if anything. Edward never touched me again.

At one of these lunches, he said: "I have some ideas about that orphanage of yours. Will you let me work at it?"

"Of course." I was puzzled but interested.

"It may take some time, – leave it to me . . . You know I have joined up? I'm off soon."

"I thought you'd go." Almost everyone was making a gesture.

"May I write?"

"Please do . . . I'll write back." We were all of us learning how much the men in the trenches depended on letters from home.

"Before I go . . ." He lowered his eyes. "There is something I want to say."

Ah, I thought, here we go. A proposal. But I'm not ready.

But what he said was: "Jameson Forsyth likes you. Have you noticed?"

"He prefers Val," I protested.

"No, it's you . . . He would not be right for you, Dorothea."

"No."

"And I don't think I say this out of jealousy." He gave his sudden, sweet smile. "Although I am jealous."

He left London the next day to join his regiment. Soon, he was in the trenches. I had the odd card, an occasional short letter. Then one day, I had a note saying that he had leave, and would I lunch with him in his chambers? He had some news for me about the Sunshine Home.

On the appointed day, I walked down the Strand towards The Temple. His clerk met me at the door. I knew by his eyes what he was about to say: "Sir Edward's been killed . . . I got the telegram this morning."

We did not speak much to each other; he was an oldish man, too old for the army, he had known Edward Coke a long time, much longer than I had and was deeply fond of him.

As I left, I said: "I suppose there was nothing for me . . . no message?"

"No, miss. Nothing."

I shall make a poor soldier, Edward had said. I believe he made a very good soldier.

However he was wrong about Jameson Forsyth. I saw him at the opera with a very pretty young woman of his own in whom he was certainly interested. Val, who knew who she was, laughed and said her name was Sally Jerrold, and although she was the granddaughter of a bishop and the daughter of a peer, she was game for anything over the sticks. I thought Val knew what she was talking about.

Chapter Five

"I love a wedding, don't you?" said Val. There she stood, effulgent in satin and blonde tulle and old lace. Golden hair and big blue eyes. She looked virginal, but she was no virgin, and I knew it, and possibly Johnny Lyonnesse knew it too. For, after all, she was marrying Johnny.

"Not really," I said, adjusting her veil. She was smoking a dark, long cigarette in a silver holder underneath the tulle and lace. "I think I prefer a funeral."

"That's a terrible thing to say, Dodo."

"Well you do know where you are with a funeral."

"And you think I don't with Johnny?"

I shrugged. "Do be careful with that cigarette, Val, or you'll catch the tulle alight."

And she did. She walked down the aisle and burst into flames. Walking behind her, as her only bridesmaid, I saw a feather of something grey and soft rising up as we stood at the altar. I gazed in horror, wondering what to do. Val seemed not to have noticed anything wrong. (Afterwards she said with a giggle: "Oh I did, darling, but what could I do? Couldn't let Johnny get away.")

As the blessing was sounded, the tulle flamed. I thought the dowager, Johnny's mother, would faint.

It was the first scandal of her married life. But by no means the last.

The second was when, as Val in her Poiret dark brown and sable going away suit was being tucked into the Lyonnesse Daimler, she leant forward and said in a soft, but as it turned out perfectly audible voice. "Oh, I've forgotten my douche bag, be an angel and pop in and get it for me."

That went the rounds of the Mayfair drawing rooms too.

I don't know what Johnny Lyonnesse made of it all, but he

was drinking heavily then, was not quite sober at his wedding. Johnny was a brave man, one has to say that, but he had not liked the horrors of the trenches, the blood, the raw guts spilling out of a man he had gone to school with and dined and drunk with all his life. War was not turning out to be a glorified hunting chase for Johnny after all.

Val, looking at me obliquely from under her lashes, as she anointed them with some new cosmetic from Paris, allowed me to know that he had been violent in his lovemaking.

"It was interesting."

"What was?"

"How I was . . . It was fun."

"Oh Val. Just that?"

"No, I was moved. I understood. He's been through terrible things."

The wedding had been solemnised, as the papers said, in Westminster Abbey. A small affair by the standards of the bridegroom's side of the house, with most of the men in uniform, but with plenty of glitter and diamonds about the women. Say what you like about these old families, they usually have some good jewellery to wear when it matters.

'The marriage of Major The Lord Lyonnesse to Miss Madden. The Prince of Wales among the guests.'

The dowager Lady Lyonnesse had offered her house in Charles Street for the reception, Honoria Madden's house so near to the city being deemed too far away and unfashionable.

Notice Val's name, She is Miss Madden. Honoria had signified her pleasure at the match by declaring Val her legitimate grand-daughter and heiress.

Numerous searches by several agencies had failed to establish with certainty which of us was her true grandchild (if either, but that never seemed to occur to her), so she had followed what she called her instincts and which really meant her own personal taste, and declared the blue-eyed, golden-haired Val, 'the living image' of several of the early Madden ladies and therefore the 'right one'.

I was to be her adopted daughter, could use the name Madden, and would receive a small inheritance, but the bulk of the estate would go to Val. We received the news in a formal interview with Honoria and her solicitor, Jameson Forsyth, who looked pleased with himself. I think he had swayed Honoria's mind. Val's whisper that she would 'share with me', I smiled at but did not count on: the Lyonnesse family might have something to say about that. In any case, we neither of us had much at the moment. Honoria meant to live a great while yet. She was deeply into hypnotism at present.

Val and I had both taken training as VADs and had over a year's work behind us in the London Emergency Hospital, more popularly known as Sister Mercy's Hospital, since Lady Mercy Pinkam presided over it as Lady Matron. It was rumoured that she had served in the Crimea with Florence Nightingale and we thought she looked old enough for it to be true. We were unit A2. The joke went round that the A2 VAD unit was the emergency, but although we had a lively social life out of working hours and were much sought after as dance partners and for theatre parties (I saw *Chu Chin Chow* about a dozen times with young officers recovering from wounds) we were not as scatty as we sometimes seemed. We were never late on duty and never flinched at what we were asked to do: slop pails, dirty dressings, gangrenous wounds, we faced the lot. If we drank and danced and laughed a lot afterwards, so did everyone.

But now Val was married, and I felt I would like a change. Not to abandon war work, no not that, but another milieu.

Time off for coffee or a rest was strictly forbidden by Matron, but we could usually disappear into the lavatory for a quick puff on a cigarette. Sometimes a gasper was all that carried you through.

I fell against the cloakroom door, closing it firmly with my body, and lit up. "O God." Then I looked across the little room. "Hello, Sally. Lousy day, isn't it?" We had lost two men on the ward that morning. Lovely men.

Sally was smoking and crying at the same time. She could do that and still look attractive could Sally Jerrold.

"Give me another ciggy."

"You haven't finished that one yet."

"It's my last and I need another . . . We lost Dandie Dinmont in the theatre."

Dandie was a young Highlander. He seemed to have no other

name and no relations and the medical diagnosis had been that very soon he must have no legs either. We all loved him.

"I didn't know you were on today." I handed over my cigarette case. Silver gilt, a present from Val.

"I stood in for Braithwaite, she's got her visitor. Agony."

"Oh, poor thing."

"No, she's glad. It was her second No Go and she was getting really worried, poor lamb. Still it's all right as it happens . . . Anyway I went in braving Theatre Sister who knew what it was all about . . ." She dabbed at her eyes. "We knew both legs were for it, but we thought he'd pull through, but he didn't."

I put my arm round her. "He wouldn't have wanted to live that way, without legs, Sally."

"Yes, he would. You know better than that, Dodo. He could have eaten, drunk, laughed, made love . . . He could have. I would have helped him."

I knew she would have done. It was something one could do. It was not talked about. But it was done. And why not?

Sally took a powder compact out of her pocket, one with a little circle of diamonds surrounding her initials. She dabbed at her nose, smiled and said: "That's over. For this time. I'm off to see the show at the Vaudeville tonight with a bunch of the boys. Why don't you come too? A girl with ankles like yours does cheer them up so."

I looked down at my feet. Yes, the ankles were trim. And you could see them too. I was shortening my skirt by the day. Val wrote from Paris where she was staying at the Meurice that 'hem lines were going up and up and waists going down'. She was shopping at Vionnet and Lelong, so she ought to know.

"I'll come," I said to Sally.

The revue at the Vaudeville was a nicely mixed blend of music, jokes, and pretty girls. The star of the show was a young American dancer called June Deland, a skinny, pretty girl with marvellous, tapping feet. I hadn't seen her before.

We were a row of six, three young soldiers, more or less convalescent, and Sally, who had brought along her cousin Elspeth and me. The theatre had given us seats in the front row of the stalls. The boy next to me, a youngster of about eighteen, quietly reached out and took my hand. By the middle of the show he had got his arm round my waist.

All right, I thought, if it cheers you up.

"This act's whizz, isn't it?" he whispered.

If the star of the revue was June Deland and her dancing feet, then the middle of the show was held up by a English star, Lotty Linden. Not particularly young, not specially pretty, but she had gusto. She could sing a bit, dance a bit, put over a line and make you laugh. She had some good material too, which I was told she wrote herself.

My young companion, Lieutenant Edward Clark – Eddy to me, a country boy, son of a small landowning family in Kent – insinuated his arm a bit further round me and whispered: "They say she's got a different lover for every day of the week. Every day, a different way, eh?"

"Do you admire that?" He was trying to shock me, testing me, to see how far he could go with me afterwards. He was about eighteen and looked sometimes younger and sometimes older because he had taken one trip to trenches before catching a 'Blighty one'.

He laughed. "She's a goer, look at her."

"Yes, really throws herself into it."

Lotty's act was whirling to an end with her feet flashing as she belted out her song. She ill-treated her voice shockingly but it was a good voice and full of music.

"Shall we go round to her dressing room afterwards and see if we can meet her?" whispered the lad.

"If you think we'd be allowed."

"Worth a try."

Lotty's dressing room was crowded when we got there. Everyone seemed welcome. Still in her stage costume, she was handing round drinks to everyone and laughing. Seen close to, she had a lively clown's face beneath a mop of reddish curls.

Eddy introduced himself and me; we shook hands, both of us said how much we had enjoyed her act and accepted a glass of champagne. It was a mixed crowd, all the men were in uniform and the girls were bright cheerful young things. It was the way we all were then. A surface gaiety with a dark pit beneath. We all fell into that pit every now and then. There was no sign of the daily lover, unless it was an older man sitting at the back wearing a dark suit.

Eddy was fascinated by her, and Lotty had an eye for him too, but he was a nice boy and did not forget that I was there. Even so, I was looking for an opportunity to disappear, thus leaving him behind to enjoy the lovemaking that Lotty might have to offer, which he so clearly wanted and might never have had: he looked virginal to me.

But suddenly we all heard whistles and the click click of rattles. A Zeppelin raid was up on us.

"Out, out," cried Lotty, waving her hands. "Find a basement. This place is a tinderbox."

She heard the rattles from the street. "They're swinging those rotten things. Does that mean gas? Percy, get the Royce round."

The dark-suited man, who might have been her lover or might have been her chauffeur and probably acted as both, got up obediently. He seemed to shovel all before him and Eddy and I found ourselves out on the street.

All the lamps were blue-shaded; along the road was a special policeman, wearing his armband and tin helmet. He was waving to us to take cover. "Jerry's about," he shouted. "Get in a doorway."

All was quiet, then I heard the throb of an engine. The searchlights swung round the sky, then crossed together, catching a small cigar-shaped object in the cross.

It seemed just about overhead, I thought, and was all for moving on. I was taking a step forward, when Eddy dragged me back roughly into a doorway.

"Here. A better 'ole." There was no joke in his voice, which was unsteady and high. He had his arms round me and was holding me against him. I could hear the guns popping away. To no purpose, I thought, having been in a raid before, and frankly, if they had hit the Zep, I should have been terrified. I thought I'd rather have a bomb than a whole Zeppelin.

Through the noise of the guns I heard a whistle as a bomb came down. The ground rolled a bit, glass popped and shattered onto the ground.

Near, I thought. Eddy held me tight to him. "Let me kiss

you, let me kiss you," he was muttering. He put his lips against mine.

"Eddy," I protested, faintly – he was pressing the breath out of me. I was beginning to have difficulty in breathing. I could smell fire. It was getting closer, I could feel the heat.

A great soft face with wet lips pressing down on mine, swelling all round me like a balloon so that my own face was held inside it, captive, like a maggot inside rotten fruit. The face was getting bigger and more hungry all the time, all mouth now.

It was opening up all round me, I was being swallowed.

An explosion shook my body and my eyes opened. The red face was gone, I was staring straight into Eddy's face; he had drawn away. In the light from the blazing building down the street I could see that he was white and shaking. He wanted to speak but words would not come.

"Sorry," he muttered. "It's the guns. Can't stand them."

I put my arms out and held him. "Steady now. I'm here with you. I won't let anything hurt you." I was talking to him like a kind old nanny. "You'll be all right. I'm here. Dodo's here." It didn't matter what I said, it was the voice and the comfort in it.

I kept my arms round him and held him close all through the raid. I seemed to hear the distant comment of that far away nurse of the Sunshine Home days: "You'll make a fine little mother yet," she had said.

When all was quiet, we picked our way through the shattered street together, not talking. A building at the end of the road was alight, but the theatre round the corner still stood. Not many people about but I heard someone say that the Zeppelin was down.

"Wish I could have you near me over there," he said as we made our goodbyes.

"I'll come over, Eddy, I promise. I'll come to Paris, and when you get a spot of leave, there'll I'll be."

There was no going back from Paris where I arrived at the end of September. Within a day, Honoria let me know she was closing the house in London because of the raids. Further, she added that Jameson Forsyth had told her that her income was greatly reduced owing to the war, and she would be obliged to cut my allowance. Of course, I would have a home with her, etc. etc. . . . In short, I was out in the cold.

And I had not been more than a week in Paris when Sally Jerrold turned up.

"Joining you," she said cheerily. "Nice little bunk hole, you've got here."

I was living in a small apartment high above the Rue de Rivoli which was lent to me by Val. I did not enquire what use she had for it when Johnny Lyonnesse had rented a large house near the Parc Monceau for her, but since the most striking piece of furniture was a large, white double bed, I thought I could guess. I had made a mental note that Eddy would never be entertained there. If he came. So far all I had had was one field postcard.

"What about Sister Mercy's Hospital?"

"Chucked me out. Matron called me in and said she had had complaints that my behaviour was not suitable for her hospital. Old bitch. I reckon I've got an enemy." Sally was a good nurse, very good. "And how's her ladyship?"

"Val?" I frowned. "I don't see much of her. This place is hers."

The truth was that Val had embarked on her first career, as an international trollop. The second and third were yet to come, but we hadn't got there yet.

Sally was not without money and position. "I know a dear little old general," she said. "He's a gunner; they're usually tiny men. He'll see I don't hang around doing nothing."

She was quite right. Within a few days, she was wearing a uniform and driving General Miller-Dove. He was not that little, or that old; certainly young enough to take a decided interest in Sally's excellent ankles.

I found it less easy to achieve a worthwhile job, but filled in time working at the British Embassy where, believe or not, Val had established herself in an office.

"I'm a kind of a lady censor," she said, which I soon discovered was a grand name for what she actually did: writing letters for soldiers too ill to write, in one of the British Hospitals for Men and Officers. But she had a delightful small room in the beautiful town house that Pauline Borghese had built. "The title helps," she said bluntly.

I joined her in the letter-writing. It meant we had to receive replies and sometimes read them to soldiers. It was a harrowing business. If you found yourself in this particular hospital, then it meant your chances of returning to active life as a whole citizen were poor: a bit of you was surely missing, and usually a major part of you.

The first thing to notice about Val was her clothes. She dressed now only at the big couture houses: Vionnet, Worth, Doucet and Poiret; these clothes were different from anything we were wearing in London, being shorter, tighter in some places and looser in others. The outline was quite different.

The second thing to notice was the sizeable collection of jewels she was collecting. Again from the best places: Boucheron and Chaumet and Cartier.

The third thing to notice was that I don't believe she paid for any of it.

And the fourth thing was that Johnny Lyonnesse did not care.

"Got a mistress of his own, dear," Val said carelessly. "Always has had. Don't know why he married me, except he wanted an heir. But we don't seem to click that way."

Eddy did come for a twenty-four in Paris, and of course, Val swept him off his feet. He quite forgot me in trying to pursue Lady Lyonnesse. In twenty-four hours even with Val he could not get far, but he certainly did his best.

He had changed; the trenches had changed him. He was stiffer, more reserved except when drunk, and apparently reconciled to his fate. He would not survive; he knew it.

I didn't blame him for falling for Val, she was such a powerful embodiment of the love and life he would never have.

"No point in going to bed as you have to be off so early," said Val. Did Eddy look disappointed at that comment? "It's late enough now," I said.

"I know where a party goes on all night. You don't mind artists and low life? Let's cross the Seine and go over to the old city."

The party was in a studio, the artist being a sculptor judging by the bronzes ranged around the room. He worked in stone as well. The room was already crowded with people of as many sexes and nationalities as Europe could produce. In no time at all I lost Eddy and Val, who disappeared across the room, whether together or not I was not sure, leaving me pressed up against a giant woman wearing a feathered hat over a very tight black dress. She was drunk, which enabled me to discover very soon that she was a he. Or was she?

"I am Victorine," she said, putting one hand lovingly around my neck. "Tomorrow I shall be Victor again. And who are you, my beautiful girl?" She spoke in English but with an American accent.

"Dorothea." That seemed enough to tell her. I was trying to edge away.

"You are the sister of Lady Lyonnesse."

"Yes, how did you know?"

"You are alike."

"I don't think so."

"Yes, you both have the same look. Around the mouth and on the brow. Believe me, I am an artist and I see these things. Let me get you a drinkypoo . . . the wine here is good, but I prefer gin. What about you?"

"Wine," I said.

Victorine disappeared into the crowd. The studio was large but dimly lit that evening; it was crowded, the air smoky so that it was hard to see from one end of the room to the other.

I turned to study the row of bronzes on a shelf behind me. They were small-sized figures, about a foot or so high, mostly nudes of men and women, sometimes alone, sometimes together. Of their technical skill there was no doubt. Of what they were about there was not doubt exactly but something to consider.

I was frowning at one. A man and woman in very close embrace. The woman had her face buried in the man, from her backside poked a pointed object over which I frowned still more. Talk about the arrow of desire, I thought. Still, you didn't expect to see it actually in bronze.

Victorine came back with a glass which she handed to me. She saw me studying the bronze.

"Lovely piece, isn't it? Be in a museum one day. Not

just yet, though," she laughed. "The moment of maximum penetration."

There was something familiar about that back, about the oval curve of the muscles down to that dimple at the base. I turned away, drink in hand. Many women must have such a back, one back was very like another.

I had not moved a foot before a figure stepped forward. Tall, wearing corduroy velvet trousers and loose silk shirt, a robust, peasant face, with a fringe of close-cropped russet hair. Not handsome, but bonny and strong.

"Know me?"

I stared, and the name burst forth, without me willing it.

"Charley!"

Then I said it again. "Charley, at last."

So there we were together again. Val, Dodo and Charley. And we had added the fourth in Sally Jerrold.

At the party, Charley and I sat down in a dark corner and talked.

"It's marvellous to see you, marvellous. Oh Charley, I have missed you."

In the distance I saw Victorine, she seemed to be looking for someone, possibly me.

I pointed her out to Charley. "Who is she?"

"Pester you, did she? Harmless. She is a respectable lady from Boston when she is at home. Over here, she acts up a bit. She will go home soon, I think. All the Americans are going home now food is short and we have the Zeppelins."

In the distance I saw Val and Eddy. Charley saw them too.

"What did you think of Val's portrait?"

"I haven't seen it."

"I saw you looking at it." Her eyes were mocking.

I was surprised. "Then I didn't recognise it."

Charley laughed. "I thought you might have known her back."

I opened my eyes wide, and turned my head in the direction of the statue of the man and the woman, so actively and fiercely engaged with each other. "No . . . not Val."

"From the life."

100

"Val!" I said incredulously. "I can't believe it."

"She hasn't changed," said Charley. "What she always was as far as I remember."

"What about me? Have I changed?"

"I can't tell," said Charley. "You're a bit buttoned up, but you always were."

I'm not buttoned up, I thought, but you are a secret-maker. "Charley," I said. "You are a tremendous success. I can see that. You have made a name for yourself. It's a long way from the Sunshine Home. How did you do it?"

Charley looked at me with that old scrutinising look I remembered. "You're an honest little soul, Dodo, and you always were. I'm more like Val, a liar and a cheat as required. I did it that way."

"You never lied."

"Let's say I twisted the truth a bit. But I have never lied when I've painted. Dead honest and straight there, Dodo."

I might have heard more of her story then, and it would have paid me to know, but across the room I saw Val with Eddy in tow; they were coming this way. Val saw who I was with and her eyes widened. She knew. And then she smiled. A great, sweet smile. Bless you, Val, I thought.

Val sent Eddy off to get her a drink, then alone, she came across and threw her arms round Charley. "You great lump," she said. "Why have you stayed away so long? We knew that was your picture in the gallery. What a turn you are, Charley."

So there we were, a group again. Val, already what she had it in her to become, Charley so strong and talented, and buttoned up Dodo.

"There's someone I want you to meet," I said, seeing a figure I was oddly glad to see come into the room. "Sally Jerrold."

I think they liked each other at once; I saw them eye each other in the way women do when they meet.

Then Charley said: "I'd like to draw you. You've got the new face, the face of the future."

Sally put a hand to her neat pointed chin. "Glad to know I've got a future. But I should think you'd want to do Val, she's the beauty."

"Val has been overdone," said Charley gravely.

101

Sally giggled; she knew about Val. "Dodo then."

"No, not Dodo. I am not old enough yet to draw Dodo, who has so much hidden inside her."

"I like Charley." Sally Jerrold gave her judgement with a toss of her head. "And I am a wise girl and know what I like."

I didn't think Sally was wise, but I trusted her judgement of people.

"I like Charley too. But I always did."

Sally settled herself into her uniform; she would be moving away from Paris within the next few days, going down the line with her General, who I had begun to suspect was certainly her General in a very physical way. That was what I meant about not being wise. To make love was Sally's way of expressing her support. If the General lost a battle then at least he was assured of a good time in bed.

"She's a fine painter."

I nodded.

"And a good draughtswoman . . . She has marvellous technique and you don't get that by luck. Charley's had professional training. Wonder where she got it."

"I haven't asked."

Sally collected her letters which were all addressed to this apartment. One fell to the floor.

"Jameson Forsyth," she said with a grimace.

"I thought you'd done with him."

She picked it up. "One does not part from Jameson Forsyth . . . He adheres."

"He's a lot older than you."

"Oh yes, and there is a younger Jameson, his son. Alike as two peas."

"I can never understand him."

"Oh there is passion inside him. Not perhaps for me, nor do I know for what. But inside him is a fire."

Val was less certain how she thought of Charley now. "I feel she has lived with vice and cruelty." Val gave a pretty little shudder. Not unacquainted with vice herself, I thought. "I sense it in her."

"I think she's good."

And I thought that Charley had had a bad time, but had come through because she was strong and now was a thoroughgoing professional artist who was respected by her fellows. I didn't think anything else mattered.

Three different views of Charley.

Charley lived and worked in a tiny studio with a view of the River Seine. She slept on a camp bed in one corner; there was no kitchen so what she ate I do not know, but there was a café on the corner whose proprietor seemed to know her well. Charley did not starve, she earned by painting portraits.

"A lot of families want their sons done, it's the war, you see, and photographs won't always do. And I have the knack of getting a likeness . . . it's a trick, but it sells."

She did not encourage visitors, but she let me call. I was studying a picture she had in hand of a young *poilu*. Very young, very touching.

"It's good, Charley. Do they realise how good?"

She shrugged. "I do honest work and they pay and I go on living. My other pictures, are a little . . . freer, shall we say?"

Somewhere, somehow, Charley had learnt to speak with an educated voice. The peasant face and strong body were the same, but the voice had changed.

Paris was crowded with people, air raids or not – and there were very few, the Zeppelins passed over and on to London – but food was short. We had our butter card and our sugar cards (although oddly, you could always buy patisserie in the expensive shops) and we had meatless days which hardly anyone observed. Prices were very high; that was the effect of rationing. Val always had what she wanted, but I hated to eat beef and butter when I knew so many people were living on cabbages and black bread.

All the same, I enjoyed it when Val asked me to lunch with her at the smartest restaurant: Vignons. I was late and Val was waiting for me. It was a hot day and the room was crowded. The war was raging. On the whole people were miserable, but the Parisians did not choose to show it. You put on your best clothes, wore what jewellery you had, and smiled. I don't know how they were doing in London, I believe they were going around with long faces as the submarine hit the shipping, but that was not the way in Paris. Not even with the rumours abounding of the big new gun that could actually shell Paris. Of course, with every fresh scare of the German advance some people fled the city, but they usually came back; the provinces were so boring.

I made my way to where Val was sitting at her table, smoking with a long silver holder. She was wearing a black silk suit, sharply tailored like a man's, with a white twill silk blouse, the cuffs just showing at her wrists. Her hair was cut short, curving onto her cheek in a smooth line. She looked immensely chic and very slightly theatrical. To my eyes she had lost something of the fineness of her face. She had developed a way of walking with the legs slightly apart: it was unmistakably erotic.

She greeted me with a kiss. "Sit down, darling. What will you drink?" she motioned to the waiter, "and then we will decide what to eat."

As I sipped my wine – cocktails had virtually disappeared because there so little gin – she said: "Look across to the window."

There in the window was a red-tabbed staff officer with fair hair. It was Colonel Lord Lyonness, who was lunching with a lady.

"That's his new mistress." She gave her husband a wide smile, which he saw. "Lovely, isn't she?"

"Yes." The woman was beautiful, with a pale skin and short hair, very elegantly dressed in a short black dress. Hardly anyone wore colours these days. But this was black with a difference. "Who is she?"

Val shrugged. "Oh everything, she makes hats, makes clothes, makes men, rides horses, rides men. If they are rich enough. Not that my darling husband is all wealthy. I think he may be her little hobby."

She gave her an appraising look. "Calls herself the Comtesse de Coulagée, but no one has ever heard of the title, not out of the Almanach de Gotha." Val never ceased to amaze me. She put a cigarette into her holder. "Not quite a lady."

"And are you, Val?"

"No, dear. Most definitely not. But I put on a good show."

"And is Johnny a gentleman?"

Val looked down at her hands, then she said slowly: "Yes, in his rotten way he is."

It happened that as we left, we passed next to the table where her husband still sat. I was ahead. Behind, Val stumbled, caught at the table to steady herself and managed, with a flick of her fur, to upset a glass of red wine into the lap of the lovely countess.

Cries, confusion, waiters with napkins, apologies, rapid departure; that was how it went.

When we got into the street, I said to Val: "That was a very silly, babyish thing to do."

"Wasn't it?" agreed Val. "But very, very satisfying." She looked pleased with herself, but was also flushed and with an unnatural bright look in her eyes.

"Are you all right?"

"Of course. Can I drop you anywhere?" She had her car waiting for her; I suppose her husband had his too, it seemed an expensive life. "No, I'll walk. I prefer."

"Oh you saint, you, Dodo."

"Are you sure you are all right?"

Val just laughed and got into her car. All the same I was not surprised to be summoned round to her house that night. Her car arrived with her own maid. "Her ladyship's not at all herself tonight, miss, and would be glad to see you."

Val was in the bedroom of the large apartment which had been rented for her from an aristocratic lady who preferred to sit the war out in the safety of Monte Carlo.

The bedroom was decorated in Pompadour blue so that Val was sitting up in a bed draped with swags of blue satin looking as if she had been painted by Boucher. Her face was still delicately rouged.

"Oh I'm so glad you've come, Dodo. I've had a horrid note from Johnny."

So the illness was more emotional than physical. I didn't know whether to be cross or relieved.

"I was worried," I said.

"He's asking for a separation." Beneath the silk and lace of her negligee I could see her breasts. If I hadn't known better I

105

would have thought she had make-up there too, pink powder round the nipples.

"It's that rotten woman."

"It may be the wine you poured all over him."

"None went on Johnny. I was very careful about that."

The room was very hot and heavy with scent. Val must have sprayed it all round before retiring to bed. She had taken a glass of wine to bed with her too.

"Have you called a doctor?"

"Yes, indeed. The British Embassy doctor, Dr Buchanan, is coming round. Muriel advised him." Muriel was the ambassador's niece.

I didn't know what to make of it. Val was never ill, nor inclined to make much of even a passing ailment.

"You're not expecting, are you?"

"Oh fiddle," she said elegantly.

That seemed to dispose of that idea.

I sat down to wait for the doctor. "You've got influenza," I said. "It's all over Paris."

There was a commotion from outside which I took to be the doctor. I stood up.

Johnny Lyonnesse threw open the door and came rampaging in. He was flushed and angry.

"What the devil were you up to today?" he demanded. I don't think he saw me. All he saw was Val.

Val got out bed in a flurry of decolletage, the soft chiffon and silk of her negligee clinging to her. A puff of scent, warm and female, came with her.

"Val!" I said. But I was invisible for her too.

Johnny grasped Val by her arms. "Don't be violent," she said with a gasp.

"I'll show you how violent I can be." The soft silk tore away from the lace as Val moved away. But she didn't go far. "Oh Johnny," I heard her say, "Johnny."

She wasn't looking at me, or conscious of me. Neither of them were.

I crept from the room. "I should cancel the doctor," I said to Val's maid. "He won't be wanted."

I felt angry and sick.

106

Val had used me. Got me there as a witness, in case she needed one.

No, she just wanted me there. She always knew what was going to happen. And Johnny was cooperating. There was something, deliberate, organised, as if they both knew the rules.

It was some game they were playing, a game they played together. With all zest and pleasure and speed. I felt sick.

I walked back to the apartment, spurning both Val's car and a cab. I don't remember the walk, just the sense of striding through the streets. The edges of my mind seemed to be fraying.

Sally was away, the apartment was empty, I was alone. I locked myself in, drew all the curtains and went to bed. I was sick. Hot and sick, cold and sick. Something was nibbling at me, eating at me. Perhaps it was me that had flu.

I fell into a deep sleep, but in the night, I dreamt that my head was on a newspaper which I seemed able to read. The *Toronto Times*. How strange, I thought, even in my dream. Then the newspaper seemed to cover me, gripping my body, folding itself into me. My body was responding, Inside me an organ opened and became thick and hard. I could feel my body vibrating.

I came awake with the movement still painful inside. I hurt.

Beastly dream, I thought, and staggered off to the bathroom where I welcomed the sight of the bidet. I let cold water sluice inside me, calming and chilling.

I crawled back in to bed, pulled the covers over my head and stayed there. Daylight came and went, but I did not move.

I heard the bell ring. I heard Val's voice, calling through the door but I did not answer. Soon after, Charley came. She shouted through the door but I buried my head in the pillow.

Then light flooded into the room and there was Charley drawing the curtains.

She didn't say anything but disappeared, coming back soon with a tray. On it was a pot of coffee and some hot toast. "You need food," she said. "Eat up."

She brought me a wrap and helped me sit up. Then she sat watching while I drank some coffee; it was hot and strong. She was right, I did feel better for it.

"How did you get in?"

"Picked the lock." Seeing my look of surprise, she laughed.

"Not the first one I've done. A child could pick that lock. Eat the toast, will you?"

I bit into it, hot and buttery, "How did you get the butter? I've had none for days."

Charley laughed. "Never ask." She leaned forward and poured herself some coffee from the little metal pot. "What's up?"

I leaned back on the pillows. "I don't know. I didn't feel myself at all." Not true, I had felt totally and absolutely myself, naked, skinned like fish, bare to the world. I had needed to be on my own to grow some covering skin back. Apparently I had succeeded. "Touch of flu really, I guess."

"Symptoms?"

"Hot, cold, horrid dreams."

Charley looked at me with sympathy mixed with some other emotion that I could not read. "You're too buttoned up, as I said to you. You push things away from you."

"Not always."

"No, not always, but you are doing so now."

"This toast is too good to waste, have some?"

Charley took a slice and leaned forward. "Don't change the subject, Dodo, that's not like you, not like what you were. You didn't have flu, you were upset . . . Val thought she might have upset you."

"I'm not going into that."

"Not everyone's like you, Dodo."

"I know that. I'm not a fool, Charley."

"Val says you never talk about Canada."

But there was nothing there. I thought of Joe, and the fire, vestigial memories of that sad boy Andrew, but beyond that was a curtain.

"What is there to say? I never think of it. Val never talks of it."

"Ah, but Val has got her own life. You haven't."

"What does that mean?"

Charley shrugged. "You've dug a moat round yourself, Dodo, and no one is allowed over it."

I went on the attack. "But you never talk about . . . well, what you did and how you became what you are. You didn't learn your skills on the top of a London omnibus."

Charley gave a guffaw. "That's my Dodo. You want to know? I'll tell."

"After the big scandal, which was nicely hushed up, but only in time for the next one," said Charley sarcastically, "which closed the place down completely, I was sent off to work on a farm. Kitchen work, sort of general slavery . . . I didn't mind, because I had no intention of staying. I stayed a month, saw the life of the land, and ran away."

"Where did you go? To London?"

"Not at first, but I ended up there. Meant to." Her eyes looked alert and amused. "It was my wonderland. I'd heard of it and knew I would find everything there I wanted . . . And so I did, in a way."

"But had you any money?"

"I had a month's wages from the farmer's wife, not that she paid me but I helped myself."

"You stole it? No, I suppose it was owed you."

"Owed? I took what I wanted. Once I was in London I knew I should find work. I could do anything, you see, and I'm very strong. A Mrs Beddows took me on. Lived in Canning Town." Charley smiled again. "She was glad to take me on because she was in business."

"What sort of business?"

"She was what they call a baby trotter. You don't know what that means? I didn't at first, although I soon found out. Not that she wanted me in her business, my physique was not right – was already on the old side."

"You've never been a baby, Charley."

"Not that sort, anyway. Then I moved on to a man, an artist. I did the housework. Scrubbing and cleaning and bit of cooking. He was a good artist and taught me without knowing it. He wanted a little slave. I was his slave. But I got what I wanted."

I wondered what lay behind this statement, what she had truly suffered.

"How's the portrait of Sally coming on?" I asked.

Charley smiled. "I am making a good thing of it. She has a marvellous face. We shall see faces like it all over Europe in the next decade."

I did not see much of Sally for some days, but when I did I never failed to notice how trim and smart she looked in her uniform which she wore with such dash. She had a well-cut overcoat, on the lines of a man's ulster, which was partnered by a rakish, tilted hat with a cockade on the side. A bit like a Napoleonic general. Her skirt finished well above her ankles, showing her high-heeled shoes. She looked very feminine.

She was driving for a new staff officer these days, her dear old General having been summoned back to the War House in London, having made several disastrous mistakes. "It's to keep him out of trouble," Sally said. "He was getting into very odd ways, bless him."

The new man, whom she called the Brig, worked her hard.

"Expects me to drive him everywhere in no time at all and at all hours of the night or day," she complained.

"You like him though."

She did not deny it. "But some of the places . . ." she made a little gesture with her shoulders.

I gathered the Brig had a varied taste in pleasures.

"How does he find the time?"

"Oh he manages. After all, he won't be posted in Paris for long, so it's make hay while the sun shines. Can't blame him."

She didn't say much more then, but one day she came into the flat, flopped on the sofa and started to laugh. "You'll never believe what happened to me today. I was nearly recruited into a brothel."

"Sally!"

"Oh well, perhaps not so very nearly, but I got an offer." She sat up. "Got a drink? I could do with one."

"Yes, Eddy left me a bottle of whisky."

"Good of him. How is he?"

"Gone back. Didn't want to, but which of them does. I don't suppose I shall see much of him . . . He's terribly taken up with Val."

"I wish she wouldn't. She just eats those young men."

I didn't answer, Val had her own way of dealing with lovers and husbands, but I handed over a weakish whisky.

"The Brig asked me to drive to one of his dubious rendezvous." She sipped her drink. "I wonder if he's in Intelligence; that might explain something. . . Not everything, though." And she grinned. "I've seen the girl who opened the door; he's taken her out once or twice and she certainly is ravishing – ready to be ravished too, in my opinion . . . Anyway, I parked down the street. Half an hour, he said, and he is reliable about that sort of thing, times himself, I suppose."

"Honestly, Sally."

"Well, there I was parked and nothing to do, but I hadn't liked the sound of the engine so I had the bonnet up and was taking a look. I heard a door on the street open, and glanced up. A woman was standing there, and she was staring at me. Then she came over. Asked me if I was English; admired my uniform. Then she asked me if I would like to join her establishment. She said she'd seen me with the car before, so I wasn't to think she hadn't given thought to the matter, but they found it hard to get good English girls and very popular they were when she could get them." Sally sipped her drink. "I tell you, Dodo, I felt a chicken waiting to be plucked."

"What did you say?"

"I didn't say anything much, because the Brig came rushing up and tore me away." She finished her whisky. "The money did sound good."

"You got that far, then?"

"Yes, after all, one never knows where one might be after this war."

I couldn't tell if she was laughing at me or not.

"But it would cut into one's social life."

"Not to mention driving for the Brig."

"Oh, I don't think he'd mind. Plenty of girls keen to drive for him. I might even meet him there . . . Don't looked shocked, Dodo, you know better than that. He's all right. Basically all right. It's the war . . . Can you spare me another tot?" She held out her glass.

"He sounds pretty energetic."

She yawned like a little cat and I saw what Charley meant. Val could never yawn like that, nor could any of the past generations of beauties, they were finished; this was how you should look now: thin, fine-boned and forever young. "Must be one of those people with a tremendous sex drive.

As a matter of fact, I know he is." She sighed. "Easy to fall for him."

"You won't fall for him, will you?"

"Don't worry, I won't go overboard." Her face changed, grew older, sadder. "There's someone else, someone I love very much."

"Who?"

"Just a poor bloody foot soldier, darling." The heavy lashed eyes blinked. "Haven't heard from him for a bit."

"Ah." We both knew what that meant: a front-line trench.

But in spite of her lightness, the episode outside the brothel had its effect on Sally. She stopped making jokes about the Brig and quietened her cosmetics.

It had an effect on me too. I felt that women were not trusted and were exploited both within marriage and without. But then I thought of Val who was probably the exploiter in her marriage.

Soon after, Sally came in to say she had got herself moved to a unit out of Paris and down at the front.

"Because of love, Sally?" She hadn't heard from her man, I knew she hadn't.

"Because of love." She shouldered her bags. "I might get to see him, or where he was, and I shall be that much closer."

"Look after yourself, Sally."

"Ditto, ditto, darling." And she was gone.

The next day, Val came rushing round. "Honoria is on her way. Telegram an hour ago. She wants to see us. Together. Something important to tell us. Same old hole, of course."

Honoria Madden was staying at the same dowdy, expensive hotel in the Rue St George that she had used on every visit since the Franco-German war of 1870. Not for her the Ritz or the Hotel Meurice.

"She arrives this evening but she doesn't want to see us today, she must rest, but lunch tomorrow."

As bidden we called together at the Hotel Sinclair. Val had toned down her appearance and I had smartened mine.

She was waiting for us in the sitting room of her suite. She was wearing a black skirt and jacket in her usual style, stiff-tailored like a man's, of alpaca and quite unlike the softer suits all were wearing, with a largish hat; she always lunched in a hat, after which it would be removed unless she went out for a walk or a drive, in which case she would change her dress. There was a dress for every occasion in Honoria's life, including tea. The room smelt stuffy as if the dried flowers I saw on every shelf had been there for years and had died in the service of the hotel. I knew we would eat there.

Honoria kissed us both, and offered us some Madeira. It was not good Madeira and tasted of vinegar. No mention was made of what she wanted to tell us, but no business was ever transacted by Honoria without food being partaken of first. We ate the luncheon that she seemed able to order wherever she was. A thin soup, followed by grilled chops, and no pudding. She was a large lady but how she did it, I had never known, since she seemed to live on very little.

Today, I thought she looked tired, and her hands trembled slightly. I thought that possibly what she had to tell us was that she was ill, about to have an operation, and might not come through it.

I was surrounded by the wounded and the mourners most of my working life but still I knew I should feel a pang for Honoria. We were not related and I had nothing more to expect from her; she had told me so clearly herself. Nor did I expect anything, but I thought I was prepared to give – she was all the kin I had. She was my umbilical cord that held me to my beginnings.

I saw her studying Val's face, and I guessed she might have heard about Val's goings-on, and that this might be what she meant to talk about. But she didn't look angry, more like a woman who had been hurt. At the meal nothing was said except how badly the war was going. But as the table was cleared and we were alone, it was clear something was coming. We looked at her expectantly. She sat up straight in her chair, then turned and held out her hand. As I was nearest and it seemed expected of me, I took it.

She was just opening her mouth to speak when Jameson Forsyth was ushered in.

Honoria stood up. I could read utter surprise in her face and she began to say his name. Then she fell forward on her face.

I found myself still holding her hand and stroking it, while she muttered "M–M––". She never got the word out.

We lifted her up, but she could not speak and one side of her face was drawn up. She had had what the Scottish doctor who arrived called 'a shock'. A crippling stroke.

She was taken into the British Hospital where she lay for days, unmoving except for her eyes. Val and I visited her daily; it was terrible to see the strong, active woman struck down.

I thought she would die.

Honoria did not die. She was taken back to London in the care of Jameson Forsyth and two nurses, but she was never able to speak again.

Val and I saw her off on the train; she was conscious and I believe still trying to say something.

"What do you suppose she wanted to say?" asked Val as we drove away in her car.

"No idea."

"She can write, so we may find out."

But she never did write, or if she did, then I never heard about it. All her correspondence from then on, was conducted by Jameson Forsyth. Val went to see her in London and came back saying it was hopeless, she was in the charge of a nurse like a soldier who must be a close relation of Sairey Gamp.

I took leave and crossed the Channel myself; I had the uneasy sense of something hanging over me, something of which Honoria knew and had never told me, knowledge now locked inside her. I thought if we met she might manage to convey her message.

Besides, I wanted to see her. To my surprise, I found I loved her. Love can root itself in very dry ground on occasion, and seems not to need rich nourishment.

London was very depressing, with troop trains coming and going all the time, and many, many people in black mourning. I got a room in a small hotel off Piccadilly, but there was no hot water and everything I ate seemed to be made of minced carrots.

Honoria Madden was living in her own house, most of which was shut up, but it was no use. I never got past the front door.

I was greeted and halted by a huge nurse, a woman mammoth. Not Sairey Gamp, I thought, but a woman Grenadier. She refused to let me in.

I tried twice, on two successive days, then I took the boat train from Victoria to cross the Channel back to what was now my life.

It was a hard winter in 1917, the war had been going on for ever and would never stop. We would all die eventually, that was clear; meanwhile we carried on.

I saw a lot of Charley. She had never asked to draw me; she said I wasn't ready for it, that I had to give up a few secrets yet.

"I have no secrets," I said.

Charley laughed. "Think about it."

"There are parts of my life that I don't think about." Bits of Toronto life flitted through my mind at intervals. I remembered Andrew and his mother, I remembered my life in the shop, or some of it. I remembered Joe and the fire, I remembered that vividly.

"I think there is something you have buried even deeper."

I didn't know quite what to make of that, so I said nothing. Val had censored part of her life too, it was something one did. Not Charley, of course, she brought everything out.

Sally did not write, but she sent the occasionl postcard which said very little. Then nothing. For weeks no word at all.

At first we did not worry, it was the way things went at the moment; in the confusion of war, letters go astray. She knew where we were, she would get in touch.

We three met every so often in my apartment to play cards, gossip and drink coffee. We were there one late summer evening when the concierge came puffing up the stairs to say that Miss Jerrold wanted to come up.

"But of course." I was surprised. Sally had lived here; I thought of it as her Paris home, she had a right to be in it, although I paid the rent and tipped the concierge.

The concierge raised her eyebrows and shrugged, sending me a message of some sort, if I could read it.

Behind her, up the stairs appeared two figures: a middle-aged man in civilian clothes, and Sally. The man was supporting, half carrying Sally.

I rushed forward, arms outstretched. "Sally, darling, what is it?"

The man said: "I'm Bill Mackenzie . . . she's bleeding badly. Give me a hand." He picked Sally up in his arms and carried her in. Her face was a greyish white and her eyes were closed. Every little while, she moaned on an expiring breath as the air was pushed out of her. We put her on her old bed.

"What is it?" said Val.

"She's in labour," said Charley who always said what no one else would.

Bill Mackenzie explained that he had got to know Sally in some godforsaken little French town near the front line, and then met her again yesterday as she tried in vain to get on a train for Paris. He had succumbed to Sally's charm, that was clear. "I'm a journalist . . . I've got a car, I was coming to Paris so I offered her a ride. She started to get ill in the night."

The concierge sent out for a midwife and a doctor. The midwife got there first but it was no use. Sally died giving premature birth to a daughter. It was very quick and violent; I stayed with her. As I watched and tried to help, part of me reached back to a bit of my own life that I hardly dared to remember, and a bit of which I remembered only in snatches, it was so full of blood and pain. Something was rising up from the depths of my mind, something I had never told anyone. I held her in my arms. She knew she was going. "Would you like me to tell the father, Sally? Who is he?"

"Goodness knows, darling, for I don't. Could be any-one of several. No, I leave it to you, Dodo, please look after him."

"It's a her, darling." But I promised.

So much blood in the room. Some blood got onto her soft blonde curls. Darling Sally. She died in my arms with blood dappling her bright hair, leaving this tiny child, as blonde as she was, and with her bright blue eyes.

There we were, the three of us: Val, Charley and me. Val had the social status, Charley had the money, and I had nothing but myself. We had the moral assistance of

Bill Mackenzie who wanted to do anything he could to help, but had to get back to his work as a war correspondent.

"We must take charge," said Charley.

"There is Sally's father." I thought we ought to consult him, although Sally might not have wanted it.

Val dismissed it. "A dried-up old widower. He won't be any help. He's gaga; I happen to know."

"But he'll have to know Sally's dead, he'll want to know."

"We'll tell him and I'll be surprised if we get much of any answer. Lord Jerrold presents his compliments and thanks you for the sad news . . . that'll be about it. And his lawyer will have been the one who sent even that message."

Parents weren't all that much then, I thought, even when you knew where they were.

"I can get hold of a wet-nurse; my concierge will get me one from her village," said Charley, her peasant stock coming to the fore.

"We must do this thing properly," remarked Val, "Register her birth here, and I'll go to the Embassy and get the right papers."

"One of us ought to adopt the child. Which one?"

Charley would make a marvellous aunt but she was nobody's mother. I didn't know about Val. Nor about myself for that matter.

"We ought to do it as a group, a team," I said.

But after we had visited the various authorities, it was soon clear that a married couple was acceptable, an unmarried woman was not.

There was no choice, none of us three would let Sally's child go to whatever was the current equivalent of the the Sunshine Home.

Charley and I looked at Val. There was Johnny Lyonnesse to consider but I knew that the British aristocracy was never difficult about taking in the odd by-blow. It wasn't something that worried them. But Val puckered her brow.

"Oh dear," she said. "I haven't told you, but I was just about to leave Johnny."

*   *   *

117

The *Daily Gazette*
10 January 1917
A report from the battle front.
Delays in dealing with casualties.
From our correspondent: William Arden Mackenzie.
SOLDIERS WHO CRY AND DIE

From the hospital in Étaples, your correspondent draws these stories.

It is a week after the last big push, and the military authorities did not allow me to write before. These stories will cause pain.

"Where am I?" called out one shell-shocked young private. "I am in hell."

That day, he died, still believing himself to be on the battlefield. He had laid there for four days before he was picked up.

Even when he arrived in hospital, it was some hours before the overstretched doctors and nurses could attend to him. That's how it is when there's a big push. Your correspondent sat with him.

"See that tongue, does it not need water?" was the cry of the Tommy in the next bed, a country boy by the way he spoke. "Give it water."

Your correspondent gave it water.

This boy died too.

Needless to say, the reports of William Arden Mackenzie provoked a flood of comment. This correspondent specialised in reporting the conduct of the war in every aspect that concerned the welfare of the soldier, and he seemed particularly skilful at getting into hospitals and welfare and care centres.

By what means did he get these stories, how did he get them out, past the censor? That was what people were asking.

Where was he?

The *Daily Gazette* said they did not know, at this moment, where their correspondent, a freelancer, was. He was not in touch.

The *Daily Gazette* was a respectable paper with a small but loyal circulation of liberal views.

A small paper with a big voice.

I was working at my desk in my office when I heard angry

shouts in full argument outside. There were often loud voices outside my offices and persons trying to get in. Sometimes they got in, mostly they did not. My secretary, to call her that, was a stalwart Amazon of a woman, a friend of Charley's as a matter of fact, who could frighten the strongest man.

I listened for a second, and then went back to work at the papers on my desk.

When I say desk, it was a long trestle table, and the office was a shed with a corregated iron roof. Sandbags protected the door, flowers grew in the sandbags, some planted, other seeding themselves. We had had one or two Zeppelin attacks, augmented lately by aeroplane raids.

I was in Étaples, the year 1917.

I had two offices and wore two hats. When I say two offices, they were under the same low roof. To change my hat, I simply removed myself to the end of the table where my typewriter rested.

Yes, I could type. I was a typist and just a little more.

I was wearing a grey wool twill suit, the jacket loose and square like a man's blazer, the edges of the sleeves lined with pink silk. The skirt was mid-calf and very plain. I had also sprayed myself generously with Guerlain's scent. The Tommies liked me to smell good. They said they could smell me coming. Those were the ones with bandages over their eyes.

The voices were going on rather longer than usual. I could hear Nadia, my large Russian assistant, muttering in reply. She was pretending not to understand English. Since Nadia was of a very mixed race in which some African blood appeared, most people accepted this and went away. It seemed this chap did not.

I went to the door to listen. This visitor, a man, seemed to be asking for William Arden Mackenzie.

"Ah ha," I thought.

He was asking in no very friendly a manner. Sharp and peremptory, I would say. A man with a commanding air who was used to being obeyed.

There were a lot of them around in this war.

I returned to my work. Nadia would keep him at bay. And if not, well . . . I looked behind me to the open window – had an emergency exit.

119

The door was thrown open so that it banged the wall with a noise hard to bear, with war sharpened ears and nerves.

An officer – a major – in Canadian uniform, stood there. I could make a guess why he was there: we had lately sent a report of a near mutiny in Canadian unit. It had not been printed, the censor had stopped that, but the story went around. Attributed to William Arden Mackenzie. A good honest story but not the sort that the army, any army, wanted to hear.

I knew him at once, but I don't think he knew me.

I had changed – hair bobbed, short skirt, and rouge on my lips. My cheeks needed nothing. Also, I was wearing a wedding ring, but that meant nothing.

Nadia appeared behind him. "Darling," she said. "I can't stop him. He is a brute."

"Don't worry, Nadia. Leave it to me. I know how." And I laughed.

Joe.

He knew me then.

He had grown a few inches, put on some weight, become a man. Three years of grinding war had drawn lines around his eyes and weathered his skin. He had seen action, I knew the signs only too well; no red tab, staff warrior, this.

But the colour melted away under the tan. He went white.

"Dodo . . . It is you?"

I didn't answer. What was there to say? When there is too much to say, how do you start? I had difficulty controlling my breathing.

Joe stood there without speaking, as if he couldn't believe what he saw. He, too, was breathing fast.

"You . . . after all this time."

I sat where I was.

He looked round the room. "What are you doing here?"

I waved a hand over my desk. "Working. As you see."

With that note of anger still in his voice, that I had heard from the other side of the door, he said: "I'm looking for Bill Arden Mackenzie."

It sounded as though he had known Mackenzie. Very few people called him Bill. I certainly did not.

"That might be difficult. He's not exactly here."

"I can see that . . . Can you tell me where he is? How can I get at him?" Get my hands on him, was what it sounded like.

I got up and walked to the window. The window was partly open but its glass substitute was sagging downwards; it had met one bomb too many. But through a crack in the oiled sheeting, I could see a line of ambulances arriving. The second today, and there would be another later this afternoon. Our supply of maimed and torn-up bodies. Well, we all knew what had been going on down the line . . . I turned round and came back and sat down at my desk.

"I'll make a note of that," I said.

"Not enough."

"If you give me a message, I'll see he gets it."

"Not good enough"

"If you write down whatever you have to say, I am sure he will to reply."

"This has to be face to face." He leaned forward, hands on the desk. "Because I want to kill him."

There we had it. I should have to be more communicative.

I thought about it for a bit. Nadia had withdrawn to the other room or she would have enjoyed this moment. I nearly called her back in as witness.

"I am William Arden Mackenzie."

Joe just stared at me. There was a long and ominous silence.

"You can't be."

I sighed. "Do I have to say it again?"

Apparently I did.

"The articles with the byline William Arden Mackenzie were written by me. I have written them, I write them now. Does that cover it?"

There was a bit of explanation behind all that, but this did not seem the time.

"I have met Bill Mackenzie. Once. In Paris, and you are not him."

"Effectively I am. Mackenzie went down the line several months ago and we haven't heard from him since. Disappeared. He's probably dead. It happens."

"Then it was you that printed that rotten lousy story about a Canadian unit staging a mutiny?"

121

It hadn't been quite like that.

My ears picked up a sound that Joe's didn't.

"We'll go into that some other time."

Joe took a step towards me. He still had not heard anything out there in the sky.

"You sit there, wearing a Paris suit, and printing those things."

Joe had changed, learnt something, as well as grown more worldly and sophisticated; he knew a Paris suit when he saw one. But the anger I had always seen in him, was still there. More so, if anything.

Yes, it was a Paris suit, a reminder of my Paris life, but I saw no harm in looking elegant.

"The men like it," I said briefly. "If all you have seen is uniforms, then the sight of a well-dressed woman bucks you up."

Then the bomb began its descent, the first of a stick of three, there would would two others.

"Better take cover." I dived under the table as the windows shook. All the glass had long since gone to be replaced by a kind of waxed paper. "They strafe us sometimes even though we have big Red Crosses painted everywhere."

There was a hiss, a movement in the air like a whip, then there was a blue flash. Then the noise. The flash always came first. If you heard the noise, you knew you were still alive. I was living proof that nothing is faster than the speed of light.

In spite of myself I gave a little cry. Joe put his arm round me. In spite of himself, I guessed. We were very close. Joe drew towards me, and I turned my face towards him.

"Joe, darling Joe."

"You said that once before," he said huskily. "I've never forgotten." I could feel his heart banging against my breast.

Then he saw my wedding ring, and moved back.

I let him go. Everything had gone quiet. The raid was over. We crawled out from beneath the table. Joe helped me to stand up. As he did so, I saw the gold band on his left hand, a continental custom not much seen at that time on an Anglo-Saxon hand.

Damn him, he was married too.

Chapter Six

Joe and I met for dinner in a small restaurant I knew in the nearest town. It was within walking distance of where I was living. I ate in it nearly every evening, there was always butter and meat, so I was pretty sure that the proprietor dealt on the black market but I shut my eyes to it. Everyone else did.

It was not an elegant establishment but the bare wooden tables were always scrubbed clean and the glass filled with the rough local wine was gleaming and polished. The owner who was also the cook was old or he would have been in the war, but Madame was his second wife and younger.

There was a table at the back in a quiet corner where I tried to sit if I could and this was where I waited for Joe. Madame Heloise poured me some wine while telling me in a low, confidential voice that she had a nice plump pheasant cooked with cider and apples for me to eat tonight. She looked after me, I was far too thin, she said. She was sturdy and comely herself, while Henri, her husband, was thin and sinewy. But a lion in bed, she hinted. They had a young son away in the war and a daughter who was an actress in Paris. The son was a donkey but brave, she said, and incredibly handsome, but her daughter was plain, plain beyond anything. She threw up her hands at this point: "And does nothing about it."

I wasn't sure if I believed anything she said about her children but I had seen a snapshot of the daughter who had what Charley would have labelled 'a modern face': angular, slant-eyed, and wholly charming.

Joe kept me waiting, but I saw him before he saw me. He stood in the doorway, a tall uniformed figure. I had left him in Toronto as a boy; now I saw he was a man. He had been Joe of Jerningham's. Now he was Joe Jerningham, but he was the essential Joe, just as gentle, and just as strong but with an assurance added. Major Jerningham, an officer in the Royal Canadian army. Promotion is won easily in a war, but I had an idea that Joe had earned his.

He saw me and smiled. He came straight over and sat down and Madame at once filled his glass with red wine as if she had known him for years. He did not apologise for keeping me waiting, we both knew we were lucky to have any time together at all.

Madame refilled my glass; she was delighted to see me with a man. I lived too much alone, she said. Men are a nuisance but necessary.

We had a lot to tell each other, Joe and I.

"You first," I said, as the pheasant appeared on the table. "Joe Jerningham . . . tell me about that."

"It's who I am now. The old man left me the shop when he died; he went before she did, just about a year before. But I'd been running it before that. He never really got over the fire, and she never really got over life."

"So it's all yours?"

"Yes, and running well. I have two shops. Of course, I've had to leave a manager in charge, but when I got back, if this war is ever over and I survive, I have great ideas." He nodded as if he was looking into the future that every soldier knew might never be there for them. "I've done a lot already. Separated things out. It was a bit jumbly then. That was the style, but it won't do for now. We have the food on one floor and textiles and clothes on the second floor."

"Oh there are two floors?"

"Three," he answered briefly. "A lunch and tearoom on the third floor."

"You've rebuilt," I said, suddenly seeing a picture of the old Jerningham's.

"Needed to after the fire . . . the old man saw that and let me have my way. He wasn't a bad businessman, you know, but she was the better of the two."

That told me something about Joe, but not all. The successful young businessman did not explain all the changes. There was more, and I should learn, given time.

Like his wife.

124

"Now you," he said as Madame produced some good brandy. She thought we were lovers. He drew his brows down in a frown. "Tell me."

I took a deep breath and told him about Sally Jerrold.

My mind went back to my wedding day. It rained, the war news was bad, I had no romantic expectations.

William Arden Mackenzie and I had been married when the baby was three weeks old. Sylvie was with her wet-nurse, well and apparently thriving.

"I'll take you on, if you'll make do with me," Bill Mackenzie had said. "The kid will have parents. I won't ask anything more of you."

I think he knew I had nothing of that sort to give, that my hard little heart, once softened, had gone back to being like stone again. And as for lovemaking, it seemed I was stone there too.

It was set up as a matter of practical business to give Sally's daughter a name and parents.

Bill Mackenzie and I were married in the Embassy chapel. Lord Bertie, the ambassador, a friend of Val, gave us special permission and speeded up all the necessary formalities. He was convinced the child was our joint product, but was too worldly and tactful to say so. He was a great figure in wartime Paris and everyone knew him and respected him. "What does Bertie think?" was always on people's lips.

Bill Mackenzie arrived for our wedding in a borrowed best suit which was tight in some places while loose in others. He said he had wanted to look the part and now felt he looked like a comedian on the music-halls. I wore a plain hat and a dark coat and skirt.

"Do you think we are doing the right thing?" Bill asked me, just before the ceremony.

"I don't know, but it's too late to stop now." People do mad things in war. "And I promised Sally to protect Sylvie."

Val and Charley attended us. There was no champagne, no flowers and not much jollity, but we had a meal and toasted Sylvie's life in wine. Then Val left France and Johnny Lyonnesse, for ever as far as we knew. What had brought about the break, I did not know then.

"As soon as peace comes," said Bill Mackenzie, "you can divorce me . . . I give the war another year or so." Which in 1917 was not a bad guess.

He was a lovely man, he kissed my cheek, brought me some flowers, and patted the baby's cheek, before departing to his war correspondent's job. He owned the newspaper for which he reported.

It must have been one of those rare weddings to take place with the divorce date provisionally set.

Then he went off, leaving the address of his paper in England and I thought I would never see him again. I don't believe he expected to survive very long the way he went out reporting the war. If a sniper's bullet did not get him, then a summary trial for treason would. He said things that the generals did not want to know.

Joe listened quietly. I saw he was looking at me with a serious, puzzled look. "A lot of girls like Sally Jerrold around. It's a sad story."

"Oh I shall look after Sylvie," I said quickly.

"That's not what is sad."

"Don't be sad for me. No sacrifice for me. It was a business arrangement."

"That is what is sad." He leaned across the table and put his hand on mine. "Do you ever think about Toronto?"

"Sometimes. Not very often." I frowned. "It seems so far away, as if behind a curtain . . ." I smiled at him. "I never forgot you, Joe, nor how fond I was of you."

"There were other things . . . Do you think of those?"

I sat for a moment. "I remember Andrew and thinking I was in love with him. Silly girl." I shook my head at the memory. "I hardly seem to know that girl any more. She's gone, Joe, she's a ghost."

"Are there any other ghosts?"

I stared at him. "No, should there be? The Jerningham's, of course." I stopped. It was my turn to feel puzzled. "Somehow, I feel as if I ought to remember more about them than I seem to."

"Do you want me to tell you?"

I sat there staring at him. Here was Joe, adult, serious, obviously a successful man. He was not a ghost, but where did he belong in my life?

"No," he said. "Forget I said that." He drained his coffee cup. "And Val, what about her?"

"I had a postcard from her last week. From Tunisia, I think. She's wandering about." What had driven Val away? One day I would know.

Madame came bustling up with brandy and more coffee. She liked a handsome well-set-up man and Joe was that. Tired and thin as he was, he was all of that and more.

She poured me some brandy. "You look so white, Madame."

I heard Joe murmur words that sound like God forbid I should do any digging up, but all he said aloud was: "Drink up."

"And now your turn." I hesitated. "Your wife is well?"

"My wife? Ah yes, my wife."

"You are married? You wear a ring."

"Yes, I saw you noticing."

"It's not usual with English men," I said, still hesitant. "More Continental."

"I married a Belgian girl," he said. "She wished it."

He didn't say where or how they had married, or how much he loved her, or what a beauty she was, just that bleak little statement. Nor did he seem disposed to go on speaking. There was silence.

I broke into the silence. "You called on us in London, at the beginning of the war."

"So I did. And got turned away." But he grinned, showing no anger and resentment. "I ought to have known better. I was a humble private then, and not at home in English society, but I've learnt the style a bit better. And the army has been good to me."

"I tried to see you in London. I hated Mrs Madden for stopping me." She wouldn't do it now, I thought. "And then, Val married Johnny Lyonnesse."

"I know of him," he said briefly. "Met him once. Violent fellow, but a good soldier, good with his men."

"So I came to Paris." I shrugged. "And then out here. I never thought it would happen but one day I had a letter from Bill Mackenzie, telling me he was in trouble with the army and the powers that be, and would I come out and take over. I fixed up a job at the hospital when I got here."

"I don't know how you got stuff past the censor."

I looked out of the window. "We don't bother with them much . . . But it's getting harder." It was over, I thought. I was not going to tell him how we smuggled the news items out to London. "They didn't take a strong line at first, but I think the paper will be closed down."

"And what about you?"

I shrugged. I might go to prison. "You've got what you wanted, haven't you? You came here to find Bill Mackenzie and shoot him, and you found me."

"No one's going to shoot you," he said gently. "Nor Mackenzie."

"I think Bill's dead anyway. I met him just once when I arrived here; he managed to get to me . . . After that, we communicated by letter." Once again I wasn't going to say more. "But there's been nothing, for weeks now."

"You're dangerous, you know, you don't think so, but you are."

I looked up, surprised. "People have a right to know of the muddles, the stupidities and the tragedies."

"But think of the men in the trenches . . . Don't you think they know, and better than you ever can?"

"It's them I think of."

"But you bite into their confidence with every story you print. They may know what you say is true, but think of going over the top with the thought in your mind that behind you was muddle and bad planning."

I sat in silence.

"I don't convince you, do I?"

"I see some right in it," I said at last. "But I see my truth too."

"Two rights, two wrongs, that's the way of it, it's life. Nothing simple. You have to choose which side to take, and in a war I know which I choose . . . And it so happens that the story of yours about the Canadian unit was duff."

I stood up. "I must get back."

Joe paid the bill, both of us ignoring Madame's quiet hints that she had a room upstairs to let.

"She thinks we're lovers," I said, as we walked out into the darkness.

"I do love you, Dodo, I always have."

"And I love you."

We stood facing each other.

"And nothing we can do about it?" He put his arms round me.

"Nothing, nothing in the world."

"We can't leave it there." Joe turned to me. He nodded towards a car parked under the street light. "Come and sit in the car and talk."

I looked. It was an open car and the air was damp and chill. "It'll be very cold." I hesitated. "Come back to where I live. I have two rooms. We can talk there."

When I said two rooms, I had a large room which was everything and a very small kitchen. But I was lucky, it still had windows and the roof was good. This was important as I was on the top floor. Underneath dwelt the local undertaker and his family. They were an incurious bunch and took little notice of me except to collect my rent regularly. The undertaker plied his trade on the ground floor so it was in some ways a sombre lodging place.

"It's round the corner, we can walk. You can leave the car where it is."

We climbed the stairs, noises from the lively and cheerful Badoit family issued from behind closed doors, together with fragrant smells of their supper in which garlic and onion had played their usual part.

I opened the door to my room. I saw it with Joe's eyes. It contained nothing but a hanging cupboard for my clothes, a wooden table, a wooden chair and a large bed. Seen through my suddenly sensitised eyes, it was all bed. One large, brass bed.

Suddenly awkward, I said: "Do you want to take your coat

129

off? It is wet." I took it from him and put it over the chair. It covered the chair, filled it. You couldn't sit on it.

That left us nothing but the bed. I felt even more awkward.

Without a word to Joe, I propped two pillows up at the end, went across to the cupboard to bring out a glass and a bottle of whisky.

"Sit," I said. "And you can smoke if you want. I've learnt to."

"No whisky. I hardly ever drink. That's the result of seeing Ma Jerningham hit the bottle."

He looked at me as if expecting a comment, but I said nothing. I drank some whisky and he took a cigarette.

"There's something I want to tell you. It's about my wife."

"No need," I said.

"I want to . . . She's a German."

"An enemy." The words came out before I could stop them. He let them rest for a moment in silence.

"Not exactly," he said finally.

"I'm sorry, I shouldn't have said it."

"Don't be . . . God knows I'm not a lover of the Hun." There was weariness in his voice.

He didn't seem to know how to go on, so I helped him. "How did it come about?"

"Through her brother."

That did surprise me.

"My work has a certain amount to do with prisoners. Those that speak English, although I speak a little German by now."

I was beginning to learn something of Joe's work.

"Some of these men have lived in Canada and the US. Gone there to take work as labourers, engineers. They've been called back to fight for the Fatherland."

He lay back, his eyes on the ceiling, looking far away, through the ceiling into a vast sky.

"I came across one such man. I visited him in hospital. A very young private, he'd been working in Pittsburgh before the war . . . but he was a patriot and he came back. He was very badly wounded and it was clear be would not pull through. He was dying, and he knew it."

Joe stopped for a few seconds. How could he explain

to her the gangrene creeping upon the boy; the fever, the pain.

"I had several meetings with him . . . I won't go into that . . . I began to like him; he told me about his sister. His mother had married again, a Belgian engineer, she was dead, and the girl was his half-sister, child of his brother and this Flemish chap. So his sister was in Belgium.

"They had always been very close. Now they were on different sides in the war. He had only had one letter from her, sent through the Red Cross . . . it didn't make him popular with his fellow soldiers."

I could see that.

"He'd been shot in the back, and a bayonet wound besides. It wasn't an accident or enemy fire."

I made a noise.

"Yes, a long way to come from Pittsburgh to have your own side shoot you in the back . . . It happens, you know that."

"Yes." It might have happened to Bill, who might now be lying buried or unburied, dead because of his undoubted powers of asking the wrong questions. I didn't think I would ever see him again.

"I promised to look out for his sister, to see if I could find her."

Joe paused again and I knew what he was thinking.

How can I explain to Dodo, he thought. Let her see how it was. "She was a thin, waif-like little creature," he began, "but attractive. Soft and appealing. Oh yes, very appealing."

A young man, on his own, he knew he looked more sophisticated and controlled than he really was. A soldier, fighting in a war that seemed less worth the deaths with every battle.

He had tracked Heloise down to the small hotel in Ostend where she was living as a refugee.

He had knocked on the door and she had answered at once and ushered him in without surprise. He had wondered at that, a girl alone. But he had explained himself and she had seemed more startled and surprised then than before, and very nervous. A great wave of colour had swept over her face. "I thought you were going to arrest me."

131

"Did I look so fierce?"

"Not when I saw your face," she smiled, still nervous, "but at first, your uniform. It's different from the ones I see here."

Yes, and I'm running a risk being here at all, he had thought, the Military Police might pick me up, soldiers aren't supposed to be travelling around on their own. But he had felt impelled. And he had some papers that gave him some support for his story of a special errand.

"Canadian regiment," he told her.

When she smiled properly she was very pretty.

"I've got bad news about your brother."

She took the news with the stone-faced calm of a girl who had seen death on every side of her. She shrugged, not shrugging off death itself, but accepting it. "I knew he was dead. I felt it."

The little hotel room was stuffy; she had the curtains drawn. There a something about the room he had not liked. So he had risked taking her our for the coffee and a drink.

It had started then.

He had felt lost himself, needing someone to love.

Joe opened his eyes. "Dodo . . ."

I leaned back against my pillow. "Go on, Joe."

"I married her. Don't think it was pity. I wanted from her what she had to give."

I thought about it with a frown. I knew from experience that marriage between a soldier and a French or Belgian woman was not easy to arrange. He read my thoughts.

"My Canadian unit was a bit easier on that than the British army would have been. My commanding officer was a bit of a rogue, he liked doing things against the rules . . . It had to be fixed . . . but it was fixed, and we were married." He sounded as if he wished it had not been fixed.

"But you're not happy?"

"I don't think happiness was ever going to come into it . . . What she didn't tell me, not at first, was that she had been working as a prostitute. That was why she answered my knock on the door without surprise; she thought I was a client."

"Oh Joe."

"I was still a bit of an innocent them, Dodo. There was still

something of the Joe you knew in Toronto hanging around me
. . . I've changed in the last year and a half; you change quickly
in a war, Dodo."

"I know that."

"I don't think she would have told me, but she had to . . . She
had contracted gonorrhoea. Sordid, isn't it. Nothing romantic
in that."

I looked at him in alarm. Once again, he read my thoughts.

"No, not me . . . it was war, I didn't want there to be a child.
French letters are not hard to come by."

I think he would have told me more – there must have been
so much more to tell – and I would have listened, but it was
taken out of my hands. A wave of sickness started inside and
I rushed across to the basin in the kitchen.

I could feel the harsh, sour vomit in my throat, as I retched
and gasped. Joe was behind me, I could hear his voice, but I
pushed him away.

Slowly the waves of nausea subsided. I let Joe help me to a
chair. "Sorry, sorry," was all I could say.

"Don't be sorry. I'm sick myself often enough. Always before
an action. Every time. Here, let me get you some water." He
poured some water from the ewer on the washstand into the
bowl and brought it over with a towel.

I let the cool water wash my face until I felt better. Then
I leaned back against the pillows. For a long time we sat in
silence. Then Joe said:

"Did it never puzzle you the way you were found in Toronto
and then whisked away?"

"No." I knew I had deep memories of that period but the
scab that covered them could not be picked away.

"It worried me." He took his hands away. "It worries
me still."

I seemed to hear a roaring outside. "There's a wind getting
up," I said. "It's blowing a storm."

"No," he stroked my hair. "It's in your head. Oh Dodo, Dodo."

We stayed together until the sky was beginning to lighten.
Joe slept, I did not, but I looked down at his face with love.
It was a love entirely without passion or joy.

Joe stirred. "I must go."

"Creep down the stairs. Not that they will wake."

He was scribbling something on a piece of paper. "This ought to find me. And I know where you are."

"I don't believe I shall be here long . . . I shall be packed off home by the army bosses. I may be in for trouble when I get back. Prison, you know the sort of charge they can bring. I don't know how we got away with it for so long."

But I thought I did know: a lot of people were coming to believe that the war should stop, that it was not worth the casualties. Such people believed also that all the lies and hypocrisy ill served the men in the trenches.

We kissed goodbye, no promises were made on either side; we knew the ways of war better than that. It was better to remain open to what the gods could offer.

I was quite right, I was ordered home, my passport taken into the care of a smooth-mannered officer who saw me as far as Calais. Put me on the boat and watched until it sailed. Just in case I got off, I presumed.

It had all been neatly done. Two men, not in uniform, but in dark suits and in the company of a French official, had arrived in my office and told me politely but firmly that I was no longer welcome on French soil.

I had had some warning when Nadia failed to appear; she had an infallible instinct for trouble and how to stay out of it. I had no chance to say goodbye to her or to anyone in the hospital.

"I am afraid your husband is dead, Mrs Mackenzie." It was still strange to hear that name.

I had thought he might be. Poor Bill.

I got no more details, no real confirmation, they didn't hand over his watch to me or any personal belongings. I had to assume that his death had been total.

Wiped out. Obliterated.

I mourned him for a good, kind, honourable man.

A new offensive opened, some bits of the army advanced, others fell back, it was all just as usual. I heard nothing from Joe; there could be nothing from Bill Mackenzie. All just as usual. War is silence from lovers and husbands.

The officer who left me on the Channel packet boat was a man of limited imagination. Otherwise he would have watched the boat back as well as out.

All I did was to stay on board and take a return ticket. Then I slipped quietly into Paris.

After all, I had left everyone who was dear to me on that side of the Channel: Joe, Charley, Sally's child, and somewhere, Val.

That was the shell of what happened when I crossed and recrossed the Channel. What went on inside that shell was something else again.

On the way to the boat, my travelling companion, who eventually introduced himself as Major Oliver, told me a little more of the circumstance of Bill Mackenzie's death. There seemed no doubt about it even though there was no body to bury.

With the aid of some peasants, Bill had got himself very close to the front line where a major battle was about to start. What he was doing there only he knew, but it was how he behaved so it was no surprise. He was right up to the German lines, so when the big guns started up, Bill caught it.

This is only guesswork because he was never found, but a work diary of his was discovered in a shell hole which the British army later took. A few clothes remained at the farm where he had found lodgings of a sort, but these the peasants had retained as rent. So there was not even the traditional watch to hand over to his widow.

They might have invented one, I thought, as they so often did. But I owned his newspaper and all related news properties, because Bill had willed them to me before he left. Of course, all might be closed down by the authorities as subversive and I might end up in prison.

Major Oliver allotted me a tiny cabin all to myself. The boat was a troop ship but as was common then, there were a lot of soldiers aboard. I sat on my bunk from which I could see the deck from a round window. The deck was covered with men in uniform, some sleeping, some standing around and others smoking while they played cards. If one moved away, another took his place. One man had a small dog with him. They looked as dishevelled and exhausted as each other.

But I noticed one thing which was true of all the men: however tired and travel-worn they looked, they were shaven and their boots were shiny.

I took this as a good sign: the British army might be a tired army, but it was not a beaten army.

A wind was getting up to which the boat responded with an unpleasant half-roll. I was not a good sailor so I leaned back in the bunk and closed my eyes. I could hear the slip slop of the water against the side. The boat seemed to rise and fall more sharply with every wave. It was raining too; inside the cabin I was dry and warm – outside on the crowded deck it must have been wretched.

No worse than the trenches, I said to myself.

A cramp started deep inside me, died away during a moment while I took a deep breath, before another spasm gripped. I turned my face into the pillow.

The movement of the boat, the sense of the heaving sea beneath, the sharp pain inside, heralding as it did the warm flush of blood, brought back memories of the journey back from Canada.

It was a memory from deep down inside me. It was a memory I did not understand, a memory that came back unbidden, always dragging a bit more of itself behind it as if it was telling me it knew more than I did.

As I buried my face this time, I heard Val's voice, worried and anxious.

"What is it, Dodo? Can I do anything? Oh you do look bad."

Val's voice faded away in my memory, the scene went with it, turning into a mutter of voices through a shifting wall of darkness, just as dreams do. Perhaps it had never happened. Now it melted away like smoke.

I heard the sound of tumbling water, the heavy thud of the waves against the side of the hull, which suddenly seemed fragile and thin, too thin to carry all its burdens to safety.

It took a moment or two for me to realise that the ship had

almost stopped. I could hear feet pounding down the corridor. Running feet.

I sprang up and opened the door. A steward was moving past. "What's going on?"

"Put your life-jacket on, Miss, you'll find it under the bunk." He didn't elaborate so I had to ask.

"What's happening?"

"We've run into a minefield. The captain's going slow." He saw I needed comfort, and perhaps needed some himself. "Don't worry, we'll get through, Miss."

Wearing the life-jacket, in which I placed no faith at all since it looked as if it had been sunk itself several times already, I paced the cabin.

The vessel was crawling forward. I could hear the engines, feel the throb. The men crowded on the deck outside had fallen silent, which gave me a measure of our danger. When I looked I saw that they were not still, but constantly milling about. It was more crowded than ever as men tried to get near the rail.

It was very dark out there so that the men's faces were just blurred ovals, with here and there the red glow of a cigarette.

Suddenly there was a flash in the sky, and sudden illumination. I flinched and drew back, but I was experienced enough in war to know it was just a Verey light, and I thought that meant we must have a destroyer escort who was sending up a flare.

Did that mean there was a submarine around? Or that there was already a ship sinking somewhere?

Another burst of illumination, and in that sudden flare I saw a man's face outside the porthole. I was staring at him and he was staring back. Not a young face, sallow, haggard, and mean.

I seemed to know that face. And what was worse, he looked at me as if he knew me.

I shivered with fear and hid myself in the recesses of the cabin, covering my face.

I huddled there, hardly aware that the ship was in motion and gathering speed across the English Channel.

I think that was why I took a ticket and turned back to France in defiance of all prohibitions. I could not share a country with that face. It was a knowing face. I tried to dismiss the idea of having seen it before.

Some men, and not the best of men, have that look, I told myself.

Chapter Seven

The cowards were leaving Paris.

No one knew me in Paris or cared about me, except the very small group of people to whom I was close.

Very few. In fact, there was only Charley and Sally's child.

But Paris was emptying fast. The German offensive had begun with success, the Allied armies had retreated; the war looked lost.

The German army was getting close to Paris, and the cowards were fleeing. There were still people alive who remembered the siege of 1870 after the Franco-Prussian war of that year, and these spread gloom and despair with stories of eating rats.

But amazingly, letters from Joe Jerningham were getting through. I answered then, but I never knew whether he received what I wrote since he never mentioned my replies. His own letters were always crumpled and sometimes mud-stained. They were the usual standard army letter-forms and had certainly been through the censor.

The first letters were addressed to me at Honoria Madden's house in London, the only certain address for me that Joe had. They were then sent on to where she was living in the country, from which someone, not Honoria who could no longer write, readressed them. I was surprised they were sent on to me at all, and I think not all of them were. After a bit, his letters ceased to come. I wrote giving an address to write to but no more letters came.

In fact, I was not living at the address I wrote from. In my circumstances that might have been a bit risky, since I thought the police, both French and English, might be looking for me. I used a convenience address in a local wine shop where the owner had a curiosity that only extended to getting his bills paid.

Joe must be lost in battle or a prisoner of war. I made what enquiries I could from some quiet secret contacts I had, men I could trust, and eventually got the non-answer that so many women got that he was 'injured and believed missing'.

I grieved in silence.

I lodged with Charley at first, sleeping on a big sofa in her studio. I think it hindered her sex life a little while I was there, guessing too that many thought I was part of it.

"You've changed," Charley had appraised after I had been with her a day or two, giving me time to sleep away the emotions of my journey. "You've changed. Not enough for me to paint you yet, but it's coming."

I knew I had changed. My face, when I looked at it, was leaner, harder, but there was hope in it. Joe had given me this hope, even though I had no expectation that I would ever see him again.

Then the great Allied push came, the Germans fell back, and in November the Armistice.

And no more letters from Joe. I found my own apartment about this time. He might always walk in. I lived for that moment.

Fog and chill on a November morning, Monday the Eleventh. The minutes passed slowly. There was one last burst of firing.

The South African Brigade which was the furthest east saw a solitary German machine gunner fire off a last belt, then take off his helmet, bow and walk backwards.

As the watch hands touched the hour, there was a moment of silence and then a strange rippling sound like the noise of a light wind.

It was the sound of men cheering from the Vosges to the sea.

"Madame Charot says that it is time that Sylvie came to live with us. She has outgrown what she can do, and anyway, Madame is leaving Paris and going to live with her daughter." Charley passed over the news one January day when it was snowing.

"We shall have to get a bonne for her." I was working now. "What's she like?" I should have been to see her, but I had never done so. I couldn't explain why. I was good about providing money, though. I found it very easy to earn these days, I seemed to have the knack.

Charley was silent for a minute. Then she said: "I wish you'd been to see her . . . She might be a shock to you."

"Something wrong with her? Plain, is she?" I couldn't believe it of Sally's daughter.

"She's perfectly lovely . . ."

I looked up.

"But she's silent, speechless, hardly walks yet . . . Slow."

"Madame Charot says children born the way she was – fast and savagely – are often like that. I suppose it's shock or something like that. Or the blood doesn't get to the brain."

I went the next day. Madame Charot greeted me with some relief. "I shall be off soon and I would like to see the little one settled. I love her but it is not right she stays with me."

She took me in to see the child.

Sylvie was tiny, with a cap of silver blonde hair as light as fluff. For a time we had wondered seriously if she was going to be bald but it soon became apparent that she would have tight curls. She had big blue eyes and she was as pretty as Charley had said. She could hear, she could see, but she did not speak.

"Does she walk, Madame?" I asked, observing the motion-less child.

"A little. But she does not play."

Sylvie could walk, but her preferred method of getting about was by a leggy crawl. She acted as if no one had told her she was a member of the human race.

I took her home with me straightaway. I did not like childen, all right everyone knew that, but this was not just any child. I began to anglicise her name, often now she was Sylvia. The home to which I took her was a working woman's home. That I could say this was courtesy of Bill Arden Mackenzie. I had inherited a suburban newspaper which had been closed temporarily but which still had a name and a following. I sold it to a Socialist millionaire, paid all my debts, then used the rest of the money to start an English newspaper in Paris.

Now that peace had come, the city was swarming with

English and American soldiers, diplomats and visitors. The Peace Conference was intending to open in Versailles. This was my market.

I knew I could sell my paper; I would be my own editor and I meant to find a local journalist who knew his way around. There was a fair amount of unemployment so I thought I would be able to hire one easily enough.

I got Mahmoud, an Egyptian, naturalised in France and without any loyalties to anyone. Ideal for my purpose. I didn't want a man who clung to national prejudices; my audience would be polyglot.

He had an American wife and a French boyfriend, both of whom knew about each other and accepted the situation. Even Charley thought that odd.

"Unusual, anyway," she said.

Mahmoud was a good journalist with loyalties to none except his current employer: me.

It was rumoured that he had been an enemy agent during the war, which I did not exactly disbelieve, but he had survived the suspicion. In short, he was man capable of much.

Paris was full of the great men. David Lloyd George from England, Georges Clemenceau, the great French patriot, and Woodrow Wilson himself from the USA.

Paris streets were a danger, so crowded were they, prices were beyond anything. All hotels were crowded. Men on leave, men with special duties connected with the Peace Conference. Press men from all over the world, from *The Times* and the *New York Herald Tribune* to *l'Humanité*. About a hundred thousand extra visitors, just come to see the show.

The British alone had taken four hotels. President Wilson, with a smaller staff, was in a palace near the Parc Monceau.

> Brass hats have small brass hats,
> Upon their backs to bite 'em,
> And bright red tabs have green tabs,
> And so ad infinitum.

In other words, the assembled general staffs of the Allied armies were there in full strength – General Haig, Marshals Foch and

Joffre and all who hung upon them. There was a reception which Mahmoud covered. He was very good at picking up gossip and turning in a good story.

I had very little money but I was managing to bring out my little paper once a week, a broadsheet, which was sold in all the smart hotels, displayed in all the bars and cafés where the Anglo-Saxons congregated and in stalls on the Left Bank. It was smart to speak English in Paris just then; if you could manage an American accent, better still, and my paper profited from the fashion.

I lived on what I had left. Wages had gone up, but I could still afford a daily bonne for Sylvia.

I had a small office near to my printer's where I worked with Mahmoud. An apprentice from a printer's who had some experience with newspaper work came in once a week to assist the technical layout side of the paper.

Mahmoud did the regular newswriting; I wrote the editorial and the reviews. We were great on reviews of new books and art. Charley helped here. We were, what was being called, 'modern'.

I began to take Sylvia into the office with me each day. She played happily but silently among the dust and books and paper. She liked paper and with a pair of scissors and a pencil would play happily for hours.

I had a surprise visitor one day. I looked up from my desk. Johnny!

Johnny Lyonnesse was still in uniform, part of the British delegation to the peace talks, still tall and handsome but otherwise changed. The war had changed him and I saw it in his quieter, gentler manners and the shadow behind his eyes. He had been a good officer, brave, uncomplaining and careful of his men.

"Sorry to disturb you."

"Sit down, you didn't. I'm glad to see you." And to my surprise, so I was. "Let's have some coffee." I kept a thick, dark brew constantly on the woodburning stove by the window.

He accepted and I poured us both a cup. Sylvia looked up with interest but said nothing. I poured her some milk.

Johnny looked at her and smiled. "Pretty kid. Is she yours?"

I shook my head. Perhaps Val had never told him about Sally. "Adopted."

"A war orphan?"

You could call Sylvia that. "Yes," I said.

Sylvia came up to Johnny and leaned on his knee. He smiled down on her. "I like kids, always have. I had a brother once, a nice little nipper. He died."

"What a shame."

"Think it was our old nurse. Gin and whisky were her tipples. I don't know if she gave him any in his bottle but I know she did me. I can remember the taste." He patted Sylvia's head. "I think she did for poor Billy, the old harridan. He had appendicitis and she called it a tummy upset, poor little beggar."

"But didn't your parents . . ."

"Oh, they weren't there. I don't know where the Guvnor was but Mamma was in Cap Ferrat. No, they left it all to her."

I was shocked. "What happened to her?"

Johnny drank some coffee. "Still with us as far as I know, tucked away somewhere at Barton." Barton was the family home.

"You didn't sack her, get rid of her?"

"Oh you don't treat an old servant like that even is she is a soak. She's been in our service for years. Her family had."

It was an interesting insight into the ways of the English aristocracy with its mixture of arrogance and tolerance.

"Wouldn't let her get her hands on a nipper of mine, though." He picked up Sylvia and sat her on his knee; he stared at me over her head.

You're a nice man after all, I thought. You've grown up.

"It's about Val." He sighed. "I haven't heard from her for nearly a year. I need to. If she's not coming back, I'll have to start divorce proceedings, but I need to know where she is. Do you know?"

"She hasn't written to me either, not a letter anyway. I did have a card." I pulled open a drawer, rummaged around and found the brightly coloured postcard. "Here."

He looked. "All it says is Tunis . . . that's not much good."

"No."

He sighed. "It'll have to be a detective then."

He stood up and put Sylvia down by her toys. "Nice child."

144

I don't think he'd noticed that Sylvia did not speak. Indeed I do not see how he would, so expressive and 'speaking' were her eyes.

"You're a good sort, Dodo. Unlike your lovely sister."

"I love Val."

"That too," he said. "Loyal as well."

Sylvia looked up at him and smiled. He smiled back. When he'd gone, I said to her: "You are your mother's daughter after all."

A few days later he sent me a letter saying he had hired a detective from London to trace Val; he would let me know when he got news. He was using a firm recommended by Jameson Forsyth.

Charley shrugged when I told her. "He should leave her alone."

"Oh Charley, why? That's a hard thing to say."

"When you dig up someone like Val you may find more than you expect."

"What do you mean?"

But Charley just gave another shrug, and changed the subject. "How's the child?"

"Coming on well."

"I'd like to draw her. It's a strange little face. A little Infanta from far away."

"She's coming back into this world, I think."

From the moment Johnny Lyonnesse took her on his knee, Sylvia had shown more interest in what went on and had begun to talk. She had always understood what was said to her in both French and English and now she began to utter coherent sentences.

"At first I thought it was a language of her own," I told Charley, "but now I can tell it is a form of English." English into which a fair amount of French had melted.

"Favour to ask you, Dodo." Johnny had slipped back into the clipped ways of his earlier London speech. But I knew the man behind the manner now and was not put off. "I've got to put up a dinner party for a visiting general or two and the odd politician. Will you act as hostess for me?"

"I don't go about much now." I was thinking of my clothes, and my hair. Money had been tight, all I had going into the newspaper, did not allow for visits to Mademoiselle Chanel and Alexandre for my hair. Now all hair was bobbed or shingled, the price of a good cut had gone up and up. And you could tell the difference between the work of a master hand and a tyro, let no one tell you otherwise. A female Parisian certainly knows.

"It's hard to get a pretty woman to help these days, Dodo," he said, making a favour of it. But I knew he was really thinking, Well, Dodo ought to get out and about more now.

"I will then. Thank you, Johnny."

"No thanks to me . . . Shall I send the car?"

"I can get a cab. Or walk."

But he wouldn't allow that, and a car with a uniformed chauffeur duly appeared. I hadn't gone to Chanel's salon although I believe I would have been welcome since my name was known to her for what I had done in the war and for the newspaper I managed. She liked enterprising women, especially if they had rich Anglo-Saxon connections like Johnny, but I managed to put myself together quite nicely.

Johnny had taken an apartment off the Rue St Honore in the Rue d'Echelle, by no means smart but in a lovely old building. I could see in Johnny's eyes when I arrived that he was pleased with me. And I was glad to have his approval, whereas once I would have walked away from it. Had he changed, or had I?

"Well, this is nicely done," he said. "It's how I like a woman to look."

"Oh come on, Johnny, don't flatter me." I knew I could not hold a candle to Val or some of the women he knew. He was supposed to be involved with a new American musical comedy star but since she was working in New York and Johnny seemed permanently domiciled in Paris, I thought it was not true.

The room was full of people. If you had been away from the world for a long time, as I had, there was something exciting and delicious in the smell of scent, cigarette smoke and the faint aroma of good wine being decanted. My spirits rose. 'Hostess, fiddle,' I thought, 'I am about to enjoy myself.' I forgot the war, the anxieties of the peace, I forgot my newspaper and I took a deep and happy breath.

146

I saw at least one general, English, another who was American and a diplomat whom I knew slightly. I was moving towards him when Johnny stopped me.

"There is someone I want you to meet."

"Oh, who?"

"This way."

By the window a figure was standing, back towards me, looking out on the Parisian scene. He swung round as I came up, as if he had been waiting.

"Joe . . ." It was Joe Jerningham. Thin, fragile-looking, but alive. Immaculately dressed too, the tailoring London. I noticed that fact with interest. So that was where the new Joe bought his clothes?

"Joe . . . where have you been all this time? You disappeared. I thought you were dead. Or one of those unhappy men who lost their memories, didn't know who were they or who they had loved."

He smiled, the old smile of Joe of Jerningham's, and shook his head.

"That is so like you, Dodo. Does it not occur to you that although I knew who and where *I* was, I had no idea where *you* were."

"I suppose I did kind of disappear."

"We only meet now because Johnny knew us both."

The two men seemed friendly and on easy, equal terms. I supposed I understood for the first time then that Joe of Jerningham's had become an important man. Johnny said to me later, vaguely, as if the truth of it was self evident: "He's so valuable to us: he keeps the Americans on an even keel, knows how to manage them."

"I'll tell you later how we met," said Johnny. "But dinner is about to be announced."

Johnny had the good sense not to put us next to each other at dinner but I was at the foot of the table as his hostess, so-called, and Joe was placed next to the spouse of a great general. We could see each other but not talk. I saw Johnny looking at us in a kind and friendly fashion. How strange to think of Johnny as being kind.

"I'll see you home."

147

I nodded mutely at Joe. I thought he might have a smart motor car like Johnny's but outside on the pavement he looked around for a cab. There was a shortage of them at the moment. Then one of the other guests, a man I knew slightly, an American colonel, offered us a lift. All the Americans had transport, it was a fact of life. "Am I going your way?"

"The Place des Vosges . . ."

"Get in." He smiled at us both. "Take you as far as Pont Neuf . . . I'd do more but I'm on duty and must get back. But I'll see you into a cab." With all the visitors, it was hard to get a cab just then.

"I could walk from there," I said. "Or get a tram." A tram route passed in that direction.

Joe took my hand. "Of course I'll walk with you."

"I hoped you'd say that."

We were soon at the Pont Neuf where the Colonel stopped the car and apologised for not taking us any further. "No can do, alas."

Perhaps he guessed we wanted to be alone.

We were silent for a while. The river Seine was on one side, and a row of shops and dwellings behind us. A big department store stretched across two blocks. This was not smart Paris, not the Champs Elysées or the Place Vendome, but it was the Paris of old buildings full of memories of the Valois, and the house of Capet and the rise and fall of the Bonaparte empire. To this Paris, the Kaiser and Woodrow Wilson were upstarts. It was a district of small squares and ancient dark churches with the distant rumble of the trams.

"Let's stand and look at the river." There was a recess, a kind of balcony on the Pont Neuf and we stood there watching the full moon reflected in the water. "I like the Thames better than this," I said.

We walked to back the Rue St Honore then turned into the Rue de Rivoli which dwindled into the Rue St Antoine. We still had a way to go before we got to the Place des Vosges.

I lived there because it was cheap. Joe said, after a bit: "It's not quite just round the corner."

I stopped. I was strong and fit and Joe, just now, was not. So I stopped. Ahead lay the Boulevard Sevastapol, then we would turn into the Rue de Birage and the Place des Vosges. "We can stop a minute." There was a stone bench against the wall of a bar. "I only live round the corner. We'll watch for a cab for you. Don't worry about me, the concierge will be waiting up."

Joe sank down gratefully, drawing me against him. "Do you ever think of Toronto?"

"Yes . . . but I never know what to think or how to think of it. It's as if it's behind a curtain. I remember bits very clearly but I think I have forgotten a lot." I shook my head. I saw him looking at me with sympathy and understanding. "But never you, Joe. Never you."

"Fellow feeling." He put his arm round me. "Perhaps some things are best forgotten," he said huskily. "I know there are things I would be glad to forget."

"You mean the war . . . your wife?"

"She's dead. She went in the flu epidemic. Poor child." I saw in his face that he had grieved more than he had expected.

"You always had a heart," I said.

Then he smiled at me. "But in a way it was a relief. I don't know what we should have done with each other in the peace."

"You have become an important man."

"Oh Johnny exaggerates. I help here and there in his affairs. But it is true the business has expanded remarkably. It was on the way before the war, but I left good people in charge."

"You've been back?"

"Of course. After I got out of hospital."

"Ah."

"Yes, that's where Lyonnesse found me . . . He was visiting a pal, and I was in the next bed. I was a bit of a crock. I hadn't lost my memory. I knew who I was and where I was . . . almost remembered how I had got there, although, thank God, not quite . . ."

"Memory is a strange thing."

"Isn't it just? Merciful in a way."

"You think so?"

"We forget what we can't bear to remember . . . I was mighty sorry for myself."

I couldn't believe that. I had never seen a hint of self-pity in him.

"And Johnny helped?"

"Dug me out of it . . ." He tightened his arm round me. "Let's walk on."

"Almost there." I indicated a tall building. "That's where I live."

He looked at it. "I shan't forget. Don't move away in a hurry without telling me."

I shook my head. I hadn't told him about Bill Mackenzie's death or the newspaper, but I had an idea he knew more about me than I knew about him.

He confirmed it. "Johnny's put me in the picture a bit." He put his hand in his wallet. "I have to go to London tomorrow but I'll be back. Here's my card, I've scribbled my Paris base on it."

It was a good address, I knew enough about Paris to guess at the rent. A long way from Joe of Toronto.

"You always surprise me, Joe," I said.

"We surprise each other."

A cab rattled along the street. I hailed it for him. "Take it. We'll meet. We must." I kissed his cheek and crossed the road to where I lived. At the door, I turned to look back; he was looking at me.

He may not have been the only one. There may already have been a figure in the darkness watching me, and had been possibly for days.

Johnny and Joe both sent me flowers the next day, roses from Johnny who was conventional, and fragile, delicate sweet smelling narcissi from Joe. It was the first present he had ever given me.

On the same day came an invitation, sent to the newspaper, to attend a grand official reception at Versailles for the Peace Conference. I'd go, of course.

Johnny would be there and I hoped that Joe would. A card came from London with nothing on it except a view of Westminster Bridge and the scrawl: 'Love, Joe'.

"I shall cover the Versailles binge myself." I said to Mahmoud.

"Oh," He looked disappointed. Mahmoud was a revolutionary, and against all governments, but he loved parties. "Going to be a smart affair."

"I know what to wear."

I knew, but did not have it. I could wear once again the dress I had worn to Johnny's dinner but what was right for a private party was not enough for a huge and very formal reception. Not if you wanted to be noticed by one person in particular.

Reason told me that Joe would be glad to see me anyway if he was there, but reason does not operate in these matters.

At the end of the day, I climbed up to the attic where I kept my trunks. Sometimes clothes, after a rest, can be resurrected. I knew there was a nice little old Vionnet there that I might do something with, and a dress from Lucille of London. The moths might have got there first, of course.

Three trunks to choose from.

The first one I opened smelt of camphor. I drew back with a shiver. This had clothes from the past in it, the longer more distant past I did not think about. Toronto.

On the top was a dress I recognised that Val had worn. A black serge skirt underneath which I did not remember but had probably worn in the shop.

Underneath was a roll of blue silk. I drew it out and let the silk run between my fingers. It was at once soft, and thick and heavy. Marvellous quality. I could not doubt its provenance: Jerningham's. Naughty Val must have stolen it, I doubted if she had paid for it.

It smelt of Jerningham's the once well-known aroma of new cloth, floor polish with a distant hint of cheese pricked my nose. I thought I could make out a touch of old Jerningham's cigars. My throat went dry.

I sat back on my heels. Faces, voices, snatches of forgotten conversation were stirring inside me. A curtain had been raised; events and people pushed back inside me were coming back to life.

I remembered Andrew's face. How strange it looked to me now. I had loved it once.

But there were other memories, even deeper down. I could feel them moving inside me. A sick tight feeling gripped me; it was almost pain.

I threw the silk back into the trunk and closed the lid.

151

After all, there were other clothes to wear. One need not wear a sere cloth.

Mahmoud offered to drive me out to Versailles: he was the only one who had really mastered the ancient car which was all the newspaper could afford.

"Been to at least two of the battles of the Somme," he said about this car.

But I refused, and drove myself, even though recklessness was the name of the game with French drivers. The French chauffeur, never lacking in dash and now no longer fearing bombs and shell holes, had been further inspired by the arrival of the Americans who drove with skill and speed. No Frenchman was going to be left behind by a Yankee, the Americans having replaced the English as the race whom every Frenchman had to beat.

I drove into the great cobbled courtyard at Versailles where Louis XIV had marshalled his horses, and showed my press card so that I could park. The place was full of shining limousines, Rolls and Daimlers as well as Italian and American makes I could not name. But there was a special parking area for the press where less opulent cars were hidden. We were not for show.

I looked down at my pretty high-heeled satin slippers and then looked at the cobbles. I made a decision; I slipped off my shoes and tiptoed across the court.

A great marquee had been set up on a gravelled side terrace where army field kitchen staff were preparing the dinner. We had been told that the retired maître chef from the Ritz was in charge. He was M. Albert Soisson, a famous name.

Army searchlights were trained on the great buildings, lighting them up with bold effect.

It was a grand occasion tonight. President Poincaré was the host to President Wilson of the United States and to the Prince of Wales and Prince Albert, and to various beautiful ladies as well. It had not been possible to get a suit from a tailor or a dress from court dressmaker for weeks now but everyone said that 'readymades' were very pretty and that the chance of seeing a twin of your dress was non-existent.

I could see that I was in danger of being sent round to some back entrance but I marched up the splendid stone staircase towards the Hall of Mirrors where the dinner was to be held and took a quick look. It is amazing what boldness will do. No one stopped me. The Peace Conference met there daily but their impedimenta of tables and chairs had been moved out and a great sweep of table covered with white linen and decorated with shining silver bowls of roses had been laid out facing the park.

Since it was such a large banquet there were three reception rooms. The most important guests, such as kings, presidents and princes met in the salon of the God of War and Apollo; the lesser guests met in the Peace salon which had been the Queen's bedchamber. There was a third reception for the press in the Venus salon. I looked in there with no intention of staying.

It was my business to see everything and I did not intend to be shut up with my fellow journalists only to receive a printed statement of what had taken place which all might use. Not my style.

So I grabbed a glass of champagne and made my way into the Queen's bedchamber where I got in because the British embassy butler was in charge and he knew my face; the salon was full of elegantly dressed men and women. I was wearing black chiffon which, although pre-war, had come from the good house of Doucet. Dresses were very floating that season so chiffon was right, the skirt should have been shorter and uneven, but I could get away with that.

I looked around for a face I knew: Joe, if I could find him. I had had no word and I thought he would let me know if he was to be there. Then I saw Johnny Lyonnesse in the middle of an animated group, of which at least three were elegant ladies. He caught my eye, nodded, and made an amused deprecating gesture to indicate he couldn't get away from this group but it wasn't a bad deal, was it, with one passable lady and two great beauties. One of them was American; I guessed from her shining hair and suntanned skin. Johnny would like that.

Then I saw him across the room: Joe, imbedded in a crowd fully as distinguished looking as those around his lordship, but in uniform, American, British and French. He saw me and moved towards me.

"I only crossed this morning. I tried to telephone but I could never get through."

"The telephone doesn't work very well." It was one of the awkwardnesses of trying to run my newspaper.

"I have to get to that bunch . . . but later . . . Do you have to stay?"

"I must put a story together."

"Do that, while I get back to my party. Then will you have dinner with me? I heard something in London I want to tell you."

"About Val?" I said quickly.

He hesitated. "Partly." He squeezed my hand and turned back.

I saw several of my newspaper colleagues in the crowd. This was the peace and I was legal now, and need not fear the police, although I suspected it would not do to press the matter and I tried to keep out of trouble. But I was known and respected by the other journalists, no longer called 'that mad Englishwoman'. My news sheet filled a purpose and they knew it.

I was nodded at and acknowledged, but I had that strange feeling you get when you feel someone is studying you. The back of my neck prickled.

As well as this reception there was the banquet for the greater souls and I decided, attracted to it by that past of mine that I did not admit, which always inclined me to the submerged two-thirds of the population, that I would get a better story in the kitchens. I wandered out into the rooms beyond the Hall of Mirrors following my instinct, drawn by the clash of china and cutlery.

The food came up the Queen's staircase, and would be carried through the Queen's apartments to the banquet. A serving station was set up in the Queen's bedchamber and a subsidiary table of knives and forks in one of the antechambers.

It was dark in these back series of interlinked rooms, making me wonder how the servants of the Bourbon kings had managed before electricity. There were candles here and there while the searchlights from outside lit up areas of the rooms, yet leaving great pools of darkness.

I was in a kind of tunnel at the both ends of which there was noise and light. Long tables laid out with baskets of knives and forks lined the wall on my left. I concluded they must represent spares and extras because surely the banquet table was long since laid out.

I walked the length of the corridor to find that hot tables had been set out nearer to the Hall of Mirrors where the plates could be kept warm and the wine ready to serve. Two rooms were linked by a short passage; the lighting was stronger here so that I could see right through to the end room. I looked towards where white-clothed and capped figures were at work on the food. Others were moving round with trays.

Most of them were men; that was to be expected since cooking at this level was a male occupation. I would like to have spoken to a woman; I knew I would get a sharper insight, a better story from my own sex. I spoke pretty good French by now even if with a strong English accent. Mercifully my admirers, and yes, I had some, thought this pretty.

No one took any notice of me: I was invisible.

There was one female. She was carrying a tray of goblets; she was wearing a tight, short black satin dress with a crisp white apron and she was swaying towards me on shoes whose heels were too high for comfort, obviously an amateur, hired for the evening. No professional would have worn them. That made her easy game for me.

I smiled and she smiled back.

"Could I talk to you? Ask a few questions? The press, you know."

"What sort of questions? Is it for an English newspaper?" She had had no trouble working out my nationality.

"Yes, but it is published in Paris, I would send you a copy."

She liked that. "Photograph?"

"No photograph," I regretted. "Just your story of the behind the scenes work, the delegates you have met, how you like them."

"Not at all," she said vigorously. "For them, I am not there. Non."

Somehow the French 'Non' sounded more forceful and decisive than the English 'No'.

"Later?" I said, following her down the corridor.

"Perhaps." She sped away, goblets jingling and wobbling on their tray, in a hurry, as if she was meeting someone. Perhaps she had a boyfriend around. There was someone at the end of the series of rooms who might be waiting for her.

She disappeared and whoever was there disappeared with her; I followed slowly. Unexpected curtains, moved by what wind I knew not, were rising in my mind.

Was it a smell, or a shape, or just a sudden sensation, causing me to frown?

The girl in black satin had turned and seemed to give me a smile as she went round the corner. Something to say after all? She was a girl of spirit that one, and I was sure that she could give me a good story about serving General Joffre and Marshal Foch and how she had seen the Earl of Derby (now the British Ambassador) and the Prince of Wales.

"I'm coming." I called and I quickened my pace.

It was dark, as I came near to the corner a figure moved forward from the shadows.

I had seen that face before. I had seen it on the cross-Channel ferry and it had worried me then. But that had been only a face in the crowd, now I saw it close to.

Some people are never forgotten. I knew him now for what he was. Older, fatter, but the face had not changed. He knew me as I knew him.

He whom I had called No Eyes.

A curtain rolled back in my mind. My body was acting out my past, without prompting, against my will.

I remembered the whole episode with him, I remembered being dragged into the wagon, I remembered the room and the bed and the smell. I remembered his smell of drink and stale cigars, I remembered his foul language and I felt again his hands on my body. I remembered my fear and revulsion and how I had had to force myself to fight. But I had fought, the memory of that was with me too. Chastity, virginity is a state of mind. But I was very angry too, I had forgotten how angry. There were details I had even thought I had trained myself to forget, like the hands on No Eyes, so red and coarse and grasping. The sweat on them that rubbed off on me. My body was vibrating with that memory, but yet another picture was imposed upon it. I wasn't here in the corridor of the palace of Versailles, but far away, locked inside another body, another time.

I had been bruised and damaged by No Eyes but I had come through that, I had won; it was what had happened later that mattered.

Hidden behind one memory another came creeping out. I remembered . . . but something hideous was pushing out that had been hidden behind layers of deep sensation.

An old drunken smell, a body stronger than mine. Old Jerningham. I was weak now. Tossed and torn. I could remember it all, faces, voices, moments of pain and shame were coming alive inside me again. Memories hidden inside woke and waved their arms and cried out.

I felt the soft skin of my vagina tear. Pain. Tearing pain. I felt the rush of warm liquid inside me. I hadn't let myself remember that. I remembered the fire that followed and Joe rescuing me but I had wiped out what went before. It was there now all right.

But that wasn't the end, I thought, that wasn't the end. Nothing ends it just moves on. You get the next bit that was planted ready for you to sow.

Just as it should, the scene changed: I could smell the sea; I felt sick, the ship was rolling, my pains were getting worse, tighter, harder to bear without screaming, a soft stickiness came between my legs. I did call out.

Val's face was there, but no body, just her face and her voice. "What is it, Dodo? Why are you screaming . . . oh Dodo, the blood."

The blood, the blood was everywhere, soiling my underclothes, the towels, the floor.

Val's face faded and was replaced by another, one of reality. I saw No Eyes' face coming closer, his mouth opening in speech but I did not hear what he said.

"I was pregnant, and I aborted," I shouted. "Not by you, thank God, but by old man Jerningham. But it was your fault, after you I smelt of sex."

He was coming closer, still uttering something which I did not hear, my ears were deaf to him in this world. He reached out a hand. The furies were out and screaming round my head; I could feel their wings beating the air. He must not touch me. Anything was better than that he should touch me.

From the table behind me, I grabbed a knife and as he came nearer, I plunged it into him. I felt nothing, not even the pressure of the knife on his flesh, not the moment of penetration, nothing.

He staggered backwards with blood coming out of his nose and mouth. He was reeling, rolling down the corridor, spouting blood and vomit over himself and over the floor.

Then he slid to it and was still.

Chapter Eight

Murder is a terrible act to have done. The worst part is that at first you do not realise what you have done. Someone else did it, not you. Never mind if you saw your hand shaft the knife, the energy came from outside.

Only slowly does this other person and you yourself come together, coincide and become one. The killer. That is you.

It takes time but it happens.

Only you are not given time, you are surrounded by policemen and taken into custody.

Then there is the Examining Magistrate with his questions to which he means to have answers and you seem to have none to give. None that seem adequate, that is.

Because of the banquet and the great people who were attending it, because I had killed in Versailles, there was urgency. The Examining Magistrate was shuttled down to the Palace before the King of England and President Wilson had finished their soup.

I was dazed and accepting.

What happens to your victim appears to be that he is rolled up inside a white wrapping and taken away. You are not conscious of this or do not allow yourself to see, but you take it in by some route afterwards. Or perhaps you imagine this bit.

The blood, however, you do not imagine, because some of it got onto you and although you ask repeatedly to be allowed to wash yourself, this wish is not granted.

The Examining Magistrate was called M. Picot and he was assisted by a small man taking notes. Inspector Laurent stood with him. I say stood because the examination took place on site as it were. In the corridor where the stabbing had happened.

This was no idiosyncracy of Henri Picot, but the way things were always done.

As I began to come to my senses, I realised that the police knew who I was and had a dossier on me. Because of the illustrious occasion, they were inclined to think my crime was, somehow, political. I was aiming, perhaps, to get the President or the Prince of Wales? I was an assassin, was I not, Madame Mackenzie?

M. Picot was tall and thin, young enough to have served in the war and by the way he limped, I guessed that he had. Inspector Laurent was older and fatter and had an agreeable, plump face with sharp blue eyes. He said nothing.

There was no roughness, nor any hint of it, but I did seem to have two bruises on my upper arms which I had no idea how I came by. I shook my head at them, they were a puzzle.

M. Picot told me sharply to listen to him and answer. But I remained quiet. "I'm thinking." I said.

He recommended me to stop thinking and answer some questions. A bit of strength came back to me. "I thought he was going to attack me. I believed he was a man who had attacked me in the past. In Canada, in Toronto."

I don't remember what M. Picot said to this, but I remember my voice.

"I want a lawyer and I want to see Lord Lyonnesse." I didn't mention Joe's name but I knew that Johny would bring him if he got the chance.

"And who is Lord Lyonnesse?" All the strong republicanism that crops up every so often in every true Frenchman showed itself in the Examining Magistrate.

"He is on Lord Derby's staff." Inside my head a voice was saying: I have killed a man, I have killed. There is no answer to that voice and the words sit inside you like a cold hard stone.

M. Picot scribbled something down, but made no other reference to my request. I swayed and someone brought me a chair and a glass of water. But the questioning went on. All the time, other figures took photographs of the scene and examined the bloodstains on the floor and on the walls. I was vaguely aware of other persons coming and going and of distant noises. The banquet still went on, as I supposed it must do. What a mercy,

160

they must be saying to themselves, that this female assassin had killed in the back premises and not on the royal staircase or the noble guests might have seen.

"We have the knife, you had it in your hand after you had stabbed your victim in the throat." So it was in the throat, was it? I hadn't known that. "Why did you do it?"

"I thought he was going to attack me."

It was true, but not enough, but it was all I could say just then, wrapped as I still was in my dark memories. M. Picot gave me a baffled look and then he and the Inspector had a muttered conversation. After a bit I picked up that there was not much love lost between the Magistrate and the policeman. I was taken away in a van and shut up in a small and smelly cell which I shared with a lady of the night. She was a decent sort though, and let me have the best bedding and advised me not to admit to anything. "Estelle Tatin," she said, holding out her hand. "Hell, I wasn't christened it, but it's what I call myself." I told her my name and she asked me what I was in for and when I said murder, she gave me a respectful look and fell silent. But before sleeping she murmured to me that all men were sensual beasts, dear, and it was best to take no notice and get on with it.

But I did not sleep that night.

I lay on my back, looking at the stained ceiling, knowing that no oblivion would come to me; I felt as if my life had gone two steps ahead of me and I hadn't caught up.

Maybe I never would. There was the guillotine for murderers in France, wasn't there?

I moved around restlessly, wishing I had a cigarette. I disturbed my companion. "Don't worry, dear," she said sleepily. "You won't lose your head. In the first place, you're English and they wouldn't want to upset the English, and secondly you're pretty, and thirdly, a crime of passion gets you a medal here. Mind you, I wouldn't want to spend twenty years in some of the prisons they've got here." And then she turned over and went back to sleep.

Twenty years, that was the medal, was it? She must know what she was talking about. And had mine been a crime of passion? Hard to say, I thought. I wished I could cry, but I felt dry and hollow.

Estelle was taken away in the morning. As she left she turned to me. "Don't you forget – there are people walking about out there without hearts. They look normal, but there's nothing there." And she tapped her breast. "Empty."

I was left alone with no very pleasant thoughts. I felt deserted.

Then the door was opened and I was taken out, down a corridor and ushered into a room.

Johnny Lyonnesse and Joe stood there. They were alone.

"Thank goodness you are here."

"We've come to get you?"

"What? How can you?" I looked round the room, bewildered. There really was no one else there, we three were alone. "I won't be let go. You know what I did?"

Joe put his arms round me. "You didn't kill him, Dodo. He died from an aneurysm . . . a blood vessel burst in his head and flooded his brain. It was not murder."

"But I stabbed him."

"You don't think that blunt dinner knife did any damage, do you?" said Johnny. "A medical examination showed it hardly penetrated. The blood on you came from his nose. But why did you do it?"

"I thought he was going to attack me."

"Perhaps it's just as well it was blunt," said Johnny.

I covered my face with my hands. Not to be guilty of a killing, not to be facing a murder charge. "Thank God."

"And the British Embassy," said Johnny drily. "And Joe, you don't know what he's been doing. I don't think the President of France or of America or the King of England have been left untouched."

"So I'm really free? I never thought that terrible man would take his teeth out of me."

"Who?"

"Égalité Picot," I said.

Johnny's eyebrows went up. "What's that?"

"Just my name for the Examining Magistrate."

Johnny laughed. "Not a bad name for him. He is an extreme

socialist. Rabid, in fact. But yes, teeth not quite out just yet. There will be charges, but you are free on bail." He looked at his watch. "Come on, there are some formalities to go through, and I am due at the Elysée at twelve. They are starting work earlier there, these days."

When I did not move, he said in a gentle voice. "Come on, old thing, you look done in."

"What is it?" asked Joe.

"I feel as though I want that simple nursery thing", which I suddenly realised I had never in my life had, "of someone putting an arm round my shoulders and telling me that I haven't been so very wicked after all." At last the tears were coming.

Joe put his arms round me and held me against him. "Dearest, dearest darling." He stroked my hair. "We all love you and admire you but me most of all. You have had a rotten time and it shall be made up to you."

I was crying, Joe was half laughing as we clung together. "We trust you absolutely, darling, darling Dodo. Don't we, Johnny?"

Over his shoulder, I saw Johnny's face, full of wry amusement. "But we still want to know what you were up to," he said.

As indeed they did.

A lawyer from the Embassy – Archibald Lomas, whose mother and wife were French – came to interview me next day. He was known as the Englishman in Paris and the Frenchman in London. A small, excessively neat man. He put my position to me.

"There will be no case made you against you. You will come into court but the charges will be dropped. The man's death was accidental and will be admitted as such."

"I'm so glad." I had not been able to eat since my release; two days had passed since I had been able to push anything down me and I felt dirty. I was always washing.

"However, there is a price to pay."

I waited to hear what was coming.

"Your newspaper . . . the authorities have never liked it. It must be closed."

"Yes," I said. But I had my own idea how to do it.

"You are advised to return to England."

I nodded.

"Also your friend Charley. Her activities are frowned upon, she must go."

"Damn."

He allowed himself a smile. "Well, she knows how to look after herself I would say. She has powerful friends. She is on terms of tutoiement with some quite surprising people."

I took another bath after Archibald Lomax had gone, putting into it a great deal of a new scent from Mademoiselle Chanel. I was beginning to feel better, but food still seemed undesirable.

Joe and Johnny called together, both of them seeing my small apartment for the first time. I could have wished it tidier. Sylvia was in another room and mercifully asleep; she had been distressed by my absence. She wasn't eating either.

"You've just missed Mr Lomax." I wished that Joe had come on his own but I knew how much Johnny Lyonesse had done behind the scenes to help me.

"By arrangement," said Johnny. "Thought we ought to keep out of the way. More tactful."

"Don't you want to know what he had to say?"

Johnny raised an eyebrow and sat down.

"Don't you want to know whom you thought you had killed?"

I was silent. I thought I did know.

"He was a private detective, he had a small bureau in Toronto, London, a bit seedy, on the edge of criminal. His name was James Dedds."

The name meant nothing to me.

"What was he doing over here?"

"He had a commission to watch one of the delegation from England. A divorce matter, I believe."

So he hadn't been watching me. Or had he? Had we just met by chance? No, perhaps chance had brought us both to Versailles at the same time, but when he saw me, then he followed me.

Sylvia was crying in the next room. I went and fetched her. As I carried her in she held out her arms to Johnny; she always loved to see him. He took her on his knee. She walked beautifully now and talked away like a little bird, but she did as she wanted. Now she was silent. She had seen Joe and he was a stranger.

164

Johnny said: "We want to know why you did it. We know you, Dodo, and we don't think you've told everything."

It was known by now that the man, who had served in the British army as a sergeant, had been a private detective of no very savoury a kind.

Did I have a very distant memory that I had heard this in Toronto? Memories were like quicksilver, as soon as I touched them they turned into something else.

But there was something that these two had to be told, and Joe anyway would understand.

"I did know him, but not by name." I sat for a moment. "He was older and he had changed, but not that much." I looked at Joe who was frowning. "You knew him too, saw him once or twice."

The door opened and Mahmoud came in. "Morning, boss. Glad to see you back. Brought some post from the office."

I knew that was an excuse, he just wanted to see me for himself, he was a loyal soul, and a very good journalist. He only had one drawback and that was that a very strong smell of garlic hung over him. Even in France which is very tolerant of such things, I had noticed that people drew away from him.

"Mahmoud . . . take Sylvie out and buy her a sherbert." He always called her Sylvie.

Both of them looked pleased, Sylvia because to have a sherbert with Mahmoud was a great treat, and Mahmoud because he would have a cup of coffee and talk to the child whom he adored. He loved all children.

I didn't want Sylvia there while I told my story.

It was hard to breathe but I forced the words out, although I could not look at them. I went to the window and talked with my back to them.

"He was the man who abducted me in Toronto . . . you don't know about it Johnny but Joe does." In halting words I told them about the man and then, in more detail, about old Jerningham's rape. I had allowed myself to forget the penetration and climax, but my body had remembered. "I was pregnant . . . it must have been very early on, but on the ship I miscarried."

*　　*　　*

165

Val knew about it, and I think used to try to get me to talk about it. I realised that I had blacked a lot of those last days out but I could never pull the curtain back . . . I didn't want to. I told myself there was nothing there, while knowing that there was.

I had a picture suddenly of Val mopping up blood and cradling me in her arms. We were both crying. We had been children really. I think I must have fainted then and almost I fainted now.

I swayed as I turned round to face them. "When I saw that man at Versailles, saw his face, it was like tearing a scab off a wound, the blood and poison came pouring out." They had seen infected wounds in the war, they knew what I meant. "And then I thought he was going to touch me . . . that was when I stabbed him."

Joe's face was white. "I would have killed him myself if I had known all this."

Angrily, Johnny said: "What were you doing to let it happen to her in the first place?"

I wasn't having that. "Shut up, Johnny, you know nothing about how it was or what we were."

Joe was gentle: "That's all right, he's just angry. I understand."

The old Johnny, the son of an old title, of a great estate, with Eton and Christchurch behind him would have replied with arrogance, but the new Johnny, out of the trenches, nodded. "I'm sorry. Clearly I don't understand how things were for you. I wish I had known . . . it would have helped me with my wife."

But I looked at Joe. "I should have tried to talk about it before, I wish I had done. The truth is always better out."

"I'm glad you didn't."

Joe started to walk about the room as if he could not control his energies. Or his anger. "Just after you two left, old Jerningham had a stroke . . . he lost the power of speech and I looked after him. But he did struggle to tell me something. I used to listen and watch. I felt sorry for him. He was trying to talk to me . . . but he died before he could."

"What about Mrs Jerningham?"

Joe gave a little laugh. "Oh her, she never said a thing. Anything she knew was locked up inside her for ever."

"And Kate?"

"Mrs Jerningham went to live with her when the old man died. I never saw either of them again except when I paid over their share of the profits. Both dead now."

"I can't believe Kate is dead." She had seemed made of oak, indestructible.

"The bottle," said Joe briefly, then continued with his story. "I took money and possessions from that old man. All I have comes from what he left me. If he had managed to tell me anything I would probably have strangled him."

"No, you wouldn't," I said, managing a smile. "Not your style."

"I'd have had a jolly good try."

"I saw that man eyeing you in the Hall of Mirrors . . . I wished I'd followed him. But you looked so beautiful that I could understand anyone staring at you."

I remembered something from that evening. "You said you wanted to talk about something, tell something, was that it?"

"No." He looked thoughtful. "No, something different. It's something you ought to think about. You should consider what happened to you in Toronto. Think about it and try and remember as much as you can."

"Pictures come and go," I told him. "Bits of them flake off and melt away. Like a dream."

"I can understand that . . . You went back to Honoria so soon after the attack on you. I don't like that woman. I wish she had no connection with you. But she does have. I feel she's there in the background of your life all the time."

I was surprised. "She never thinks of me."

"Don't let's talk about her now. I couldn't then, you looked so lovely."

"I don't feel beautiful at this minute."

"But you look it. You always will. There's a goodness and sweetness inside you that will always make you lovely."

"Oh Joe . . . you only say that because . . ."

"Because I'm in love with you? Whatever that means," he added under his breath.

"I think it's rather because I am in love with you . . . whatever that means."

167

Joe stopped his march up and down the room to come close. "When I was in hospital, I couldn't talk but I could think. And I thought about you and I thought that if I had the luck to see you again I would ask you to spend the rest of your life with me."

"Glad to, Joe," I said huskily.

"You're crying."

"I noticed."

"Come and sit down." He drew me to the sofa and put his arms round me, and we sat there together.

I had never felt so close to anyone in my life before, so sure of total love. I had never had such love before. I had always had to grab at what bits I could get, taking what was on offer. Val loved me, but Val's love had her brand on it and was a commodity all her own.

Funny thing about sex, I thought, this doesn't feel like an urgent thing; it feels comfortable and warm and happy. I ought to have picked up the warning signal then. "I feel so close."

"We are close, Dodo. I should have done this years ago. Crossed the Atlantic, found you somehow, found out how you felt. You do love me? In love?"

"Always have been, Joe." I raised my head: "Where's Johnny?"

"He's been gone for a long while . . . he took himself off to a sherbet with Sylvia."

I dried my eyes: "And Mahmoud, he can't bear Mahmoud." It was the garlic, Johnny hated the smell.

"They thought we ought to be alone."

"I wish you were out of uniform."

"I will be soon. A quick visit to Toronto and I shall be out of the army. They have had enough of me."

When Johnny came back, bringing Sylvia but not Mahmoud with him (Gone back to the office, Dodo), he agreed that we ought to get married as soon as possible and he would be best man.

Getting married in France is full of difficulties if you are a foreigner; possibly it is complicated for those of French birth too, you must have the right papers, the right certificates.

I had none. It was not, as was pointed out, as if I even had

168

proof of the death of William Arden Mackenzie. It looked insuperable.

I was ordered out of the country and Joe had to get back to Toronto, but we wanted to get married at once.

"There's one advantage to an Oxford education, a bit of English history does rub off on you," said Johnny. "I spent three years at the House and this one thing I brought back: you must have a handfast marriage – it's what the Anglo-Saxons did and I believe you can still do it in Scotland. Or you could. You just go into a roomful of people and say you are married. That does it. I'll give you a party at the Embassy and you can do it there."

So we did, and it was to be the cause of endless trouble later on. What you have to remember is that we had all just come through a terrible war . . . we were a little mad.

The clothes for my wedding became of immense importance to me. Important because not only was it to be a great occasion in my life but it had to look like one to the audience. I had to come in looking truly like a bride.

So I went to Mademoiselle Chanel. Johnny had been a customer for one or other of his ladies since her shop in Deauville in 1915 when she sold only hats, but she was now established in Paris, producing her soft jersey suits trimmed with rabbit fur. But with the peace she was adding short, youthful chiffon evening dresses as well.

I bought a suit with a short skirt and a soft jacket in a kind of mouse-coloured bouclé jersey. Chanel liked soft neutral colours. But I also chose a flowered chiffon evening dress with a petal skirt and a low cut back. I had a pretty back.

I had my hair done at Antoine's and bought a hat from Reboux. Chanel was teaching us to go bareheaded but I knew for this wedding day and for this audience, there had to be a hat.

Johnny organised the party which was small in numbers but carefully chosen: Lord Derby himself was unable to be present but his secretary came; Sir Charles Mendl came, one of the Vanderbilt ladies, and a whole bevy of English beauties – Johnny always had a supply of lovely ladies. But several of his fellow officers came and a group of grave-faced men who claimed to know Joe very well.

Joe and I came in together as if we had just left our wedding ceremony. I found it amazingly easy to believe that I had married. There were flowers and music and champagne. A good deal of champagne had been drunk by our guests before we got there which made them very jolly and disinclined to ask questions. There was no cake to cut, the three of us having tacitly decided that this was a point to which we could not go. No one asked for cake.

Charley was there of course, in company with a dark-clothed, spectacled French woman of a severely intellectual appearance who could not be a gatecrasher, so distinguished did she look but whose appearance surprised Johnny. But he was so impressed to meet her that he was delighted, calling her the most influential art critic in Paris. It was my first intimation that inside every landed gentleman is someone who knows his old masters because he has always lived with them.

Charley hugged me and said she wished me well. She was in on the secret but ceremonies meant nothing in her life, she had long since emancipated herself from the laws of the land. Any land. Yet I noticed she always kept within them. I was more reckless than she was, there was a peasant caution inside Charley.

"I wish Val was here," I said as we embraced.

Charley shrugged. "This might not have happened so easily if she had been."

I rejected this at once. "Val would have wanted me to be happy."

"But she liked to arrange things her way. You marrying Joe might not have been her arrangement."

"You've never liked Val."

"Yes, I have, liked her and often admired her. But she's different, that's all. And she would certainly have had a try for Joe. He's attractive and a richer man now than Lyonnesse."

I made a little sound of protest.

"Or didn't you know that? Fortunes are made quickly across the Atlantic, Dodo. What an innocent you are, what shall I do with you?"

But it would be wrong to call Charley mercenary, simply she put a value on herself and the world must pay it.

"I wish I knew where Val was."

"Does anyone know?"

"In North Africa somewhere. Johnny is going to hire a detective."

"He is wasting his money then; Val will be found easily enough if it suits her."

And not if it doesn't. I had to admit she had the truth there.

"But I must rescue Madame Rousillion from his lordship."

I took a look. "She seems as if she could rescue anyone as well as herself."

Joe came across, he had met Charley a few times now, and they had studied each other. "Charley . . . nice to see you."

Charley took a step back and scrutinised us both. "I am going to paint Dodo as a wedding present. Her face is just right for me now."

Joe knew the prices that Charley was beginning to earn. "That's a handsome present . . . but I still want to pay its market value. More, if I can recognise it." He had been perusing Charley's work and knew that a portrait was not a photograph.

"Oh you will recognise her. But no money, there is no price for Dodo."

Joe gave a little bow. "Thank you."

And with this remark, the wry, amused relationship between Joe and Charley was set. She thought he was a prude, but honest and good; he thought she was rakish, but honest and good. Also alarming and a dangerous friend for me.

People were drinking our health, Johnny made a little speech, Joe answered, and then we were getting into our car and driving towards the Channel. I held Joe's hand.

I thought: this will make me happy for the rest of my life.

Part Three

Chapter Nine

Well, of course, it didn't. There was a major hiccup straight away, although it was one I kept to myself.

We crossed the Channel, then travelled by train to London. Joe had taken a set of rooms at the Savoy. A sitting room where we had dinner and where our bedroom overlooked the river. I recall standing there and drawing back the curtain on the first night and seeing a tug drawing a string of barges downstream.

London was grey and cold, but there was more sense of vitality, of cheerfulness and optimism than in Paris. The generation that had come through the war wanted to enjoy itself. The war had been expensive, taxation was up, but many people up and down the social scale had prospered greatly so that there was money to spend, and on every side were signs that it was being spent.

But I felt the change with the London I had shared with Val when we were growing up in Honoria Madden's house. It was brasher, speedier, less mannered. And not many horses. No carriages, or very few, but motor cars and taxi cabs everywhere.

We had a week alone, Joe said, before he had to go to Toronto. I could go there with him, or stay here and find a house for us. He intended to extend his operations to England. There was already a beginning in New York which must expand with the life that was going on in the US; we might be obliged to live there for some months of the years.

He was full of hope. Business was going to boom, he said, later, it might go back, one must be reasonable, but he meant to establish a firm base now from which all future advances could be made.

Jerningham's was big business. It not only had its chain of multiple stores, but supplied others, a double platform for prosperity.

But bed and lovemaking was our business then.

"It's our future now," said Joe, kissing my lips, my neck, my breasts. I held myself ready for him.

My body, which was willing even eager to make love, prepared itself without being told; the muscles relaxed, I was warm and moist. I was entered and enjoyed. I opened myself in the expectation of sharp, bright pleasure . . . but then nothing . . . nothing.

I did not plunge into that world of bliss that I had expected; I acted as if I did, but it was a pretence, and a politeness.

So this was married love, I thought, as I looked up at the ceiling. I wished I had Val to talk to. I felt I understood her cheerful plunges into violence, perhaps it was necessary. But not for me though, I thought, surely not for me.

Joe looked hot, sweaty, and happy. At least I had given him content. But it was not total happiness for me.

I discovered that Joe had a very practical approach to lovemaking. He saw that the room was warm, the room dusky but not dark, that it was quiet, that we might drink some wine – in this luxurious hotel it was easy to arrange.

It crossed my mind that in that part of his life when I had not known him, Joe had not been without experience of lovemaking. Possibly even in Toronto in those early days, he had found someone. And I also thought that in making his so practical arrangements for making love he was acting out a picture of an ideal that he had nursed for a long time – in Toronto as a raw boy whose love session might have been in odd corners, or as a man in the trenches where he could only dream of it.

I found this touching.

It took me right to the boy who had met us on the docks in Toronto that first day with his meticulously turned out buggy and pony and said, I am Joe of Jerningham's.

One day I must ask him what his real name was. If he knew.

He was amusing in bed too.

So I thought, when there is so much love, so much tenderness, so much laughter, what can anything else matter?

We had a week together in London, after which Joe set sail for Canada. "Look for somewhere to rent," he said. "A short lease as we don't know what we shall want. Furnished. This gives us freedom."

I didn't like the idea of living with someone else's furniture so I made up my mind to ignore this ruling.

He had talked to me about his two shops in Toronto, a plan to create a chain of shops; he already had a big outlet in New York. "Jerningham's is class and quality; that's what we sell. Silk and leather, this what we specialise in. Silks from France and Italy, leather from Paris. There's this Frenchman who has been coming over to buy Canadian leather and doing amazing things with it. I shall deal with him."

He was sitting on the edge of the bed while I drank coffee. My life in France had innoculated me against the usual English breakfast of bacon and fried eggs. All I wanted now was coffee. "You're selling luxury?"

"The idea of it, anyway. That's the sharp edge of our selling. Of course, we have solid a underlay of reliable old goods that we have always dealt in."

"No food?" I was thinking of the cheese and the windows of tinned fruit in the old Jerningham's.

"Certainly. But top quality stuff, sold in a specially prepared and decorated part of the store."

"Where did you learn all this, Joe?"

"I think I always had a feel for it, but I took myself on a tour of the high-class stores in New York and Chicago and Boston. I learnt a lot, I can tell you."

Men had their worlds as I was realising and women did not always step into them. Johnny Lyonnesse had a large London house which he wanted to sell and an estate in Hampshire. He would be back soon and immersed in saving them in the new world of peace. I regretted my newspaper left behind in Paris, but Mahmoud was a good custodian and I had no intention of losing control even though I now took little money out of it. Not that there had ever been much to take. I had an idea that Mahmoud would remedy this. On his own initiative, he had made a small change to the name of the paper, had moved his office by a street or two and found new printers. Nadia, my old assistant from the battle days, had appeared from nowhere having dyed her hair red and lost a stone in weight and had joined forces with Mahmoud. She was busy gathering advertisers.

"I'm coming back to bed." Joe took the cup from my hands, and threw back the sheets. He smelt of bath soap and clean water.

After we had made love, he said: "Before I go I ought to tell you something. It's been on my mind since I was last over here. I nearly told you that night."

No need to say what 'that night' was, we both knew.

"I think you ought to see Honoria Madden. There seems to be a story that things aren't quite what they should be there."

I wondered how much he knew about Honoria and my relationship with her. I hadn't said much. Nothing, in fact.

"She won't want to see me. Val was the one. I do write and she never answers. Well, a card of acknowledgement."

"Oh, you get that?"

"Doesn't mean anything. It's just that Honoria has a certain code of conduct. Good manners. She wouldn't not answer a letter. But Val was the loved one. I was a just misbegotten little bundle who came along with the packet."

Joe sat up. "That's the bitterest thing I've ever heard you say."

"I didn't realise I was bitter until now. Unhappy, often, yes. All right . . . why should I go to see Honoria?" I was wondering how Joe should know about Honoria Madden. How could their two worlds have crossed? And he sounded as if he minded about her.

"How do you know about Honoria?"

"I've kept myself informed about Honoria Madden as soon as I was able to do it."

"You mean you had her watched?"

"No, not watched, but I built up my contacts. Men do, you know. And I used to find out about her. Don't you think I worried about you and Val?"

"Did you know where I was all the time?"

Joe smiled. "No, you were harder to keep track of, you and Val, you moved around, changed your name. She stayed where

178

she was. And being in touch with her, I felt I was in touch with you."

After that we made love again.

Within a few days of his departure, Charley arrived with Sylvie, who had made it plain she wished to be called Sylvie but would submit to Sylvia. "Let you get the honeymoon over. Success, was it?" She didn't wait for an answer, that wasn't Charley's way, she thought she knew the answers and very often she did. She knew now. I could see it in her eyes. Not a total success, her eyes said.

She was in a good mood, not minding at all that she had been obliged to leave Paris, and not intending to stay long in London. New York was her destination. But in London she would paint me. "It's a good thing this child doesn't talk much," she said, depositing Sylvie on my bed. "Or she'd get a shock with the language perchance."

"She's speaking beautifully now," I said indignantly.

"Yes, a kind of Anglo-French." And it was true: Sylvie – Sylvia was fluent in a mixture of French and English with the odd German-sounding word thrown in. Or might have been Dutch or Flemish. One of her nursemaids had been come from Flanders.

Meanwhile, Charley soon found a studio in Chelsea that she could rent. To be near her, I took a small house on the edge of Belgravia. I had the whole house painted white from top to bottom, and the uneven old oak floors polished. Charley offered to do a mural for the dining room which I refused. Joe was somewhat conservative in his artistic taste.

Together Charley and I toured the antique shops of Chelsea and Knightsbridge, buying small pieces of furniture and some antique kelims for the floors. I didn't spend much money, only the bed from Peter Jones was new. Joe had been insistent on the state of the bed. He said that a man who had spent the last four years in the trenches (not to mention six or eight before that in the stables at old Jerningham's, although I did not remind him of this) wanted to be sure of his bed. He would have nothing to complain about in his own home.

"Nice to be rich," commented Charley, touring the house with me. "You've bought this sweet little house, made it very pretty . . ." Pretty was not necessarily a word of praise on Charley's lips. "And you can drop it the minute you've had enough."

"I won't do that."

"You will, of course you will." She looked around my sitting room with its rich coloured rugs and the pale linen curtains. "You don't think you and Joe are going to live like this for long?"

"I'm not thinking."

"You'd better, Dodo, you'd better."

But I did go to visit Honoria Madden. As soon as I saw her I knew I had been right to go: she did want to see me.

Or perhaps it was not that she wanted to see me as that she *needed* to see me which in itself was odd. That she let me see it, was even odder.

I had known for some time that Honoria was back from the country, that the place in Surrey had been sold, and she was living in the London house.

Of course, I knew there would be changes but I wasn't prepared to find it so run down. Neglected almost.

I don't think Honoria walked around it much, so probably she didn't know. The room where she received me (one always thought of it as a reception in the case of Honoria) was comfortable enough. The curtains looked the same, heavy red brocade, and the carpet was the well-remembered deep red Turkey; neither showed much signs of wear, but then everything in the Madden house had been bought to last. There was a bit of dust about; I noticed that as a sign of the times that would not have been allowed in the old days. And I had been admitted by a parlourmaid. No butler, no footman – all gone to the war and never to come back.

She was sitting in a big upright armchair. Physically, she did not look much changed, but mentally she must have been because she was pleased to see me. She could speak again but it was slurred.

She was not alone. In one corner, a dark one, whether from choice or because this was where Honoria had placed her, was a small, grey-haired woman.

And of course, Jameson Forsyth had come into the room with me. I remembered him and he had not altered except to grow fatter and older. Not nicer. I suppose that hardly happens with age.

"I am glad to see you, my dear," said Honoria, offering me her soft, powdered cheek to kiss. "I was pleased when I got your note."

I had taken the precaution of writing to say I would call, and I was learned enough in the old ways to call in the afternoon.

A maid staggered in with a silver tray heavy with the apparatus for tea. So that still went on.

The grey-haired lady crept forward from the corner. "Shall I pour, Honoria?"

I knew from her look that she was one from that strange world that Honoria dabbled in; they all had the same air to my mind. Mystics, hypnotists, the readers of dreams, but all not as we are.

They were not all good people and nor was this one. I could almost smell what she was and it surprised me that Honoria could not.

"If you will, Grace." Honoria was always polite, but her manner to Grace had a carefulness to it which convinced me that Grace had a hold on her mind.

The tea was hot and weak as always, but I sipped it politely while crumbling a slice of the rich fruit cake which seemed to have survived the war and rationing unscathed.

After tea and some polite remarks from Honoria and Jameson Forsyth about Joe and my marriage, the real subject emerged.

"I would like to see Valentine, she never writes. Does she write to you."

"No. Oh I had a card or two but there was never an address. I think she's in North Africa somewhere."

"Egypt? It would be easy to locate her there . . . one knows people."

Probably why Val was not there. "No, I think not in Egypt. Tunisia possibly or Morocco."

Honoria looked to Jameson Forsyth, who was eating fruit cake. "It would be possible to check in both those places. But what about her husband. Cannot Lord Lyonnesse give us help?"

"I am not in touch," said Honoria sadly. "He, too, does not answer letters."

But Johnny did not know any more than I did where Val was. The odd card was all that had come his way.

"I think he means to try and find her."

"I think he should do," said Honoria severely. "It is his duty. A husband should know where his wife is."

Grace spoke up. "If you could give me something that her ladyship has worn lately, I could consult the cards."

They all looked at me. So all they wanted from me was a scrap of cloth: a lace handkerchief or a bit of fur.

My spirit revolted. "If I hear anything," I said evenly. "I will let you know." I left soon afterwards, kissing Honoria's soft, powdered cheek. That was different too; she never powdered before.

As I did so, she whispered: "You see there are certain settlement . . . Val is my heiress. I need her signature to release certain funds . . ."

Ah money. I knew that would come into it somewhere. But all the same, she had wanted to see me.

I recalled the grip of the cold, old hand. And as I left she had whispered: "Come again, just come. There is something I want to say . . ." I waited, hopeful of elucidation, but her voice trailed away. "I will remember . . ." she said.

Jameson Forsyth took my arm, muttering words about having heard about Joe in the City. As he held the big, heavy door open, he paused and helped me with my furs; it was a cold day. "I understand you are his common-law wife," he murmured.

I shuffled my furs about my shoulders. "You are well informed," I said coldly. "But it is no business of yours."

It was, of course, if he chose to make it so.

Chapter Ten

Joe came back from across the Atlantic and was immediately immersed in buying large, empty premises in the City, because that was where the money was. There would also be another outlet in Bond Street because that was where the spenders were.

I had met him off the boat train from Liverpool on a foggy day. I had bought a small motor car which I drove myself. The traffic alarmed me, especially at such points as Hyde Park Corner and Oxford Street. Bond Street was quieter and Cork Street tolerable.

It seemed you bought business property by long meetings in dark city rooms, by studying plans and discussing railway routes and access to the docks. Only at the end did you actually look at a building.

I don't know how Joe had learnt to do this. Perhaps he had inherited the knack for he certainly had it.

Johnny said not, that he was a marvel and self-taught. "You know he has no idea who his parents were and never will have."

Johnny had come back to sell his London house in Mayfair for as high a price as he could get, then to put the money back into his debt-ridden country estate. I would have sold the country place and kept the London property but English gentlemen don't do that sort of thing.

So Joe was buying and Johnny was selling. It's known as the whirligig of time bringing in its revenges, except that the two men were surprising friends.

"I'm sending a private detective out to find Val," Johnny said. He saw my face. "It's all right," he said quickly. "No connection possible with the man who attacked you. I am using a very respectable London firm."

"There were two men in Toronto," I said thoughtfully. "Eyes and No Eyes. They were connected. And it was because of the older man, the one who came to the shop, that we came back to London. I had forgotten that. Honoria Madden must have employed the older man. Perhaps this man is now dead too."

It was a horrible thought.

"Good people can make use of evil people without knowing it."

That was certainly true of Honoria, I thought, she had a gift for picking up weird people.

"Honoria is not worldly," Johnny went on. "Why not ask her?"

"Not now, not ever. She has no memory . . . things come and go." I had recognised that when we had met. She had known me, but only as a shadow on a shifting sand of memory.

Then occurred what came to be known as 'l'affaire Charley'. The newspapers called it this, since Charley had come from France and they preferred to believe she was, anyway in spirit, French.

It began in the smallest possible way. I called on Charley in her studio on a wet morning to find her surrounded by packing cases.

She hardly had interest to greet me. "My paintings . . . just arrived from Paris."

"I looked around. "You've been working hard."

"No jokes please."

"Let me help you unpack."

"No, I prefer to do it myself. I may undo all of the pictures."

A lot of trouble might have been saved if she'd let me help; I would have known better what she had there.

"What are you going to do with them?"

Charley sat back on her heels. "I'm going to show them, but God knows where."

God didn't come very often into her conversation which perhaps explains why he didn't help in this matter.

Joe has just bought a couple of empty shops in Cork Street which he is meaning to convert, but not just yet . . . You could use one of them."

Charley was pleased; Joe agreed, although he knew nothing of the style or content of her work, and I helped her paint the inside of the shop a soft grey and put down cheap hessian floor covering. It looked good in a bleak, modern way.

Then I helped her advertise it and send out invitations.

Her pictures certainly livened it up: I ought to have known from the early picture which Val and I had seen in the gallery before the war.

But Charley had been secretive and jokey in the phallic motif then. Now, she was quite open about it.

Everything was open. More than I would have thought possible. Nudes, men and women, lay, walked, straddled, seemed to swim through the air. It goes without saying that they were good paintings, even elegant, but they stunned you. Not all were figures, but even Charley's landscapes seemed to suggest something active and sexual.

There was a group of straightforward portraits, no one I knew, I judged them to be ordinary men and women of Paris. A coal-heaver, a girl of the streets, an old woman with a young child. These portraits I thought excellent, and if there was a distortion here, an exaggeration there, I could understand why. These were ordinary people but Charley had seen inside them to what they truly were. The coal-heaver had sad, wild eyes, and might have been a lost scholar. The prostitute had been a dancer, one knew it from the way she stood, the old woman was a mystery.

Charley used the violet symbol in the corner, smaller than before.

On the walls, the effect of all this was staggering.

The private view was sparsely attended since Charley was not well known in England, although this was to change. Visitors came, drank our wine and studied what was on the walls. One or two left rapidly. There was some muttering, but one man, an eminent critic, came to Charley to congratulate her on her bravery.

"Marvellous brush work, but you run a risk."

Charley grinned. She knew it, of course, and I was beginning to feel it. There was no doubt she was a major artist in the making, but she was also dangerous.

Someone, we never knew whom, complained to the Lord Chancellor, who was disposed to be liberal but was impelled by his position.

Next day a vanload of uniformed policemen headed by a detective inspector and a detective sergeant piled into the shop, arrested me and Charley and took us to Bow Street police station. They cleared the shop, taking away all the pictures which they considered indecent.

"I say, what an arse," said one of the constables as he carried out a picture. "Wouldn't mind bedding her. But she can't draw this Charley. One cheek is fatter than the other."

That was when Charley hit one of the policemen and that was why they took us away.

The pictures were stored in a cellar and the rumour went around that they were going to be burnt.

We were bailed out by Johnny who thought it all a good joke and said he'd been stuck in Bow Street himself after a drag hunt dinner, and that this was the second time he'd had to visit me in prison and would I give good warning next time because he'd been in bed. He didn't say with whom.

Next day Charley and I came before a magistrate accused of causing public offence and being a danger to the morals of the United Kingdom. At least I think that was what it was called.

Joe was also in trouble as the owner of the premises.

We all got off with a caution, but Joe was not pleased. He blamed Charley more than me, after all I was his new bride and he did love me, even though I suspect I was a disappointment to him in bed. But he sold the shop where we had held the exhibition, and I took this to be a sign of something. He sold it at a profit, of course. At that stage in his career, everything Joe touched turned to profit. I was hopeful that I would in the end.

Of course, Charley and I did not get away unscathed. We were harassed. Somehow Charley's address was discovered. Ordure through the door. Shouted at by well-dressed matrons in furs, that was the way it.

Johnny said: "The detective I sent out wired me that he had found where Val was living. Not too difficult, I guess, Val would never be easy to hide, but she would not see him. He couldn't get in. I want you and Charley to go."

That was only an excuse, of course, to get us out of the way, while the press and the British public got over its fit of morality.

"It seems she is in Damascus. She has rented a house there. Old and beautiful, the detective said, but with a high wall and a locked gate."

"Can't you write?"

In a dry voice, Johnny said: "It seems that in Damascus you need not receive your letters unless you wish. At any rate, she has not received mine, nor answered them."

I could see that silence would be Val's way out.

"I don't know if Charley will go."

"Of course she will, if you ask her."

I gave him a sharp look. "Charley doesn't feel that way about me."

"Certainly she does, and always has done, I should guess." He laughed. "But don't worry, Charley is, in her way, a gentleman."

And this was true. All of it was true. I asked Charley, who thought for a minute because she said she had planned to go to New York, and then said yes.

So Charley and I were shuffled off to North Africa. Overland to Marseille and then by boat. It took us two weeks and we got there as the summer was hotting up.

There was cholera in Damascus.

Chapter Eleven

There was always cholera in Damascus.

Damascus was a magical city. It was also a secret city; beyond the crowded narrow streets its true life went on behind the courtyards and walls of the houses.

The streets were noisy and dusty with pedestrians, horsemen and camel drovers, all pushing for position on the cobbles. It was very hot and I pitied the Arab women who were shrouded to the eyes in black draperies, but perhaps they were cooler than they appeared. The men strode past festooned in what looked like floating rags in some cases, while others were dressed in dazzling white. Young children seemed to wear nothing as they darted in and out of the traffic. All of them, men, women and children, had sparkling black eyes.

It was a city of mixed heritage: Greeks and Turks as well as the Bedouin had contributed to make it what it was. You could sense the history and feel the touch of ancient Greece and Rome. Now the French were here to add their cosmopolitan gloss.

As well as cholera there was typhoid, the plague and something called 'jumping fever'; these diseases were endemic.

Charley and I stayed at a small hotel run by a Swiss family. It was in a relatively modern building with what we hoped would be safe sanitation. Charley did not fear disease and nor did I but this was no time or place to take sick. The Swiss proprietor advised us to wear a little mask over our mouth and nose to avoid infection; it came from the dust, he said. Dust there certainly was and in abundance. Also a strong smell of horse and camel dung.

I remembered how London had smelt of horses in those days before the war and how it no longer did. Smells do bring back memories. I began to think of the Sunshine Home where Val and Charley and I had first come to know each other. I could remember the smell of strong soap and disinfectant that had hung over the Home.

Had we been such wicked, evil girls? I asked Charley over our first breakfast in Damascus. I wanted to clear my mind before we saw Val. We had her address and surely she would see us?

"Do you think we should engage a guide?" I asked Charley. She thought not. "We can find the way. There are cabs." Cabs, carriages, equipages of a battered sort plied for hire outside the hotel. The men who drove them looked wild but we could take their honesty on trust the hotel manager assured us. Two women on their own would be respected. "We will do better if Val knows we are on our own."

We discovered that Val's residence was well known. Lady Lyonnesse was a figure in the town: she gave parties, held entertainments and went about herself as a guest to Arab and European households alike. If the Europeans kept her at a cautious distance, the Arabs loved her. She was beautiful, rich and generous.

So much our driver told us.

Val lived down a narrow alley which was lined with high stone walls. A narrow gate gave entrance to a courtyard, beyond which lay the house. But you had to get into the courtyard and the gate was locked.

There was no bell, no knocker, nothing. I could see how Val had remained inviolate. Perhaps you were meant to shout.

I looked at Charley who was laughing. "Just like her, isn't it?"

I rattled the gate, and to my surprise an old man, wrapped in dusty robes, appeared from a crevice and looked at me. I demanded to be let in. In English. I gave my name.

He stared for a moment without moving.

"Lady Lyonnesse," I said. "I want to see her. Let me in."

He thought for a minute more then gave a shout. A small boy appeared from across the courtyard and the old man spoke to him. Instructing him, I thought, because the boy nodded and strolled away.

The old man shouted at him; the boy began to run.

"That made him get a move on," said Charley with satisfaction. "I think we're in."

As she spoke, a woman appeared in the doorway of the house. A wrinkled, grey-haired figure.

"Val's got plenty of servants."

The woman nodded to the old man, the gate was opened and she beckoned us to follow her.

The house was cool and dark with shuttered windows. We were led through several rooms into another courtyard. This courtyard was small, private, dappled by the shade from several trees, and cooled by a running fountain in its centre.

Under the trees a couch was heaped with pillows. No sign of Val, however.

Here the woman left us, without a word. We were beached, stranded.

"Nice here," said Charley. "Trust Val. Good light, good colours, I could paint here." She sat down on a pile of cushions, drawing her sketchbook from her pocket. "Just a few notes."

Across the courtyard was a room with an open door. I strolled across to look. A large room, and at the end of it a couch, with cushions like the one outside. And on them lay Val, her arms fondly round another figure which she was kissing.

I made a sound and Val sprang up. She was wearing soft blue robes, almost as if she had adapted to Arab dress, but looser and silkier. Very becoming, I thought, Val always knew what she was doing with clothes.

Val put her arms round me and kissed me warmly on both cheeks. "Hortense didn't tell me who you were."

"I thought she had," I said bluntly. "I told her."

"Well, I was just coming."

Across the courtyard, Charley had seen us and stopped her sketching.

I stood where I was. She was herself, only more so. Val had thickened, put on weight, flesh covering the fineness of her bones. Her skin seemed darker and she had lined her eyes with kohl; she had tinted her lovely hair with henna so that it was reddish.

She was still beautiful but her beauty was more suited to the land in which she lived. Perhaps Val, the instinctive performer, had felt the pull of a different taste and had responded to it.

I thought of her in Canada; there she had been bright and sharp, the New World girl.

In London she had been moved with womanly grace, all softly elegant, flounces, pleats and tucks. Her hair had been carefully composed about her face. It had been a static look but strongly feminine. Perhaps she had always bent herself towards the world she lived in, shaping herself to what it wanted.

Now here she was female rather than feminine, voluptuous and seeming to offer rich attractions. It was a secret look. I felt the secrecy.

I looked towards the figure on the couch. He still lay there. Val took my arm and turned me away. I let her move me.

"Oh, Val, he is not your lover?" He was so young, so very young. But I had seen the way she had bent towards him.

"He is my son."

"Your own child?"

Charley was walking towards us.

"But not by Johnny . . . That young man in Paris with the skin like ebony."

"Now you see why I had to hide. In law, he is Johnny's rightful heir. The next Lord Lyonnesse." In a half-amused voice she said: "Johnny wouldn't like it."

Charley was almost upon us.

"Are you coming back? Do come Val, somehow things can be worked out."

"I can't, really, Dodo. Anyway, I couldn't come now, the boy is ill, he has a fever." She moved the hair off her forehead. She looked flushed herself. "You'd better go yourself. I'm glad you came – I wanted to explain, but of course, I wasn't going to speak to the man that Johnny sent. I couldn't trust him."

"I see."

"And I wanted to see you, Dodo," she said. Her voice was softer.

"What about Charley?"

"Oh yes, Charley." Once again she sounded amused. But tired. There was fatigue in her voice.

Charley had come right up. She was studying Val with that cautious, amused gaze she wore with someone she found interesting. She came right up to Val and kissed her on the cheek.

"Thank you, Charley." Val accepted the kiss with dignity. "I

191

am touched you should kiss me, especially as you have never liked me."

"I may not like you but I have always admired you."

Val laughed. "Come on, no flattery. I am too old for that ... Nor is it your line, Charley. Tough honesty, that is what you go in for. In your painting as everything else." She flicked her eyelashes at Charley and smiled. "I know all about you and your shocking paintings. I get the English newspapers. A day or two late, but I read them in the end. I know more about you two than you know about me."

"Always the case in my opinion," said Charley gruffly. "But my God, you've improved, I could draw you now."

"I don't accept. Keep your pencil for Dodo. Have you done her yet?"

"I'm always trying but she won't agree."

Val led the way forward. "Come in, come in." She led us into an inner room which was cool and scented. Everywhere were piles of large, soft cushions. She sank down on one. "Sit down. More comfortable than you would think once you get used to it."

She clapped her hands and called out: "Hortense, tea." Presently, Hortense appeared with a tray of little cups filled with a pale liquid and a little saucer of sweetmeats.

"She is French," Val told us, as if the woman was not there or could not hear. "But she prefers to dress like the Arab women, as I do myself. It is more convenient. And really cooler."

We sipped the tea while I considered what to say.

"Johnny wants you back."

Val shrugged.

"Or a divorce," I said bluntly.

"He can have that."

"He needs evidence."

"Ah."

"You must come back, Val. Honoria wants to see you too."

That got a small, cynical response. Val raised an eyebrow. "Something about money, I expect."

"Yes, I think it is."

"Oh Dodo, you must realise how far away from Honoria and her world I have moved."

I heard Charley make a sound somewhere between a snort and a laugh.

"You owe her something, Val. You are her only descendant, her heiress."

"All the more reason for not letting her see me now."

"She settled money on you," I said. I felt cross.

"And on that I am living. I don't touch Johnny for anything . . . Or not much."

It was impossible not to laugh. "Oh Val, you are hopeless."

"Not at all, I am full of hope, and you must be for me, but just at the moment I am very tired . . ."

She looked it, I thought. Goodness knows what her life was really like.

"Come back tomorrow and we will talk about Joe and that business in Versailles . . . oh yes, I know about it. More tea? No?" She kissed us both. "Tomorrow. Go sightseeing, there is so much to see. Roman ruins, Greek temples, Crusaders' castles. And go down into the souks. Don't touch the jewellery, it is usually rubbish which they swing on visitors but you might find lovely brocades and damasks."

"That was the authentic Val speaking," said Charley as we left.

"I hope she will agree to come back when we see her tomorrow."

But when we came back the next day, the gate was barred and no one answered. I shook the gate and shouted while Charley watched.

"She means it this time." I sank back in despair. "Oh, Charley, what's it all about?"

"She is play-acting. Val always is." Charley shrugged.

I shouted through the gates: "I'm coming back, Val. Don't think you've got rid of me all that easily."

Charley said nothing; she was looking down the street and then back at Val's house.

"Oh come on, let's go."

"No, I want to watch. Come across to that little café and drink some coffee."

It was a tiny, shabby but friendly establishment which soon

provided us with tiny cups of the bitter, exceedingly strong coffee that was imbibed in Dasmacus and which even French coffee had not prepared me for. I liked it, although it hit the stomach like a hot bullet. With it came a glass of water and a little saucer of dark jam.

"So?" I said to Charley. "What are you watching? She isn't going to let us in."

"Think about Val and what you know of her. Is it likely that she is here just because of her child?"

"Don't you believe her?" I was looking at my cup and wondering when it was last washed and how.

"Rub the edge with your handkerchief," said Charley irritably, watching my face. "Yes, I believe her as far as it goes. But what else keeps her here? Or who else? Have you ever known Val without a lover of some sort."

I sipped my coffee which was thick and sweet. "So you think she has someone here?"

"And that is why she will not receive us now . . . He is either there or is expected. I am going to wait and see."

"We may have to wait all day."

But we did not; I was on my second cup of coffee when there was a flurry of horsemen at the end of the street. A troop of half a dozen clattered up. All wore the flowing Bedouin robes of the nomadic Arabs. They reined in outside Val's house.

"Six of them," I said, horrified.

"Look at the one in the middle."

He was the leader, a tall, dark-skinned man with the shining dark eyes of his tribe. And it was he, who was admitted to the house. The rest of the band, saluted and wheeled away.

Charley was satisfied. "So now we know. And he's rich too, those are superb horses."

"Yes, no doubt there. He's Val's lover. Oh dear."

"Don't worry." Charley was amused. "She can't marry him. He's probably got six wives already."

"That might not stop Val. She'd edge them out."

Charley laughed. "Wife number one, eh?"

I felt sad. "Perhaps he is the love of her life."

We went back to the hotel where I stayed in my room. I had a headache. I was finding the heat and smells of

Damascus unpleasant. Undaunted, Charley had gone out with her sketchbook to see the sights.

She came back in the late afternoon and found me resting on my bed. I raised my head from the pillows. "I've brought you some coffee," she said. "Do drink it."

"Thank you. That was well done. I am thirsty."

"Drink up," she said, watching me.

"I shall go back tomorrow."

But she handed me a note. "This was waiting down below." It was from Val.

'Darling Dodo and Charley,

I cannot see you now. The boy is too ill. Go back home, Damascus is a pest house just now. I promise you I will write as soon as I can and follow my letter back.

All my love,

Val.'

I handed the letter to Charley who read it slowly but as if she knew already what it said.

"Is she telling the truth?" My mouth was very dry.

Charley folded the letter, and handed it back to me. "I think she's right. This town is boiling with sickness. We'd better go."

I leaned back against my pillows. "Charley, I think I am pregnant."

"All the more reason to go."

She said this too as if she knew already. Perhaps Val knew too. Did everyone know more about me than I knew myself?

Chapter Twelve

I did not have typhoid but one of those nameless fevers that Damascus bred. I felt ill enough as we travelled home, but I refused any suggestion we break our journey in France. I was still, I suspected, *persona non grata* in that country. Mahmoud kept my news-sheet going, taking his own rake-off of the profits, and passing on what he thought was my due, but my name did not appear as owner. The police knew better, I expect, but provided I kept away, allowed the fiction to go ahead.

On our first day back I had lunch with Johnny at the Ritz to tell him about the trip. I edited what I told him about Val and her life in Damascus, not mentioning the child.

"But she will be in touch. She promises you your divorce."

Johnny received the news with a wry smile. "She'll do it in her own good time, I suppose. Val always does what she promises one way or another. That virtue I will allow her. I am glad you saw her. I suppose I ought to go myself but I don't think she'd see me, damn her."

"No, I don't think she would."

"Thank you for going. You're a good sort, Dodo. Are you all right? You don't look well."

"A bit recovered today but my temperature goes up and down."

"I recommend bed. Thorough rest."

He never rested himself, being one of those healthy English gentlemen who cured everything with a good gallop.

He had finally sold the house in Charles Street. It was going to be turned into a club. Johnny did not care too much, like most Englishmen of his class and generation; it was the country house that counted. He said it was small and not too difficult to run. "Only sixteen bedrooms and the gardens and park not too much of a worry." Agriculture was enduring a depression which lowered his income from the estate, but Johnny had other resources; his mother had been an heiress of a great banking and brewery family.

"I want you and Joe to come and stay in Lyons Court." This was his house in Dorset.

But my next duty, unwell as I felt, was to call on Honoria to tell her about Val.

The house smelt stuffy and sour. I remembered it when it had been well staffed with servants who kept all the furniture well polished; I recalled the old butler and the doorman. Where were they now? Long dead, I supposed. The house itself was dead.

Honoria no longer owned it, the lease had run out during the war, and she now rented it from a City company. I was never sure if she took this in.

I was shown into see Honoria by a maid I had never laid eyes on before. She was grey-haired and her uniform not as trim as I would have expected but she was polite enough.

"This way, Madam," and she pushed open the door to the big drawing room, always Honoria's favourite place for receiving visitors and holding audiences. I had chosen the old-fashioned afternoon visiting hours which Mrs Madden had once held so sacred. You called then. Or not at all.

For once she was alone, sitting in a great chair by the fire. The room was overhot and airless.

I told Honoria about Val but she raised her head to stare at me absently; she seemed to have forgotten that she had asked me to speak to Val.

She had somewhat regained the power to speak after her stroke, but her memory seemed patchy. She had a newspaper on her lap as if she was reading it, but I noticed it was unopened. Of course, she was as beautifully coiffed and dressed as usual.

I felt sorry for the proud old woman who had given so much, but never love. She was gentle though, the sharpness was gone.

"Thank you, my dear daughter," she said, taking my hand.

I said nothing.

"I am Alice Sit By the Fire now." She saw my puzzled look. "It is a play by Sir James Barrie which I remember seeing. I cannot remember what it is about but I remember the name. Words, you know, make great companions, and it is what I do now. Sit by the fire."

She had never been a clever woman but she had been an active one, prompt to carry out her own ideas. Now her life seemed managed for her. There was no one with her but I felt the presence of someone in the background.

I saw her tongue pass across her lips as if she was thirsty. Normally by now a maid would have brought the heavy silver tea tray, loaded with pot, hot water jug and delicate blue and gold Worcester china. Or Honoria would have tugged at a bell and it would have arrived with speed.

"Would you like tea ordered?" I asked.

"Tea?" She looked around vaguely. "Yes, order it, my dear, if you will."

I rang the bell. No answer. I gave it a long, hard tug. Still no reply.

Honoria seemed unsurprised.

"A minute," I said. "I'll see what is happening."

I went out into the hall. I stood for a moment, thinking. Then I opened the door of what was the library, then the dining room, then the little morning room. Behind every door was an undusted room and an air of neglect.

I pushed the green baize door and stood at the top of the stairs that led down to the kitchen. No one around.

I marched down the stairs to find a circle of servants, comfortably tucking into a large, cooked tea. They looked up in surprise.

"I rang."

"Well, Madam," said the woman who was probably the cook, she was the fattest and reddest of face.

"No 'well' about it. Your mistress needs some tea. Now."

I turned on my heel and went upstairs.

In a quicker space of time than I would have expected, a tea tray appeared. I saw Honoria drink her tea and eat a scone before I got up to leave.

I rang the bell again. This time I got a quick answer. The woman who had let me in appeared.

"I am going now, but I shall come again. If I find your

mistress is not well looked after, I shall sack the lot of you."

Then I left. When I consulted Joe, he said I had better see Honoria's lawyer, old Jameson Forsyth.

"I'll go tomorrow. I suppose I have his address somewhere. Or you could get it for me."

We were at home in the London house I had decorated so carefully, and where I was now creating a nursery.

Joe looked at me in a worried way. "Don't take too much on. You don't look well."

I blamed a lot of my sickness on my pregnancy now I was safely home in London. Joe insisted I rest and even engaged a nurse to watch over me. A child, possibly a son, would be marvellous.

"I never had anyone," he said. "I know nothing of my family. I lived with a family in London who told me they had adopted me. Then I was shipped out to old Jerningham in Toronto. I was eight or ten or older . . . I've never been really sure of my age or my name."

"Jerningham does well enough." Although, in truth, it was not a name I was proud to bear, but that was not Joe's fault. It was one of his little insensitivities that he was still willing to use it even now he knew all that the old man had done to me. I was learning about Joe all the time.

"It makes one thing urgent," he said.

"What?"

"We must be married properly."

I had almost forgotten that we had not.

"But I have had a good firm of lawyers working on it," he said. "And they've got the documents together."

Joe had managed to get proof of the death of our respective spouses. Joe knew that the girl he had married had died of influenza in 1918. I knew that Bill Mackenzie Arden had left his billet in Flanders at the time of a big push, had gone out into heavy shelling and never been seen again. He was missing and presumed dead; one of the great unburied of the Great War.

A good man and I mourned him with Sir Edward, and the young Eddy who had gone one day to lead his men over the top and had never come back. You never get over such deaths, they are there inside you for ever. Sally was there too, but I had her living representative in Sylvie.

She was growing, looking more like her mother every day. The child inside me did not grow, however. It seemed that a high fever could inhibit development. Eventually the doctor who examined me informed me bleakly that 'there was nothing there' and recommended what he called 'a scrape'.

A scrape to tidy me up, to clear what was left of what could never grow.

Joe minded more than I did. The maternal hormones had not had time to grow either. Sylvie did not call them out; I loved the child but I could not mother her. She had a good English nanny and lived the life of an upper-class English child, which, after all her mother had been. But I think she had been happier with the wet-nurse in Paris and with outings with Mahmoud and his family. She spoke beautifully, still in both French and English, sometimes a mixture of both, and was promising great loveliness.

Joe and I had a very quiet, anonymous marriage ceremony in Caxton Hall, then the fashionable place for secular weddings. No church seemed to suit us both.

But we plighted our troth to each other with love, and with Johnny as a witness, and to protect the future of that infant who had already signalled his departure.

Then we went to stay with Johnny in Lyons Court. This was a dark, quiet old house with clear evidence of its medieval beginnings. Johnny was both a proud and devoted owner.

"We have a Roman mosaic in the grounds. There was a Roman villa and perhaps a temple, and there's evidence of a building even before that. There has always been a house here."

He showed us round the park and gardens with pride. I found it hard to think that Val had ever been mistress here even for a fleeting few weeks at the start of the Great War. She had left no trace, there had been no time for a portrait of the lady of the house. Gainsborough, Romney and Sergeant had painted her predecessors, but there was nothing of Val, except a wedding photograph.

"I haven't heard from that damned woman," complained

Johnny. "Supposed to be getting in touch about the divorce, wasn't she, blast her?"

In the weeks before the ceremony, Charley had attempted my portrait. I say attempted because she claimed herself that I was going to be very difficult to achieve.

"You change, you disappear sometimes." She picked up the charcoal with which she was marking out the canvas.

"I am always there," I protested.

"No, you only think so. The real you goes down a rabbit hole somewhere."

"Thank you."

"But you have settled into your face now." She worked away. "When I have finished this portrait, it will be my gift to you. I shall go away. Don't burn it or throw it away; it will be valuable one day."

It was a good portrait, though, even if it did make me look some ten years older than I was.

"That is how I see you," said Charley. "That is how you will be."

Joe did not approve of the portrait when he saw it first, because it made me look older than I was, but he learned to appreciate it later.

"You may never see her like that," said Charley gravely. "But you should."

Charley announced that she would leave for New York soon afterwards, saying that from all she had heard she would do better there than in London.

"What about Paris?"

"No, I have used that up. I might go back to Syria, but New York first. I see my future there."

Joe studied the picture with a grave face, said he did not like it but he saw its power. He hung it in the office he had established in the City and I knew it meant he was proud of me.

Charley superintended the hanging of the picture, checking to see it was placed at the right height and that the light on it was how it should be.

"Watch that woman," Charley said to me. "She has the mouth of a procuress." Miss Gilroy was certainly no beauty; I could not

201

accuse Joe of choosing a beautiful secretary. "She is no friend to you."

"You do say extraordinary things."

"I think them too," smiled Charley.

Miss Gilroy might not be attractive but her young sister who managed the telephone was one of the prettiest girls I had ever seen.

Two days later, Johnny received the letter from Damascus that he had been waiting for. But its contents were not what he had expected.

I got a telegram from him, asking me to meet him in the Ritz for lunch.

He was standing waiting for me when I arrived. "Sit down." He handed me a letter. "Read it."

Inside was a letter on thin paper in a spidery hand. It was from Hortense. She said Her Ladyship was dead. She had died of fever two weeks ago.

Hortense presented her compliments and passed on to us the certification of the death. A thin slip of yellowing paper, printed in an evil type which was difficult to read and typical of French provincial officialdom at its worst, fell out of the envelope.

I sat there, unable to take it in. Val was dead.

I had a picture of her with her beautiful hands, henna-tipped, resting on her breast. Wild, wrecked, her great blue eyes gradually growing dim. Darling, darling Val.

Chapter Thirteen

These were almost the same words that I had cried out as I had left Joe behind that time in Toronto, but my picture of him was changing. All those characteristics I had seen in him then were there, the warmth, the affection, the generosity, but now I saw other traits too. They must always have been there but they were masked by his youth. He was very ambitious, he could be aggressive, he valued money and was mighty good at making it. I am not saying these are bad things but I had not noticed them before.

He also had remarkable powers of assimilation: he had absorbed much of the manners and ways of the world in which Johnny Lyonnesse moved. It was done naturally and without effort and with no show. It happened so easily that it was not until I looked at him one day, sitting at the fine old desk in our London house, wearing his suit from Mr Davidson in Conduit Street and his shirt from Turnbull and Asser in Jermyn Street, that I saw what he had become.

Such powers of – I will not say of imitation, it was far and beyond that – adaptation to one's background made me wonder about the Joe of Toronto. What had he really been then?

"This house will be too small in a while," he said looking up at that moment and smiling at me. "There will be children eventually."

"Soon, I hope." There seemed no reason why not. I had conceived twice. That part at least seemed something I could do successfully.

"We might as well settle here. You will never go back to Toronto."

"No." He knew how I felt about that city so full of living ghosts.

"And it is too soon for New York."

"Too soon?"

He was serious about it. "When we live there we must live there in a certain way and with a certain income. And I am not ready yet."

"I don't really understand."

I had a three-storey house with a basement in Knightsbridge in which I had an inside staff of a cook, a parlourmaid, a housemaid, and nurse for Sylvie. I had given several dinner parties where I knew most of my guests, I had my clothes fitted at Lucille's, the best London couturier, and we had been invited to a private dance where I had seen the Prince of Wales. I was imbedded in London domesticity; I did not see how we could move.

"It's the way of the world, love, and of that world in particular." There was a hard, clear note in his voice as if he was listening to a voice I could not hear. "Oh Joe."

"Darling Dodo." He came across and put his arms round me. "You're still grieving for Val."

"Yes, I am. There's an emptiness. No funeral, no grave."

"Johnny is trying to discover where she was buried. He says he will bring her back and bury her in the family vault."

"Do you believe that?"

"I think he will try. Mrs Madden says she wants a memorial tablet in the city church where the Maddens worshipped."

Mammon's Temple, I thought. "How do you know?"

"Her solicitor wrote to Johnny."

"I expect he's glad she's dead and wants to make sure she is firmly embedded in a piece of stone."

"I think Johnny was quite touched by the letter."

"More fool he then. Forsyth dislikes me and he didn't like Val either, I'm sure of it." I turned on Joe. "You didn't trust him either."

Joe examined his hands. "I checked as far as I could. He has certainly looked after Honoria's estate. She is richer than she ever was."

"So it's all well then, is it?"

"I believe the son is managing the firm now."

"Then he will be the same."

204

"It's true there are stories in the city about them. They hunt in couples."

"What does that mean?"

He shrugged. "Young women. Girls, the younger the better."

I got up and walked to the window. The usual London late afternoon scene. An organ-grinder at the kerb, winding away at a tune from 'The Maid of the Mountains', an errand boy cycling along and whistling. Two women dressed in furs getting out of a taxi and the postman with the last letters of the day.

He came over and kissed the back of my neck. "You don't like being made love to, do you?" he said softly.

"That's not true."

"I can feel it in your throat."

I turned round. "Leave it."

"That's hurtful, Dodo."

"I'm not pushing you away."

"It feels like it."

"Nothing personal, Joe."

"It's a personal thing."

I turned back to the window. "I don't think the Prince of Wales liked me."

"I didn't know we were talking about him."

"Or there again, perhaps he did like me. He asked for me to be introduced. Sent one of his aides across."

"I didn't know that."

"You were dancing. With that very pretty girl with red-gold curls. You wouldn't have noticed. But then the Prince had to leave. He had one of those sinewy little women he likes with him and she ordered him out. Lovely emeralds she had. If they were real."

"I expect they were."

"She had him on a chain. But then we're all on chains of one sort or another, aren't we?"

"Dodo!"

"I'm thinking about odd things." About love and infidelity and death and the loss of confidence; they were all surging around in my mind and sometimes I seemed to see old Jerningham's face, and sometimes the man I had knifed. Not really, of course, I wasn't mad, but they were in the back of my mind, locked up and struggling to climb out.

"Val?"

"Among other things . . . Val deserves to be remembered. Something more than a couple of lines in *The Times* and the *Morning Post*. Not even a proper obituary. A service of remembrance would do." Better than nothing. But Val would have preferred a party, with champagne.

"Organise one then, You are a great organiser. The girl who hung on to her little newspaper, who still hangs on to it, can organise a memorial service."

"I couldn't do it on my own, and you are overworked as it is." He looked tired and thin.

He ignored that comment. "Get Charley to help you."

"She's packing to go to the US."

"She hasn't gone yet. You're right. Val should have a proper service."

"With no body? If Johnny brings her back, then I will."

I saw Johnny off on his journey a few days later, driving him to the station myself in my little open car.

"Look after yourself, Dodo."

He was fond of me, I knew he was. I also knew he was seeing a famous musical comedy star, and there was certainly that girl in the country who rode to hounds so well that she might kill herself any day. Or her horse. So perhaps it was as well Val was dead. But gossip said he would not marry the star.

Next day, I saw Charley off to New York. She had several packing cases of her work and almost no personal luggage.

"Do you remember the Violet Adventurers?"

"Of course, I do. You don't forget that sort of thing. Silly girls, we were."

"No we weren't. We were fighting for survival, Dodo, and don't you forget it . . . Show me your arm."

I rolled up my sleeve and held out my forearm. "It's a bit swollen and sore today. I don't know why."

"I do. It's because you are remembering."

"Show me your mark."

Charley obliged; her scar was thin and old, hardly visible.

But when I put my hand on it, then I could feel it, a ridge of flesh on her bone.

I waved her off on the boat train. She was all on her own but there was never a sense of loneliness about Charley. I wondered if I would ever see her again.

So it was all partings.

But Johnny didn't bring Val back. He said he had found her grave, plain, unmarked, in a small plot on the edge of the village, but it had been quite impossible to dig the coffin up and transport it back.

Local feeling had been intense. "They would have lynched me," he said. "They don't like you touching the dead there."

"What did she die of?"

"As far as I could judge, she had malaria. And drink – that was a factor." His voice was quiet but there was pain in it. She had been such a beauty.

"And was no one with her?"

"She had the maid you met . . . and there was a young boy. They arranged everything."

"And where were they?"

"Gone. I couldn't find them. Nothing left but a pile of debts. I settled those."

Poor old Johnny, he had a lot of tidying up to do.

"You can marry again now, Johnny," I said.

"What makes you think I want to?"

"Oh I don't know. Someone said so. Your mother, I think." When Val first took herself off, and in no very pleasant a tone.

"I expect she said I ought to. For the sake of an heir."

He had a legal heir, if he did but know it. The young lad who had taken himself off with Val's servant. But better to keep quiet about that.

Then he handed me my share of the tidying up.

"See to Honoria for me, will you? Tell her everything. I can't face her."

I wasn't sure *I* wanted to.

"And I suppose I ought to arrange for a memorial service for Val. It's the decent thing. You might tell Honoria for me."

"She's having a special tablet put up in her church," I said. "But I don't know if she wants to come to any service. She's old and ill now."

Odd as well. Odder than ever the last time I had seen her. I called regularly now, sometimes seeing her and sometimes not.

But you never knew where you were with Honoria these days. She had changed her mind about Val and her death. No memorial tablet would be prepared.

Honoria's eyes looked pale with a hint of film; she stared into the distance as if not seeing anything.

At intervals she remembered that there was something she wished to tell me, or something she had better tell me, then she forgot what it was.

I was not sure she even remembered Val. Or possibly she thought I was Val, because she was friendly and gentle to me, holding my hand in her soft, damp old one. I had to dry my hand afterwards.

But then she shocked me.

"Miss Parrott does not think Val is dead," she said.

Miss Parrott was the new lady figure; there was very often a new one.

"What I said was: 'Your granddaughter is not dead'," fluted Miss Parrott in high agitation.

Honoria ignored her. "I have made a new will. In it, I say that if my granddaughter is dead, then I leave everything in trust with Jameson Forsyth. For charity. He knows which I support." She paused for a moment, then added, "I will not be coming to the memorial service."

But she did come. Hobbling in on the arm of Miss Parrott.

Flowers and organ music do not a memorial service make. In spite of Johnny Lyonnesse's desire to have the service in his country parish church, the memorial to Val took place in the elegant profundities of the edifice where she had been married. There was a horrid resemblance between the two affairs.

"There should be no flowers," said Honoria. She had complained about the flowers at Val's wedding but then it had been the sparseness of them, it being a winter wedding in wartime.

Now I had provided too many, been too lavish, made too

much of a show. On an impulse, I had brought the child, Sylvie. At the moment she insisting on this name, bless her. I did bless her. Honoria seized on her at once. "Who is the child?"

"The daughter of a friend of mine; she died and I adopted Sylvie."

"No relations at all?"

"There was an old grandfather but he's dead too." And we had never told him about Sally's child. He'd been senile for years, and there was no money, never had been.

"I could see she wasn't your child, no resemblance at all, but I thought she might be a bastard of your husband."

"Mrs Madden, Mrs Madden," bleated Miss Parrott. "You mustn't . . . you shouldn't . . ."

"I shall say what I like, Parrott." She turned on me. "Where is your husband?" She was in a sharp mood, and although Miss Parrott was trying to restrain her, she would not be stopped. She had never met Joe, had refused to do so, but now she wanted to see him.

I was half amused, half annoyed. "He's coming, He's been in Scotland on business and is coming straight from the train."

"Oh Scotland, everyone knows what people mean when they say Scotland."

And she hobbled in on the arm of Miss Parrott.

How senility and old age peel the layers with some people. Once Honoria would never have spoken in that gibing way, never even have thought in those terms, but underneath, all the time, was that very person who could say such remarks out loud.

Sylvie and I waited outside for Joe so that we could go in together. I heard the organ sounding.

I gripped the child's hand. "We'd better go in, I shan't wait any longer."

A taxi drew up smartly. Joe jumped out and he kissed me. "Sorry to be late, the train was delayed." The taxi drew away and I saw, sitting in the back, the pretty, flushed figure of the junior assistant from his office.

Life does not record every question, every hesitation, every doubt about someone you love. You bury them.

The first undue, unexpected lateness, the first forgotten

arrangement, the first 'late train from Scotland', the first air of abstraction; these are swallowed in the workdays and festivals of life.

Surprise is an element of knowledge.

I ignored the first letter. Blinked, shrugged and tore it up. It was not, after all, explicit: "DO YOU KNOW WHAT YOUR HUSBAND DOES WHEN HE IS NOT AT HOME?"

This was all it said. Nasty. Anonymous. To be torn up and burnt. Not even mentioned. I did not mention it to Joe.

I did not forget it though, and the second came as no surprise. If I had recognised the envelope for containing what it did, then I should have torn it up unread, but it came in the pile on my breakfast tray (which I now took fashionably in bed); it was just one among the numerous circulars, advertisements, pleas for charity and invitations from people I hardly knew.

There was a letter from Mahmoud, quietly cheerful about the paper in Paris. He was a getting a lot of advertisements and selling more papers, Paris being full of expatriates of one sort or another. He had long since abandoned my crusading style of journalism, but I recognised that those times were past for me and that Mahmoud was an excellent businessman.

There was a postcard from Charley in New York saying something indecipherable in her foul handwriting which was beautiful to look at but impossible to read.

Then I opened the letter. A business envelope, typed. Nothing to alarm.

"CAN YOU COUNT THE PRETTY LADIES IN YOUR HUSBAND'S LIFE. OR DO I MEAN HIS BED. WHY NOT ASK?"

I put the letter aside, ate my breakfast, held my cheek up to be kissed by Joe before he left for work.

"Not on the lips?"

"No lips."

He didn't see what I meant.

I saw Sylvie at her lessons with the newly installed nursery governess; I kept my appointment with my hairdresser, and I had my nails painted the new, fashionable dark red. I felt red nails suited my mood.

Then I took a taxi to Joe's City office.

Miss Gilroy his senior secretary was there. She stood up at once as I came in. Something in my manner must have alerted her. Or perhaps she had been waiting, ready. Afterwards, I thought she had been.

"Mr Jerningham is not here."

"I know that."

I threw the letter on the desk in front of her. "Did you write this?"

She hardly looked at it. "No." She had large white teeth which showed when she spoke.

"I don't believe you."

"That is your affair, Mrs Jerningham."

"Where is your assistant? She's your sister, isn't she?"

"Working with Mr Jerningham." She smiled her crocodile smile. "I believe an emergency meeting has called them to Paris. He asked me to telephone you."

"I don't like you, Miss Gilroy, and I think my husband would be well advised to get rid of you. I think you did write those letters. Those lying letters."

"Lying? You think so?"

"So you admit you wrote the letters?" I turned my head away, I couldn't bear to look at her, a little bead of spittle had appeared at the edge of her mouth. "You and your sister had better go."

She laughed. "Open your mind, Mrs Jerningham."

"What do you mean?"

"Ask him about the little actress at the Vaudeville, or the girl who sells scent in Selfridges . . . she's going to work for him."

I wanted to hit her in the face, my hand felt warm and ready. But I took a deep breath and walked out of the office.

Joe didn't come home that night. Instead, he telephoned to explain himself that he had to take the boat train in a hurry.

"There will be an aeroplane service soon and that will make my life easier."

"Splendid."

"What's the matter. You sound odd."

"Not odd at all."

211

"I'll see you as soon as I get back. Is there anything you want from Paris."

"You could look up Mahmoud."

There was a pause. "I don't believe I will have time for that."

Of course not. "Where are you staying?"

Another pause. "The Lotti."

Later that night, I rang the Lotti. They were not there.

There were flowers all over the drawing room when Joe came back. The whole house smelt of them.

He kissed me. "I brought you this."

It was a bottle of L'Heure Bleu from Guerlain. Their shop was on the corner of the Place Vendome so I reckoned they had been staying at the Ritz.

I opened the package. "Lovely." Somehow the bottle slid from my fingers and emptied itself on the floor, cracking the bottle.

Joe picked it up with a puzzled frown.

You're nervous, I thought, you're bloody nervous.

I had stabbed a man once and I thought I could do it again if I wanted to.

"You didn't stay at the Lotti. I telephoned, you weren't there."

"No, in the end I stayed with the manager of the Samaritan . . . he has a flat over the shop. We had business, it was more convenient."

"And the girl? Your secretary?"

"Somewhere, I'm not sure where. He arranged that."

"I don't believe a word of it."

"Dodo . . ."

"And if it is true, what about the girl from the Vaudeville and the one who sells scent."

"I don't know what you are saying."

"Ask that sabre-toothed secretary of yours. And after you have, I should sack her if I were you. She talks too much."

"Dodo, this is fantasy."

"Oh is it, I am given to that, am I? I suppose in your heart you think that all things that happened to me in Canada and Paris were fantasy. I expect you have thought so all along really. A man would."

"Dodo." He tried to take my arm but I wrenched it away.

"Thanks for letting me see into your mind." I went to the door. "I shall leave or you can." And I slammed the door.

It was Joe who went, silently packing a bag and getting out.

Some weeks passed. I wrote to Charley telling her all, or nearly all; she sent back a cable saying I was mad. I wrote to Mahmoud, not exactly telling him the position but letting him know that I might be taking a more personal interest in my paper. He did not reply. I did not tell Honoria, but she got to know anyway, and summoned me to a meeting.

"You are not my granddaughter, I have no grandchild now that Val is dead, but I have a responsibility towards you."

I was tired, and it was cold and uncomfortable in the room where I sitting with her. I felt sour; she pulled me towards her with one hand and pushed me away with the other. "No responsibility, I am grown up now."

She ignored this.

"You know the story, of course, of my daughter. She married a man I could not approve of, violent, and rash as he was. We quarrelled and she cut herself off from me and all her friends. It was later, much later, when I found out how she had died and where, that my dear Friend and Adviser—" She seemed to put those words in capitals. "Used a detective to find my grandchild. He succeeded."

Oh yes, I thought, and one of those detectives tried to abduct me and force me to marry him. Was that in Mr Forsyth's instruction?

She passed over this, although she certainly knew about the man and what had happened in Versailles. The incident may have been hushed up, but Honoria knew. Or was it one of the things her patchy and selective memory had suppressed?

"At the time, I did not think it wise to let you know what more I knew, what Jameson and the detective had discovered: that he had identified your mother."

I looked at her sharply. "You mean you have known all this

213

time, who I was and who my mother was, and have not let me know?"

"It seemed wise, especially during the period when I had to decide which of you was my daughter's child, that you should be cut off from the past."

It was so like Honoria Madden and her insufferable air of knowing what was best.

"But I think it my duty to tell you now. I shall die soon; Miss Parrott tells me that this recovery in my memory and mental powers presages my death."

God bless Miss Parrott, I thought, but all the same, some feeling for Honoria made me say: "I shouldn't believe that if I were you. You look better, Honoria."

In a way, she did. Spryer and more alert.

For a moment, she softened. "You are a good child. Wilful and hasty but loving, I think . . . Your mother was an actress, Alice Morton. Jameson tells me that she still performs."

I was silenced by what she said. "Are you sure?" I managed eventually. She bowed her head in assent: Yes, in her belief, Alice Morton was my mother. "I have heard of her." Met her once, long ago at the beginning of the Great War. "Yes, she still performs. She's a star." Or she was. Perhaps she still was.

Theatrical fame meant nothing to Honoria, she was retreating into the past again, I doubt if she really heard me. She stretched out a hand. "Goodbye, say goodbye to your old friend and mentor."

Friend or enemy, it was hard to know which, but she was a good woman, although strongly streaked with silliness. I leant forward, put my arms round her; she was very thin beneath her layers of clothes, the solid flesh having melted away. I kissed her cheek.

"Goodbye, Honoria. I will come again soon."

Of all the reactions to my crisis, Johnny's was the cleanest. He took me to dinner at the Savoy and let me talk. He was still Joe's friend and he let me know that too.

"Did you know about Joe?" I asked. I suppose I was looking for a confession. A peep through a keyhole into a masculine world.

Deliberately, he poured me some more wine, then drank some himself. "There are two sorts of men, Dodo. Those who talk about their relationship with women and those who don't . . . Joe was not a talker, and neither, for that matter, am I."

I suppose I ought to have felt rebuffed, but somehow with Johnny Lyonnesse you never felt ill-treated.

"Have you heard of an actress called Alice Morton?"

"Yes. She's top of the bill at the Vaudeville. Not as good as she was, but still pulling them in."

The Vaudeville did two shows on Wednesdays and Saturdays so I had a choice of an afternoon performance or an evening one. Probably better for a woman on her own to go to a matinee; a lot of lonely women did so, taking a tray of tea on their laps in the middle of the second act.

I suppose I had thought that I would look at all the girls in the show and suddenly say: Ah, that's the one, that's the girl Joe's been after.

But it didn't work like that. All the girls were pretty, or seemed so in stage make-up and with stage lighting. Most of them seemed talented as well, trilling away like birds while they danced. I couldn't pick one out from the others. Red-heads, blondes, dark-skinned brunettes and honey-coloured ladies.

But Alice Morton dominated the show. She had all the best songs and delivered them with brio; her costumes were a marvel, glinting and swaying as she moved. And if she sometimes moved a bit stiffly and the songs seemed the tiniest bit old-fashioned, well – who could wonder?

I studied her face, trying to find a resemblance to my own. It was hard to think of her as my mother. Or as anyone's mother. Honoria had spoken with such assurance that I had believed her at once, but she might be wrong. It might be part of a smile fantasy.

I pictured myself going backstage, knocking on the dressing room door and saying, Do you know me mother?

If I hadn't been so miserable, I could played it for the comedy. But you need an audience for that sort of joke.

Alice had her following who applauded her enthusiastically, but the really wild clapping was for a slender creature with a mop of curls and a clown's face who seemed to draw the whole audience into her own world. I seemed to know her face.

Perhaps she was Joe's girl and if so, I could but applaud his taste.

As the curtain came down. I made up my mind; I walked round to the stage door, which was crowded with excited fans, several holding flowers and others clutching books. A telegraph boy came marching in with his yellow envelope and the telephone in the doorman's office was ringing.

"Miss Morton?" I said. "She's expecting me."

The doorman reached out for the telegram and turned towards the telephone at the same time. "Go through. Speak to her dresser."

Was there a thoughtful look in his eyes as he turned back to his duties? Hindsight suggests there probably was.

I found Alice Morton's dresser outside her door, an elderly woman carrying several costumes over her arm. She had just closed the door with a bang.

"Can I see Miss Morton?"

"You can see her all right."

"She's expecting me."

"Is she now? Well, you go in and see her then."

I was right, the woman was angry.

I pushed open the door and went in. At first, I thought the room was empty. Then I saw there was a figure stretched out on a sofa, eyes closed.

"I told you I wanted to nap, damn you. Go out again and don't slam the door this time." The voice was thick.

There was a tea tray on a table by the sofa, but also a bottle of gin and a glass.

I cleared my throat. "Miss Morton?"

Alice opened her eyes, raising herself on one elbow. "Who the hell are you?" She was slurring her words.

I didn't answer that because I wasn't sure who I was. "I came to see you?"

"Well, you're seeing me." She picked up the glass and took a good swig. It seemed to wake her up. "Here I am."

I took a step backward to the door. "Perhaps I'd better come back later."

"You think I'm drunk, don't you? I am a bit tiddly. But I wouldn't advise coming back later. I'll be proper sloshed by then."

I didn't say anything.

"Anyone would be, sharing the billing with that little cow. That's what I'll be doing next week. The management is pushing little Billee up, and yours truly down."

I felt I didn't blame them.

"Everyone liked you," I said, wondering how they would like her evening performance.

"Oh I got a good hand, I always do." She picked up the bottle of gin.

"Oh, should you?" I said before I could stop myself.

Her eyes stared over the top of the bottle. "What's it to you? Oh, I know, you think I won't be able to go on for the next show. Let me tell you, I'll be as sober as a judge the minute I set foot on that stage . . . I may fall on my bottom as soon as I get off it, but on it . . ." She started to laugh.

I believed her, but it did not seem the time to start my 'Here I am, my darling mother, this is your child', speech.

The door opened and her dresser came back. She rolled her eyes at me and held the door. "Thought better of it, have you? Wish I could."

The air on the pavement was cool and damp. A taxi was coming round the corner and I waved my hand towards it.

"Dodo, my girl," I told myself. "You're short on husbands and mothers, so it's up to you."

Next day I was paying bills at my desk when the doorbell rang. I was alone in the house so I answered it.

A tall, elegant woman stood there, elegant even though it was pouring with rain. A bag at her feet.

I took a deep breath.

"I thought you were dead."

"As you see, I am not," said Val.

Val stepped inside.

Chapter Fourteen

Val moved in with me at the Knightsbridge house, taking up residence in the suite of rooms we had made ready for guests. Val made approving noises as she looked round at the cool blue and green room. "Nice. You've done well." She walked around distributing her bags. I noticed she had a jewellery case with her but few clothes: Val always went for essentials. I could see I would be lending her lingerie and nightgowns. Furs too if the weather got cold.

"How you've come on," she said, looking at the small bathroom. "Sophisticated colour scheme."

"Charley helped."

"Oh she's still around, is she? Well, she's come on too, then." She touched the central heating pipe. "Quite American-style comfort. Just like New York."

"You've never been to New York."

"No, but I'm going. That is my intention."

"You'll find Charley there then."

"Ah. Will I? How is she?"

"Exactly the same."

"Only more so I expect, one could see that happening."

I flopped onto the bed. "Now you can do some explaining, Val. Why you played dead and why you're now alive."

She stretched out beside me. "Lovely bed. You can't think how heavenly it is to be back with the cleanliness and comfort of the West after the dirt and noise of where I was."

"You chose it," I said. I didn't feel like letting her off this particular hook.

"I had my reasons, and you know them."

"Yes, where is the lad?"

"He went off," she said evasively.

"He had his reasons for that, I suppose?"

"Don't be sarky, Dodo, not your style."

"Well, come on. Explain what happened."

She looked thoughtful. "I loved where I was of course, and Prince Saludin was a marvellous lover . . . he wasn't a real prince of course, not by our standards, but he was the head of his tribe. Well, he wanted to take another wife. He thought it was his duty really, a matter of prestige. He had one already but I didn't mind her, a little dark old creature. But the new one . . . she was very young and she came from a very important tribe."

"A political marriage then," I said.

"Told you not to be sarcastic, Dodo. Anyway, she was jealous and her family got in touch with the local police. Nasty little Frenchman ran that outfit; I wouldn't have anything to do with him, the little pederast, and he hated that, so he was glad to make trouble . . . and then there were debts."

There would be, I thought.

"So?"

"So I decided to move out into the desert until things cleared up."

I wondered exactly what she meant by that but decided not to ask, it would come out in the end. Probably there had been a riot, pitched battle between two sets of tribemen and the police.

"And then when my maid fell ill and died, the boy identified her as me. It seemed simple, a good idea."

"And then not such a good idea?"

"Well, here I am, so it didn't work badly. I am sorry if it upset everyone here. I didn't think you'd get to know."

"Oh but we did. And we had a memorial service for you." In spite of myself I began to laugh. "Oh Dodo, we did praise you and several people cried and Johny wore black, and all the time you were alive."

Val was laughing too and we reeled back on the bed drunk with pleasure and mirth. It was lovely to have her back. She was wicked, wicked, but I did enjoy her company.

I raised myself on one elbow. "And what about the boy?"

"Oh he's all right. He went off. He knows how to manage."

"And so do you . . . you haven't been alone, have you, Val? There was someone."

"One needs looking after," she said. "Such a nice man, and asked for so little in return."

"And where is Mr X now?"

"Signor X it was, as it happens. Gone to the family estates near Lucca. Such a boring place to live, I feel for him." She leaned back on the pillows. "There, I've told you everything."

Not nearly everything, I thought, but it would come out by degrees, it usually did with Val.

"And Johnny? What about Johnny?"

Val took a deep breath. "I'll deal with Johnny later. But not until I've had a hot bath with some of those Roget et Gallet bath salts you have there and something to eat and perhaps a glass of wine. I'm sure you have good wine."

"Not bad." I got off the bed. "I'll see about it."

As I moved away, Val gripped my wrist. "And then you shall tell me about yourself . . . There is something, I can see it in your eyes."

I stood still for a moment, then went to the door. "Have a bath. See you in a little while, Val."

When I returned with a tray on which I had arranged a little smoked salmon and a half bottle of champagne, with two glasses, Val came back from the bath.

She was naked and not worried in the least. Her body was pink and fuller than before but still lovely. "Got a bit of cover for me?"

I put the tray down. "Didn't you bring anything with you?"

"Just my jewels. It was what you might call a speedy exit."

"Open the champagne." I went away to my own room and returned with a satin and lace negligee which Joe had bought back after a trip and which was more Val's style than mine.

She draped it round herself. "Wear this and you won't have any sex problems."

She had opened the champagne and filled two glasses. I took one and sipped the wine. "How did you know I have?"

"I can tell. I may not be able to read minds but I can read bodies. Yours looks deprived."

I took a long drink. Then I walked to the window. I drew the curtains, soft heavy green silk, but took my time about it. It was easier to tell her without looking at her.

A few sentences did it. You never had to explain that sort of thing at length to Val.

I turned round to face her. She stood there in the silk robe looking flushed and lovely. But I could read her face too and knew she had her miseries. It hadn't been all bliss for her these last few years however bravely she spoke of it.

"Are all men the same, Val?"

She sat down on the bed. "More or less. Pretty well. As far as I know. Does that cover it?"

I couldn't laugh, quite, but she was a marvellous relief, Val.

We agreed that she would spend a few days hidden while we decided what to do about Johnny Lyonnesse, (who was in for a shock), and Honoria who might find it even harder to grasp, but who might have forgotten that Val had ever died.

As if he scented Val's arrival, Johnny called next day. He looked round my drawing room with a questioning eyebrow raised as if he knew somehow that Val had just hurried out.

But he didn't say anything and neither did I. He had come to tell me that the newspapers, one paper in particular, had picked up a story about Val and me and Joe. They had been investigating in Toronto and Paris. A lot might come out.

I knew I ought to tell him about Val but still I did not. She had to speak for herself.

"I saw Joe. He looks rotten."

I said nothing. It was my belief I did not look too good myself. Only Val seemed to rise above misery. For that matter, so did Johnny, who looked fit and handsome. Perhaps you had to have aristocratic blood.

"He'll manage," I said finally, to break the silence.

"I'm sure. On past history, he always does . . . You don't know much about his very early life, do you?"

"No." For me, Joe started in Toronto, in Jerningham's.

"I've learnt a bit . . . he was an orphan."

"We had that in common then." But I had thought as much.

"He was sent over to Canada with a boatload of other youngsters, boys mostly. Human cargo . . . to work on farms: servants, farm hands. Joe went out with another little creature and after a while they couldn't stick where they were in Ontario. It was hard, rough work, and not much food. Maybe a bit of mistreatment, through poverty and lack of imagination, not ill will. It was a hard world for them all, adults as well, and remember they were very young."

"I can imagine."

"They ran away. Lived on the streets in Toronto . . . Joe decided to set up in business – he always had ideas. They had no money but they had one asset – the other youngster had a voice."

"Singing in the streets?"

"Yes, and in bars too probably, and Joe banged away at some home-made instrument . . . they were both Scots, or he thinks they must have been because of the way they spoke, although both soon lost the brogue. So they sang Scottish songs, because there were a lot of immigrant Scots living in the city then . . ."

"Still are," I said.

"They did better than some, with coins tossed in the hat. Joe took this money and used to buy apples which he sold from a rudimentary stall. He had noticed that the apples in the market were not selling; he got a barrel on the cheap and sold them dear."

"How did he do that?"

"He polished each and every one, till they were shiny and sweet-looking."

It sounded like Joe. A salesman from the word go.

"It wasn't a fortune but they were surviving. Only the street traders didn't like it and one man attacked the pair. They were both badly beaten up . . . old Jerningham was in the market and he stepped in. Took the two back with him. That was how Joe got there, and why he felt a loyalty to the old man."

"What about the other boy?"

"Did I say boy? It was a girl. Joe thought she might have been his sister . . . but nothing was ever made clear. She had TB. I don't suppose singing in the streets helped there. She died."

A silence fell in the room.

"And then you don't know much about the war and what he did?"

"I know he got married."

"And so did you, Dodo."

I shrugged. "True. So I did and you know why."

"You did a good deed when you married, and so did Joe. But it doesn't matter. People act out of character in a war. Joe joined up almost as soon as the war started, although he already had plenty of business ties to keep him at home, and he certainly didn't owe a debt to England. But he took one of the Jerningham horses and joined the Fort Garry Horse, it became the First Canadian Cavalry Division. But he didn't stay with it. He turned out to have special skills and he was sent on errands that not everyone could do. It was dangerous work." He paused, then said: "You know he has a gun."

"I've seen it. A lot of men have now, left over from the war. You have a gun, several, I expect."

"For sport . . . I don't like his having one."

I turned away. "I know why you are here, Johnny. And don't threaten me with talk of guns, Joe would never kill himself or me. You're a messenger."

"Give him a chance."

"I can't."

"Can't or won't, Dodo? You have a hard little heart."

He wasn't the first to say this. Years ago in that rough sunshine world, a nurse had told me so.

"It's been beating inside me for years."

Johnny picked up his stick and went away. I expect he said goodbye, he always had impeccable manners, but I didn't hear.

My hard little heart was causing me some pain.

The missive next day was a variation on the anonymous letters. I suppose now I had guessed that Miss Parrott was the sender; there was no point in them. Something else was needed.

The address was typewritten but I had a feeling that I wasn't going to like what I saw inside.

Not a bill. Not a circular. Not an invitation.

"Well, you've covered the field," said Val, across the breakfast table. "Now open it."

I slit open the envelope and tipped the contents onto the table. Three photographs fell out.

It showed Joe and the pretty secretary girl walking towards the hotel in Paris. Not the Lotti or the Ritz but the Meurice. Well, it must have done well enough. She was hanging on his arm, as if she might fall if she didn't get support. I couldn't really see Joe's face. Just as well possibly.

The next photograph showed his tall figure bending over her and kissing her. I recognised her hair. Couldn't see his face.

The third photograph was just a blur. But what I could make out I did not care for.

Val looked at them and then at me. She shrugged.

"I should take no notice."

"I can't quite manage that."

She picked them up and looked again. "Well, ask yourself why they were taken."

"To inform me."

"Exactly. And not for your good. Anyway, I don't think they look like Joe. They could be anyone."

"The one outside the hotel is Joe," I said.

Great joy and great sorrow sometimes hang together, the one the product of the other.

I brooded all that day, not exactly sulking, but silent and morose until Val said she would take Sylvie to the zoo or anywhere until I had got over my mood.

"Have a hot bath or get drunk," she called over her shoulder as the two of them left. Sylvie did not remember Val but seemed happy in her company. Sylvie did not like the zoo, which she said smelt and was cold but then I did not believe that Val meant to go there. A tour of Bond Street shops then tea at the Ritz or Gunters was more in her style.

I took some of Val's advice. That is I was almost drunk and was on the point of having a bath when I heard the heavy front door bang.

Only one person banged the door like that.

I picked up a robe and went onto the landing. I looked down the curving stairs to see Joe running up.

He was as disconcerted to see me as I was to see him.

"I thought you'd be out," he said.

That's a lie, I thought. You couldn't know whether I would

be in or out. Unless you've been watching the house. But that wasn't Joe's style.

What was Joe's style, as I was coming to see, was not to admit he wanted to see me.

He got to the top of the stairs, breathing heavily. I drew back into the bedroom and he followed me. "Dodo," he was saying.

I had the photographs on my dressing table. Now I picked them up and threw them on the bed.

"Look at those."

He gave me a questioning look, walked to the bed and stared down. Then he turned to me. Joe always had a quick temper and I could see anger gathering now behind his eyes. But I didn't care, I was too angry myself.

"What's this?"

"You can see for yourself . . ."

He picked up the three photographs. "Where did you get them?"

"In an envelope, through the post."

"You're a fool." He plucked out one picture. "This is me and my secretary. The girl stumbled. I remembered that. Who took the photograph?"

"I don't know."

"You're a fool," he repeated, "the others are nothing to do with me. This is what they are worth." He tore them in two, then threw them to the ground.

Tears started to pour down my face; anger always makes me cry, and my hand shot out to hit him on the cheek. He caught my wrist.

The flesh has its own language. The silk slid off my shoulders, did I help it or did Joe pull it? I don't remember. But without intention we were on the bed.

There was no foreplay. Joe was gripping my shoulders, my buttocks, my breasts; I was screaming.

Nothing like this had ever happened to me before. I was shivering, trembling, vibrating. But there was nothing of the rape about it, my God I was as eager as he was. The energy and force were equally mine.

Oh God, words I did not know I knew were rippling from my lips. Then I seemed to turn inside out.

225

I think I slept briefly, Then a noise from Joe woke me. I raised myself on my elbow. Joe was making choking, gasping noises. "Darling," I said. "Darling."

I sat up, noticing for the first time that his clothes were in a heap on the floor.

I put my arm under his head and raised it. "Joe?"

I heard a breath of sound. "Dearest Dodo."

"I'm here, I'm here . . ." I had to get a doctor but his head was heavy on my arm.

Too heavy.

I hated Val. She had come back into my life and Joe had left it. I was full of anger and violence. When she came into the room, I attacked her.

Part Four

Chapter Fifteen

We were the wild ones, the wicked ones, the ones who had sat at the back of the class. Some of us were less evil than others, and one and all we were pathetic.

Not that we understood that, of course – we were tough and defiant and some of us thought ourselves rather clever.

I was imprisoned first in a police cell in central London. After being sentenced I was sent to Holloway Prison for Women. Later, much later, I was moved further north.

There was no getting off the hook this time. Death is death to the British police and violent death is a serious business.

Charley was one of my first visitors. Even before the trial, she said murder was quite justifiable under such circumstances and for women especially. It was strange to see tears in her eyes, Charley never cried. Of course, she thought I might hang.

They still hanged women, but the fact I was so recently widowed (together with other factors) saved me from the gallows. Some people said I had suffered enough. Other people were quite keen to see me swing.

I had very few visitors. Honoria, of immense age now, was senile, with flashed of lucidity which did not usually include me, but she did her duty and tottered in. Darling Val came as often as she could be admitted while Charley asked to draw me in prison, meanwhile she sent me drawings of the world outside.

Johnny was a regular visitor, which was good of him. Sylvie was kept strictly away from me which was right and proper: she was in Johnny's charge. She wrote me little letters with illustrations. She seemed to think I had a serious illness. I suppose I had really, it was called My Life.

Val came to see me from the hospital as soon as she could,

which was very good of her since it was her I had attacked first. "You were crackers, darling," she said, "I never took it personally for a moment. He should not have done either. It was his punishment."

But of course 'He' was dead which did make a difference and I had meant him dead too.

She also was seriously concerned about the death penalty.

The legal profession was very wary of me. After all, I had killed one of their own, hadn't I? I think the judge was for hanging.

The day after Joe's death, when he was still unburied, I had sent messages to the managers of all his concerns that the business would be carried on. I didn't know how, but it would have to be done.

Val stood by me that day in a way I could never forget. She was tender, loyal and gentle. She let me rage and weep. I had hit her in the face in my first madness and she was already in pain from an illness which was to sweep her into hospital, but she gave me all she had.

Val had to manage her renaissance with Johnny Lyonnesse herself. I don't what was said, she never told me, but she said that Johnny stood dumb for a minute, and then that great upper-class English laugh, bred to ring out across hunting fields and battlefields, burst out of him.

I heard the laughter in the next room. Val came to lie on the bed beside me in my own room to tell me. She was smiling herself, half ruefully. "Johnny says he's glad to see me, never liked to think of me buried abroad but it's no go between us. I never hoped for that, Dodo," she said. "Never wanted it." She sounded assured although I wondered. "He says divorces are easy to get these days and we'll get on with it . . . I expect he wants to get married again. He's always been in love with someone. Do you know who it is?"

I shook my head. Perhaps he was waiting for Sylvie, it had occurred to me.

"By the way, love," said Val. "No hard feelings about the whack on my face. You were just hitting out at the world."

I reached out and took her hand. "It's a debt."

"I'll call it in."

Or life would. It does, I've noticed.

I had inherited everything that was Joe's and in addition, I had inherited his London solicitor, a small plump man called Henry Carbonnie, from Carbonnie, Fisher and Dalhousie, who was Johnny's solicitor as well as most of the nobility. A City firm dealt with his business affairs and a third in Toronto dealt with overseas arrangements. I was to find there was yet another in New York. But Carbonnie, Fisher and Dalhousie were for my personal use. Mr Carbonnie had told me that I inherited everything and Johnny Lyonnesse was executor.

Johnny took over calmly. I could see he was trying to protect me, even from myself but I was past all that.

I was mad with grief and rage, but I reserved one job for myself. Joe's office. I knew how to do it too. I put on my most elegant clothes, bought in Paris earlier that year and not outmoded, and picked up the sable wrap that had been a wedding present. I sprayed on scent from Guerlain (Jicky, I remember, I was never to use it again) and marched into the office.

Marched was the word. I was an avenging angel.

They were both there, the young one and the older one. I don't know what they were doing or pretending to do, the two Misses Gilroy, niece and aunt. Or was it sister and elder sister? I was never sure.

"I thought you might have gone," I said.

"No one has given us notice to go," said the older one.

"I give you notice now. Clear out. Take anything that is yours and go."

"We were packing to go anyway." She was sullen. Afraid, I think. The young one said nothing and would not meet my eyes.

I watched as a few moves were made. I was a cat, waiting to pounce.

As they took a step towards the door, I put my hand on the young one's arm, I gripped it hard. "Stop. I want to know why you sent those photographs."

She didn't answer but her eyes flicked a glance at her sister-aunt.

"Let us go."

"Tell me. Or you will get no references and I will let people know you stole money."

"No one will believe you."

"Enough will. Sufficient to stop you getting work."

The postwar depression had already begun; I knew what I was talking about.

"You won't dare do that," said the older one. "We know who to go to for advice."

"Mr Forsyth . . ." said the young one.

I tightened my grip. "Good," I said. "You are a lying, treacherous, mercenary little bitch, but you know when to open your mouth. Go on about Mr Forsyth."

I knew he hated me.

"Hold your tongue," her sister snapped.

"Talk," I warned. "Or I will break your arm."

"Then we will scream."

"Fine, scream, then we will get the police in and I will say you attacked me. Accuse you of blackmail."

I might do that, anyway.

"He hates you."

"I know that."

"And your mother before you."

My mother? God help us, what does she mean?

"Old Mrs Madden's daughter. He wanted her and she wouldn't have him. But he got his own back. She died and so did her husband and he had you traced and followed to Canada. He would have had you there but you escaped."

Eyes and No Eyes, I thought. Jameson Forsyth had employed them. One bad man and one middling good. How we had escaped destruction and been taken back to England, I could not understand. Honoria must come in it somewhere, but that the man who abducted me in Toronto and who had died in Versailles, had been paid by Jameson, I could not doubt.

Paid to destroy me as my mother's daughter. There was a joke there somewhere when I could laugh.

I let them go too. They would get no references from me.

But Jameson Forsyth, Jameson Forsyth . . .

*　　*　　*

I had only one piece of preparation to do and I did it without thought. There is no doubt I was either out of my mind or exceptionally in control of it.

I took my own car and drove it to Forsyth's office in the City. I deliberately chose a route which was not far from the gallery where years ago I had seen Charley's picture on the day when Joe had come calling on Honoria's house. I thought of that day as I parked my car and decided life had a sort of neatness about it.

I swept through his outer office where a startled clerk leapt to his feet; I went through to the inner room where father and son were talking together.

They stared at me. They looked surprised but there was no surprise in me. I felt as though I had always known him and as if I had been born to live this day.

Jameson Forsyth and I had come together in a congress of hate.

"Mrs Jerningham," began the son. But I ignored him. I shouted at the old man.

"It was the other one, the other one, not me. You have persecuted and destroyed the wrong woman."

Then I shot him.

I don't recall events very clearly after that, but Val tells me that I drove straight back home and told her what I had done. At first she did not believe me. However, her doubts did not last long as the police soon arrived. Val was feeling very ill herself then with an internal infection and would shortly be rushed off to hospital for an operation.

But events moved fast. I admitted what I had done, I was committed for trial where I pleaded guilty.

This kept the stir to a minimum and inside my cell I was oblivious of it. Since I had pleaded guilty I was found guilty. But I am told there was immense sympathy for me as my story got around so that the death sentence was commuted to life imprisonment. Mahmoud organised a campaign in the French press where there was also much sympathy for me, as well as the usual dislike of Angleterre. In America, suffrage groups took me up as a woman who had been victimised.

They little knew. I was not docile, I was not gentle.

Prison was like a Sunshine Home for adults. The behaviour I had learnt there, the covert insolence and resistance all came back.

"You can't just kill people like that, you are too violent by half, Dodo."

"I had a right."

She shook her head. "It's odd. You seem so rational, just and loving, but there is something hard inside."

"Yes, it is my heart. My hard little heart." I could hear that nurse from the Sunshine Home saying; "You have a hard heart." And so I had; it had softened and then turned to stone again.

Val shook her head.

"No, not hard, just badly damaged. But it will heal. Remember shell shock? You're shell-shocked."

But I didn't want my heart to soften; I knew I was better off where I was, with my heart of stone.

It was amazing how I adapted to my life in prison. The past sloughed off me. Gone was the protected wife of a wealthy man, gone was the sophisticated Parisian who had owned and run a newspaper. Thrown off was the debutante who had run away from London and had gone to war, thrown away even the shop assistant of Toronto. All shed like skins that had dried and died. I was back to the girl who had lived in the Sunshine Home.

That was who I really was.

I wore prison uniform with no discomfort, I was accustomed to the feel of rough and not too clean cotton; my body was used to it. Did I mind that my hair smelt sour and that there was one bath a week, and the water not hot?

I accepted it.

There was Alice and Doris and Phyllis and Mary, and every one of them could have been found in the Sunshine Home.

I suffered a certain amount of bullying: my food was upset, the contents of a chamber pot were thrown at me (and missed, dousing a warder which did not make me more popular) and I was shoved and jostled.

I accepted this too, knowing it was the way of institutions full of the imprisoned and the deprived.

But there was no need for it to go on for ever. One established one's place – in the hen run, it was called the pecking order.

A large, blonde woman called Betty was the worst. I think there was some personal feeling behind her attacks; I irritated her.

Betty could be quite vicious to those she disliked while being generous to those she patronised. She was in with the wardresses who feared her; she was no woman to be alone with in a cell or at an odd corner in the corridor. She had the knack of giving you quite nasty bruising blows without being seen. She got me several times before I learnt how to avoid her. I was cleverer than she was, if less cunning. One day she would go too far and I would get her.

That day came not too soon, but not too late either.

I was working in the kitchen. It was an easy job, clean and warm, which counted in that place, and I was not sure how I had earned it because I was far from the most popular with the warders, any more than I had been popular with most of them at the Sunshine Home. There it had been because, at first and before I learned better, I was too rough and tough; here it was because my accent was too prissy. But I was losing that accent, it was growing less polished every day.

I was in the kitchen before the big stove with its glowing hot plates over the coal fire. They were still burning coke; within a few weeks it was to be replaced by a gas-fired range, and later still by electricity.

My job that morning was to peel, then cook – boil to smithereens was the approved technique – several great pans of potatoes. Next to my pans of potatoes was a great flat pan in which odd pieces of fat were being rendered down into dripping for cooking; it smelt rancid and was spitting onto my arm. I reached out to lift it away – my hand was on it – when I saw Betty approaching. Sidling towards me without looking my way.

I knew exactly what she was about: she would bang into me as I lifted that pan of fat so that it spilled over, boiling hot. I might be lucky to live through that dousing.

She approached on my right, her head down, like a rhino charging. With my left hand, I lifted the fat pan.

As she came up to me, my right hand came out from under my apron to grip her wrist. I lifted her hand and put it down on the red hot plate of the stove.

For a space of time, I held it there. I waited until I heard her scream, then I released it.

"Oh Betty," I said, "that was a nasty fall, right on the hot plate, you'll have a bad burn there."

With her uncooked hand, she reached up to hit me across the face.

I caught her right hand. "Want that done too, Betty?" I asked.

She was a day in the hospital, returning with a bandaged hand in a sling. To do her justice, she did not report me to the wardress. They all knew of course, but did nothing. Perhaps they thought Betty had asked for it.

Some days later, she asked me if I would be her biddy. There was, naturally, a good deal of sex of one sort and another inside. I said no.

But I was treated with caution and some respect after that episode, by both prisoners and prison staff.

"You look better," Val said to me on the next occasion when she could visit. "Not so bruised."

"I won't be in future," I said.

"Only inside?"

I shrugged. "We all have those." I looked at Val. "Even you."

"I don't know why you say 'even me', I think I've had my share."

"You always seemed . . . so invulnerable."

"Impervious, you mean."

I smiled. "Resilient, anyway."

"Of course, I wasn't." Val reached out to touch me, forbidden of course, I saw the wardress on duty looking, but Val managed it. "I wish you weren't in here, Dodo."

"I wish it myself."

"Do you regret what you did?"

"Not regret, no, but I wish I could have done it some other way."

Val moved restlessly. "The air is dead in here. I suppose if I stood up, they'd turn me out?"

"They might." The rules for visitors were strict.

"And you don't want that?"

"Of course not. You are my lifeline. I breathe the outside world through you."

"And I breathe this one."

"So you will stop coming?"

"You know I will always come."

I did know. "Have you thought that we've all three got bags of violence inside us? You, me and Charley. Does it go back to the way we lived in the Sunshire Home? With Charley it comes out in her painting, although when I first knew her, I thought it would come out in her life. With you . . ." I hesitated.

"It comes out in sex," Val finished for me. "And no, I don't blame the way I go on – and I still do, by the way, when I find someone – and yes, it's not the way a granddaughter of Honoria Madden should behave, although between you and me, I think my father was a dangerously violent man, but I claim a later infection."

"You call it an infection? You don't blame yourself?"

She countered with her own question. "Do you blame yourself?"

"Yes, I think I do. It would be wrong not to. I might do it again in the same circumstances. But it was still wrong." Then I said softly, something from my heart. "When you have killed someone, you are never the same again."

"You're a moral soul at heart, Dodo. Are you sure Honoria Madden is not your grandmother after all?"

I laughed. "How is she?" Of course, she never came or communicated with me.

"Not proud of me since my renaissance and then divorce, but astonishingly still alive, and occasionally articulate."

"So whence comes your infection, Val, my dear?"

"I never told you everything that happened to me in Toronto, any more than you told me."

"You know all now. So what about you?" I drew in a quick breath. "Not old Jerningham again?"

"No, not him – his wife, Mrs Jerningham." Val looked down at her hands; she began to speak quickly. "I came in one evening, not long before we left, suppose I was a bit drunk . . . I did drink then, you know."

I did know, and knew she still did, on occasion.

"She was drunk herself, of course, far and away worse than I was. Did she tell you about her life in England? About being an Urning?"

"She told what she could."

"But not everything . . . and did not show you."

"Show? No, I was shown nothing."

"I was shown." Val's voice dropped. "She lifted her skirts and showed me what they had done. You knew she was shut up by her parents in an asylum?"

"Yes, and they only let her out when she agreed to marry old Jerningham."

"Not only that. Not quite only that. They did more. While she was there, they gave her some chloroform, and opened her legs and clipped away at the soft folds of flesh at her entrance . . ."

I put a hand over my mouth.

"But she came awake before it was done and started to scream, but they carried on. So she says. So she says . . . It was done by a surgeon, on medical advice, to quench her sexual longings. They meant well, she said."

"But she didn't believe it?"

"Probably didn't believe it. Anyway it didn't work, she carried on just as before. Only the worse for poor old Jerningham. But she felt the need to show me, and she did. She showed me her scarred and chewed up self; she had healed badly . . . And it had this effect on me, you see," said Val simply. "That I never forget it, and when a man wants to make love to me, I see it, and I can only feel desire myself, only act back as I should, if I am angry and rough. So I offer violence and receive it back – it is the only way it works."

"I see." I supposed that I did. Poor Val.

"And of course, Johnny, when I married him, was a violent man. The war changed that; he is changed."

"And you?"

"No, I am not yet changed." She smiled. "But I live in hope. At the moment, I am almost celibate."

Only almost, I noted; Val didn't change. There must be a number of badly bruised gentlemen in Belgravia and Mayfair. I wasn't the only one to bear my bruises.

*   *   *

238

In spite of my brave words to myself that this was no worse than the Sunshine Home and even though I had had my victory over Betty, I had still not truly understood that I was here for life.

Whatever that might come to mean. A hope had been held out to me that after a term of years, I would be released, but the number of years still stretched ahead into infinity.

So I was in a kind of limbo, not quite grasping that this was all the life I would have for years and years, but not believing in release either.

Then I was very very low, and would not eat and could not sleep. Judging by the noises I heard in my insomniac nights, I was not the only poor sleeper. There were shouts and moans and even bursts of singing.

It was not until I fainted into a bowl of mashed potatoes (they were not wasted, but tidied up and served later), that I was taken into the hospital wing.

A silent nurse whose apron was starched so crisply that it moved before she did and crackled as she bent, the doctor a tall, thickset woman who looked as though she might have been a sergeant in the British army before she changed her sex. If she had changed it.

"You are not eating," she said. "That is wrong." She made it sound worse than infanticide.

"The food is disgusting." This was true, it was badly cooked, greasy and usually cold when served.

"You will eat what you are given." She turned her head. "Nurse, see this woman eats what she is offered."

Then she told me I could have one day of bed rest and then back to the cells.

But she must have been kinder than she looked because the food I was offered was palatable and hot. I had milk to drink and some fruit. Also the bed was warm and clean (cell sheets never seemed quite clean, the last occupant always seemed to have left a ghostly imprint), and the ward was quiet.

The only other patient was a pale young woman who had just had a baby; she had been delivered in the hospital ward outside on account of the baby's birth certificate, but they were both together now.

239

"I lost a lot of blood," she confided in a hoarse whisper, "that's why I'm still here." This explained her severe pallor; her hair hung dankly about her face, she had a cast in one eye, and her nose looked as if it had been broken at some time. I didn't ask her what she was in for, but she told me anyway.

"Robbery with violence," she whispered. "Extreme and excessive violence, the judge said." She sounded proud of it.

Looking at her frail body it was hard to believe she could have managed extreme violence. She clutched her baby to her as if it was the most valuable possession, perhaps the only valuable possession, that she had ever own.

The nurse who had been so silent while the doctor was there, had burst into speech as soon the door closed behind her. Or him, it really was hard to be sure of that one's sex.

In a flow of words, she told us we could have a bath, and we must not steal nor eat the soap nor use it for any of the foul purposes which she knew we could put soap to. We ignored her.

"I'll wash your hair for you," I said to the girl. Winnie was her name.

She looked pleased, and even the nurse seemed to think that was a legitimate use for the soap. Nurse's flow of conversation had now moved on to the water for the bath, its temperature, quality and quantity. The water would be hot but not too hot, the water was hard so we must clean the bath of the deposit it left, not to mention our own dirt which she did not wish to see on the sides of the bath when she next viewed it; materials for the cleaning were to hand, and we must not use too much hot water, we must not think we were the only people in the world.

It was a marvel that she could draw breath in the flow.

But she was kinder than she seemed because she took the baby quite tenderly from its mother, saying that while we certainly could not bath at the same time because who knew what we would get up to, I might go in and wash Winnie's hair which she would be the first to admit it needed it, and she had a few curling pins I could use to set it afterwards. Her own hair set in rigid waves like a ploughed field.

"What sex is your baby?" I asked Winnie as I rinsed her hair; it was coming out quite a different colour.

"A little girl," she whispered. "Daughter."

"What do you call her?"

"No name yet."

"Ah." That didn't sound too promising; even a baby in prison deserves a name. I knew enough not to ask about her father. "Baby then, how is she doing?"

"Baby," agreed Winnie. "I don't think she thrives."

"I'll curl your hair really tight," I said. "It will suit you."

I said goodbye to her next morning, the baby still asleep; it slept all the time which might be a good sign or a bad sign. Winnie held the baby clasped to her and sat there on the edge of the bed with the curls in her hair already beginning to flop over her ears.

When I got back to the wing where I lived, I found I was still accorded the respect I had won with the victory over Betty, but with some sympathy also.

There was a flow of sympathy between us women in there. I saw it a few days later when we were joined by Winnie.

"I didn't expect to see you. I thought you would go to the annex with the other women with babies." A woman was not parted from her child until it was weaned.

"Died," Winnie whispered. "She died." .

I wondered if the baby had been dead all the time I had been in the hospital.

But the women were tender to Winnie. Muriel, who shared a cell with her, comforted her in the night when she could not sleep (sleep was hard to come by) and told her funny stories of her own life in the markets where she had been a trader.

Winnie did not laugh, the stories were not very funny, but she felt the kindness, and when Muriel tried to sing her to sleep, Winnie did not complain, although the rest of us did.

All the same, there was no false sentiment in Muriel. "I reckon she killed her kid."

"Oh no, surely not. She loved it."

"That would be why. What sort of life, eh? Hand over the face, that would do it."

I didn't believe it, but Muriel knew better how the world wagged than I did, because one day, as we took our exercise in the yard, Winnie said to me, in that thready voice of hers: "Murder isn't murder if you do it out of love."

She waited for me to say something, and when I did not, she asked: "Was it that way with you?"

It so happened that we were the only killers in our wing at that time, so I suppose she had no one else to ask.

"No," I said. "With me it was hate."

She considered. "Is that worse or better?"

I could see she wanted to be reassured. "Oh worse. To kill from love, why God does that. Did that."

"Did he?"

I could tell that God did not come into her life very readily. "Oh yes, think of the Crucifixion and all the martyrs . . . He could have stopped it if He wished."

She gave me a nervous look, and after that she kept away from me. I was dangerous company.

I had just made myself comfortable in my cell when I was moved. I was put in a small side wing with only half a dozen other prisoners. These were long-stay ladies like myself, or else the wives of such violent and dangerous criminals that they had to be kept apart.

We were strictly segregated here, but with the advantage that we did not share our cells and that there was a small kitchen that we might use to make tea or coffee. Toast came into it too, I remember, and Marmite which was laid on toast so thick it burnt the tongue. Someone said we needed the salt; I think we just needed the excitement.

I was amazed at the comfort some of these ladies arranged for themselves. One was the wife of a highly successful bank robber, who although inside himself, had tucked away a good part of his spoils, I had to assume, since Loo, his wife, had a mink coat brought into her to keep her warm in the winter. And mink was mink in those days.

Nor was she the only one. Edie, a large, blonde lady with an enormous bust, had covered herself with a great silver fox cape. A whole covert of foxes must have died for that cape.

These treasures did run the risk of being stolen by other inmates or the staff, because we were incredibly light-fingered, but these two ladies were protected by the violent reputations of their spouses.

But I did hear, after I had moved away (such was the nature of the prison administration that I had no sooner got myself dug in comfortably than I was moved on again), that Loo lost her mink, or someone put boiling oil on it, the details that filtered north were not clear. It may have been that whoever stole the mink, got the boiling oil.

Suddenly, I was told to put my possessions together and be ready; before dawn I was on my way north. No reason was given. There never was. Rumours you picked up later sometimes told the truth. This rumour said that Edie's husband had plotted to spring the whole wing.

A variation on this rumour said that those girls Edie liked would get out with her, and those of her enemies would get a bullet.

I profoundly believed both versions. In prison, if there are two sets of stories, take both on board, for each will have some truth in it. This habit was to save my life later.

The northern prison was cold and hard, I was closely watched. Perhaps they thought I was one of those who would have escaped, but I think I was considered more likely to have received a bullet. Edie had called me a stuck up cow and accused me of eyeing her husband on a visiting day.

I was unhappy and depressed again, but I soon settled down. I was like a foot soldier who knew it was going to be a long war.

After a few months, I was moved from the laundry to work in the library, and in case this should go to my head as being too agreeable, I was made one of the team that cleaned the chapel. You might think a chapel might not need much cleaning but this one did. Somehow the women who filed in made their messes. Cigarette papers, soiled sanitary towels, we found them all.

The chaplain was a plump man, just past middle age, with spectacles and a very beautiful voice.

On a visit Val said: "What's up with you?"

"Me?" I was startled.

"You, Madam, you look different."

I put my hand up to my hair, smoothing it; I did not answer.

"Yes, your hair is shinier and so is your skin. You look . . . if I didn"t know it couldn't be, I would say you had a lover."

I did not answer.

In an incredulous voice, Val said: "You *have* got a lover!"

"Yes." It was all I could manage to say.

Val leaned back and took a deep breath. "Only you could manage it in prison, Dodo."

I forbore to laugh; she was more innocent than me these days, poor Val. You could manage anything in prison if you paid the right price.

A thought came to Val, I could see it coming. "Dod . . . it is a man?"

I didn't laugh. "Yes, Val, a man."

I had literally bumped into him – we collided as I was carrying a pail into the chapel; his arms went round me at once, gripping me like an octopus. You don't expect a clergyman to have such strong arms.

"Sorry." I dropped the pail.

He said sorry too, but still held me. It was dark behind the screen. Without forethought, our lips came together and we kissed. Gently at first, and then more strongly, roughly.

Each to each. I was doing my share.

No more that day, but as time went on, we got more adventurous. It was silent, nameless almost, but strong and warm. It became no secret, there were no secrets in that place, but there were circles of relationships and if you kept your activities within that group, then a shroud could be dropped over them.

As a relationship, it was joyous, friendly, secret, and, in spite of what I said to Val, largely innocent. Largely. How could it be else?

It was so tender and innocent, romantic even that I was not ashamed nor, I believe, was he, but we didn't talk much. I learned that he had a wife, but she was barely a shadow to me. And I am sure that I was nothing to her.

I didn't mind being nothing. You are free when you are nothing, you have no duties, no responsibilities.

But, in the end, I suppose the conspiracy of silence was broken. He was moved away, or retired, or died, I never found out. Nothing was said to me, but I was sent south again. I was a bit of dust, swept under the rug.

I had learnt how to make the best of prison. By now I regretted, not perhaps what I had done, but the life I had bought myself. But I had learnt to live it. There were tensions of course, sexual and social (you could have a social life in prison if you knew where to look for it); I had friends and I had enemies. The trouble was both served their sentences and moved on, whereas I was there for ever.

What wore you down in the end, made you thin of spirit, meagre and dry, was the pervading sense of meanness. Of course, there were some generous souls, there are saints everywhere and I knew one or two, but even they got worn down and thin in the end.

The world outside seemed very far away, but I kept in touch. We heard about the Jarrow marchers, we gossiped about Mrs Simpson and the Prince of Wales. I received a number of business letters and knew that my affairs were surviving the great Depression and that I was a rich woman. It seemed so distant. My friends were good, but I suspect that to them, too, I began to be not quite real.

It was a protected world. We did not have to worry how to make a living, or what we should eat, it was provided for us; we need not ask ourselves what we should do with the day, our work was laid out for us. But we could not be shielded from everything: we knew when war came, we were told about Munich, we heard about Dunkirk and the loss of France; we knew about the air raids by being bombed.

By then I was in a large prison near a big industrial town where we heard the bombers going over. "They are going to Birmingham, they are on the way to Coventry," we said as they went over.

I was in the hospital wing with suspected appendicitis when it happened. The hospital ward was no place of peace or comfort, presided over by an overweight monster of a nursing sister, Elsie Mangan, who had trained in hell. She knew how to make a bed so that the sheets bound one into a shroud, how to offer food so chilled you could hardly push it down, and drinks so hot that they burned the mouth. She was subservient to the doctor and rigidly brutal to us. She was a bitch that woman.

I saw her one night, refusing a drink of water to a woman who was plainly dying and who was dead in the morning. "You'll dirty the sheets," she'd said.

The sheets in that place were clean but with a kind of elderly cleanliness that looked as though they had been washed so often that dirt was part of the laundry.

We heard the plane overhead, its engines loud and throbbing; we didn't hear the bomb, they say you never hear the one that hits you. But there was a blue flash and then the noise so near, so close, that I wasn't conscious of it all, just the movement of the air, a great shudder.

I remembered those earlier bombs which had fallen near me in that other war. But this was closer, I could feel the warmth, smell the explosives.

After the noise there was silence, just for a moment, and then the sinister, quiet crumbling of the building settling down upon us.

It was the last thing I heard.

It was not a bomb as such, so I was told later, or not the sort that whistles down, but the kind that descended on a parachute; they called it a land mine.

I came back to consciousness to find myself pinned down by a weight on my feet, anchoring me to the ground. Whatever was there was sharp and hard, but I found I could move my feet. But I also became conscious that something soft and heavy was lying across my chest.

After a moment of bemused thought, my mind not being very nimble just then, I recognised by the smell of sweat, cigarette smoke and drink, Sister Mangan.

I could also smell and then see fire, a tongue of fire, just above me in what had once been the roof. Or had it? The world seemed upside down.

Once again a fire in my life.

*   *   *

246

"So you're the little heroine," said Val, by my bedside; she was holding what she could touch of my hand.

"Don't think I wanted to save her. She's a bitch, that woman. A pig. But I could hardly let her fry."

"Fried bacon," said Val wickedly.

"In any case, she was lying across me. To save myself, I had to drag her out too."

"But you were badly hurt."

"Burnt." I looked down at one side of me; arms, body and leg were wrapped in bandages. Val was on the other side of me. But even there a few bandages had sprouted on my arm and hand. Every time I looked there seemed more, but the doctors assured me there were not.

It was true I had rescued Sister Mangan, even now lying in a bed down the ward, true that my left side was badly blistered, the skin and flesh eaten into by the heat and flames, but it was also true that her stout body had protected me. She had burnt first, and worse; they said she might not recover.

How hard I was now – my hard little heart had come back again.

I was worse after Val went away, a fever set in. Apparently your kidneys get worried if you lose too much of your body surface and once they begin to act up you are lucky to survive. I didn't know this when I spoke so cheerfully to Val. But Sister Mangan found out before I did and looked like pioneering the way to hell.

It would be hell for me, I could feel the approach of damnation, all burning and chafing and fevered as I was.

In this fevered state I seemed to read letters. Letters to Hell.

"Dearest Dorothea."

No one had called me Dorothea for years.

But it seemed to be Joe's writing, although I did not recognise it. But I could hear his voice.

He seemed to know all about Charley, Johnny, Sylvia and Val, and he was telling me their history, what they had been doing while I had been 'away'. He called it that, although of course, he knew where I was. I could tell from the manner of his writing, he was tender and discreet, not asking me questions but telling me much as if he knew the outside world was beginning to be a mystery to me. Or anyway, foreign territory.

I seemed to read it as a list.

Charley was a successful figure in the New York art world, not rich yet but prospering, but I must not believe all she told me: she was not a happy woman. She had been a born a village girl, one from the farm; now she missed the English countryside – she was not as urban as she had thought. The rusticity, even the roughness of the scene she had left behind, was pulling her back. And she missed me, I was part of it. She had always been in love with me, did I know?

I had known, I allowed, but had thought better of admitting it.

News about Johnny came next. (The list was to be alphabetical, I saw). Johnny was a very rich man now, did I know that? No, was the answer, although I could have guessed; he had always respected money. It would be a mistake to think the English aristocracy did not know good value for money. Think of their history, they were bred from men who had succeeded, never mind how many centuries ago.

It was Johnny who was superintending the management of my affairs, and who was creating a large fortune for me when I should emerge. This proved that Joe knew I was 'inside' but was being tactful about it.

It's the dead's business to be tactful, isn't it?

Sylvie was in Lausanne where she was at school; she had been told as much as possible of her birth and upbringing. She regarded Johnny and Val as her guardians. In spite of wavering in her loyalty to the French spelling of her name when France fell, her admiration for Charles de Gaulle had returned her to Sylvie. She meant to go and work in New York with Val as soon as she had left school. Val thought it would be a good idea if she took a degree at Brynmawr or Wellesley. She hardly remembered me.

Val was being a great success in representing several British companies in the US. She was helping sell various luxury goods. She saw Charley sometimes, and was doing a good deal of praying. Surprising, eh? She would never tell me herself. She had her son with her, did I know that fact?

No, I did not.

Mahmoud was not mentioned. Joe had never met Mahmoud in life as far as I knew, so would find it easy to overlook him beyond the grave.

Then the voice changed and it was another letter, this time from my mother, but I did not recognise her voice. She began to say that I had got it all wrong; I had not solved the mystery.

As I struggled to the surface, I thought: All me really, I was talking to myself.

But what mystery?

And if there was any mystery, then was there something I knew but had not recognised?

And then I came more fully to myself, and knew my head ached and that I felt sick.

Sister Mangan died. Since I was still laid up, I was not obliged to go to her funeral which, as the prison heroine, I might otherwise have been obliged to do. I understand she was cremated, so I really saved her for nothing.

After I recovered I was given a cushy job in the library and that was where they found me.

Part Five

Chapter Sixteen

He was a small, neat man wearing a brown tweed suit; he might have been a farmer. Perhaps he was, in another life. He was called Major Gold, which was not his real name. Nor was he a farmer. I discovered later he was a successful dramatist, well known in Hollywood. Acting and disguise were always his business, you see. Not to mention lies, sudden death, fortitude and courage.

It was a lonely kind of courage he dealt in, had displayed it himself, so he could demand it of those he recruited. Afterwards. when we got to know each other well (as well as you could know him; no one knew him completely), I called him the Recruiting Sergeant. He had the ability to change his appearance without any obvious devices of make-up. When I saw him, years later in Hollywood, I hardly recognised him, but he knew me. He never forgot a face. This double ability to change himself yet forget no one must have contributed greatly to his survival in the field.

He knew all about me, which he let me know in a detached way. No emotion. He had emotions: anxiety, guilt, fear, all of them, but at that stage in the war he had to bear them as his war burden. You do rotten things in a battle and he was fighting all the time.

He had scouted me out, knew about my life in Paris, knew my contacts and employees there and had come to offer my freedom.

At a price.

The price was possibly imprisonment with torture and quite likely death. There was a strong chance I would be exchanging one prison for one much worse. A delightful prospect.

Of course, I accepted.

I didn't do it because I was brave or very patriotic, but because

I could never resist the lure of the next step, and the next one after that.

Mind you, I did not, at that time, know exactly what was expected of me.

I was a released on a chilly, misty day in the New Year; there was no one to meet me but I had been handed an envelope in which were train tickets and an address with instructions on how to get there.

Since there had been a night air raid, all the trains were delayed or missing altogether. Val was in Washington working at the Embassy there in some undisclosed capacity. Sylvie was with her, but in any case I was not to let anyone know where I was, and letters would be forwarded in some underhand way. No one knew I was out.

"Clapham Junction got hit, Ma'am," said the tired railway guard. "And that puts us all out. I believe Euston got it too, they know where to hit, those buggers. Still, it's nothing to what we're doing to them now."

The period of the great day raids over Germany had begun.

I managed to get a seat on the train when it eventually arrived and was at Paddington by dusk on a cold February evening. I took the underground train to Victoria, then walked to the address given.

It was strange to be free and walking around like anyone else. But I felt as if I was on a lead and holding the end of it was the Recruiting Sergeant. The address was a hotel, not the smartest of establishments but it had a solid look. I had been told to ask for Colonel Warren.

After being kept waiting in an outer room for almost an hour, I was finally led in by a tall, thin woman who smiled but said nothing except: "I'm Diana, but you can call me Di." That seemed to mean I was going to be accepted. "Oh – and I am . . ." I began, when she interrupted me: "No, don't bother, don't tell me, you won't be using it here, Miss Brown."

When I got inside the room, the man sitting at the desk in the otherwise empty room was, of course, the Recruiting Sergeant. I was to know him as Colonel Warren for a while and then many other names as well; different places, different names, and the same went for me too. I went through Mary, Petra, Valerie and Rose, with assorted surnames. Just remembering and answering as I should was a test. In all I was to have about half a dozen different names before I was dropped into France as Angelique Duval.

Practising to jump from an aeroplane was something difficult in itself, and I came close to breaking my leg. Limping into a training session one day, I said to my instructor, that I supposed that if I had broken it then that would have been the end of my mission.

"Not at all, we would have patched you up."

This was my first hint of the ruthlessness with which I was being used.

I had various other techniques to learn: codes, and radio transmission and receiving. Suspicion and caution they could not teach me; I had them already.

My final course was in an old country house in Oxfordshire. I had known The Grange in happier days. I had stayed there with Joe, visiting some friends. They appeared to have moved out, or been removed. But the Salters had left possession around that I recognised from that now dream-like past. I did not tell the Recruiting Sergeant (who appeared here once) that I knew the house: I had already learned to keep quiet about what I knew or did not know.

One afternoon in early April, I went into the library at The Grange. There was a man sitting by the fire reading the newspaper. It was not an English paper but a Spanish one, and I did not wonder how he had come by it. Such speculation was better avoided.

He looked up and saw me.

I looked at him. He was thinner, greyer but I knew him at once. He knew me, although I don't think he had expected to see me there. But who to tell? It was the house of secrets, and some people, of whom he might be one, knew more than others.

We didn't name each other. No names, not real ones, were ever used and false names were changed and changed again.

Still I knew him. I was the first to speak.

"Aren't you a bit old for this war?"

He stood up, he was wearing no uniform, but the sturdy old

tweeds he had always worn in the country. It occurred to me that I had probably seen those tweeds many times before. They hung on him a bit, so my idea that he had lost weight was right.

"There's always a part to play . . . and I've turned out to be goodish at languages."

In his talk, I knew this meant he was bloody good.

He showed no surprise at seeing me there, which meant that he probably knew in advance, which meant in turn that he was high up in the organisation. But given his rank, age and experience there was nothing odd in that. At that first moment, I thought it might have been he who had put my name forward, suggested me, used it as an excuse to get me out of prison. But later, for a good reason, I knew it was not.

Another trainee came into the room then and I walked away to choose a book from the shelves, but we met later, as strangers, at the evening meal which we ate at the same long table. We were a curious mixture of people, thrust together in tight intimacy but who dared not become close to each other.

But the secretive club of which I was now a member had found ways of meeting when it so desired. The local pub, called The Barleymow, had a pleasant bar and a small dining room where you could eat and be quiet.

We met there, by arrangement, and he was waiting for me when I arrived. Always good mannered.

"Johnny . . ." I held out both hands.

He put his arms round me, hugged me and then kissed my cheek. I looked in his face. You are not old yet, but on the edge, I said to myself. I knew that my own looks had changed – prison is no beautifier – but since I had been out I had taken full advantage of a good hairdresser and decent cosmetics. I was still a rich woman, and could spend some money. I had clothing coupons in rather a generous measure.

"You're beautiful, Dodo." He stood back, looking at me. "More so than ever."

"That can't be . . . but thank you for saying so."

I was shy with him, wasn't that ridiculous, and what he said did not help me.

"I mean it."

I knew he did. I looked at him sitting there, tall and solid, with fatigue etched into his face, but calm and determined with it. He knew the way he was going, it was built into his bones. Not remarkable, I thought, that his family had helped shape England over the centuries.

I had been radical, even egalitarian in my philosophy but life in prison had changed me. I noticed there that some people always sunk to the bottom of society, seemed to have an inherited disposition to do so while others stayed firmly on top.

"How you've changed." I said, thinking of that energetic, violent, selfish youngster I had known all those years ago.

"You mean how much nicer I am."

"That too, but I noticed that long ago . . . It's more – what a man you've become."

"If I have, it has been due to Joe."

I was silent. Darling, darling Joe.

"I never forget him," I said.

"And due to you too," he added.

"What about Val?"

He smiled. "In one way, I shall always love Val. She's in Washington now, you know, beguiling them all. But no one was ever improved in character by knowing Val . . . Not like you, Dodo."

"I can think of at least two people who were the worse for knowing me," I said thoughtfully. "They died of it."

We walked together through the drizzle. Then, as if it had been decided beforehand, I took him back to my room and we went to bed. My body was warm and welcoming and ready.

"Darling, darling Dodo . . . I don't know, I don't know."

I cradled him in my arms. "Don't say anything." What was it he didn't know? I didn't care.

I felt joy.

I fell asleep, felt him beside me, turned to him confidently and slept on.

In the morning, he was gone. Quite, quite gone.

We did leave silently, and with no loving messages, in that place. It was the rule.

Paris was not much changed, not so much changed as wartime London. London was bombed and burnt, buildings were boarded up, roads sometimes blocked with fallen debris. On bombed sites there were great square water tanks against fire bombs. Little yellow brick walls everywhere. People looked grey and tired.

In Paris there were German soldiers but the cafés and shops were operating. The women looked different though; I don't know why, perhaps you do look different if you are female and the enemy is walking around in your city. I thought I must look different, but no one seemed to notice. I wore a pale stone raincoat, a soft felt hat and clogs. That was one thing I had noticed about the still stylish Parisians, the women were badly shod and a lot of them wore clogs with immensely high soles. Mine were of just medium height, but I had to practise wearing them.

Mahmoud had taken off my leather shoes as soon as he saw me, and bought the clogs.

"They'll shoot you if they see those leather shoes."

"They are French," I had protested. I had been well kitted out.

"Too new, and too old-fashioned; they must be old stock."

I did not feel at ease as I walked down the Boulevard Hausseman, and it would have been dangerous if I had. "Never feel relaxed, always be on the alert," had been drummed into me at The Grange. "There is always danger."

Two weeks before I had been dropped into the Norman Vexin, close to Richard I's Château Gaillard, from which he taunted the French King.

I knew what I had to do, it was simple. I had to identify someone I knew well, or had done in the past. This person was very important now to the coming invasion of Europe but he had to be certified as genuine. He could have been replaced by a look alike, or he could have been turned.

I was promised that as soon as I had done this job, then I would be lifted out. This was an untruth and we all knew it: they would get me out only if they could.

But the truth was even more ruthless: if the person concerned was not genuine in all ways, then I would never survive to get back. I understood why Johnny had been so miserable to see me, he knew even before I did, even as he put forward my name. If indeed, he had done.

If they didn't hear from me in a certain way at a certain time, then they would know the contact had gone bad on them. I was expendable and I knew it. I wasn't the only one, there were a lot of us in that great game, secretly written off before we departed.

I landed with identification documents, money but no map. They assumed I knew my way.

The Resistance man who met me was exceedingly nervous, which was no help to me, but he showed where to get a bus to the nearest spot to board another from which I could reach a suburban Metro station.

"It still runs?"

"Of course."

He was glad to be rid of me. I don't know how long he lasted but I shouldn't think too long. No man who showed nerves as clearly as he did could escape suspicion.

That was how I thought then, before I discovered how remarkably stupid the occupying forces could be. Capricious and nervous, yes, but mercifully not always clever.

Looking back, I wonder if so late in the war, they hadn't given up and were longing for a quiet exit. Most of them, anyway. You always get the obsessed.

Once in Paris, I walked to where Mahmoud lived. I had memorised my contact there; I would need it if I was ever to get my information about Mahmoud back to London. This contact was in a beauty shop in the Place de l'Opera.

Mahmoud knew who I was when he opened the door and even why I had come.

"Get inside, or we are both in trouble." He lived alone; he had sent his wife and children into unoccupied France.

He lived above the office as he had done for some time. The whole place looked different, but smelt the same, because Mahmoud smoked the same vile cigarettes and doused himself with the same strong scent.

"What shall I do with you? How am I to explain you? Don't you suppose the old harridan below who acts as concierge did not watch you as you came in?"

"Of course she did, and I smiled at her and said I had come to see my cousin."

"And you think she believed that?"

"Naturally not, but when you tell her that you met me when you visited your wife in Vichy and I have come to visit you for a few weeks, then she will think we are having an affair."

He grunted. "The Gestapo will sniff around, they are always very suspicious of cousins from the country . . . she'll tell them the next time one comes in. Our local chap's a bit thick [this was not the word he used], but he's not past putting two and two together. He's got his own skin to think of."

There was a certain sympathy in Mahmoud's voice, as if he knew that they had something in common under the skin.

"I know why you've come," he continued, "to check on me. I suppose you understand that if I am false, you will not be around long. I shall inform on you."

I was the tethered goat, the sacrifice. I had known it for some time, but I could not stop the cold chill I felt at his words.

"And if I am not, then we are both in danger . . ."

"Yes, but as soon as I have satisfied myself . . ." I had been given instructions, what to to watch for, how to check, I suppose he knew that too, he seemed to know everything. Was that suspicious?

"And if necessary, then I shall not hesitate to sacrifice you. I am more important than you."

I fear he enjoyed saying that to a woman and one who had employed him. And with my record, he did not have a great respect for me.

But amazingly, I sensed a sort of affection.

Of course, the Gestapo man did come; he called in one afternoon. I knew this was the moment of danger and verification: if I survived this, then I would give Mahmoud a clean bill. I had prowled round the flat and had found no evidence that he was talking to the Gestapo, and only in touch with local gendarmerie as much as his job obliged.

The only suspicious thing was that he was still being allowed to publish: he ought to have been closed down. I could see what made the security people in London suspicious. But he had always been a wily beggar so I was not as surprised as I might have been.

He was capable of being a double and even a triple agent, I knew this well, but I thought I was reading him right at the moment and what I saw was loyalty to the Resistance.

The Gestapo man called himself a historian-turned-journalist who was writing a history of this part of Paris. It was hard to see why he thought this story was a convincing cover that would make his victims relax, but Mahmoud said he was a stupid man and that it was the man behind him that you had to watch.

I was introduced as Mahmoud's cousin from Vichy; the information was handed over with a leer so that the idea that I was really a sexual object in Mahmoud's life was introduced to his willing mind.

Mahmoud gave him a drink, then got rid of him with some skill.

"Fortunately, he does not like women," he said, thus wiping out a small secret fear that had nestled inside me. "It's me he's after."

"Oh, don't you mind?"

"I mind nothing that will help me to stay alive. However, it won't do to get too close. One day this war will end and if I am still alive it won't do me any good to be known as his boyfriend."

"But your friends in the Resistance will know your true part."

He laughed. "You do not know my friends. Their knives will be out and sharp with the end of the war, and anyone's back might get it . . . But that's tomorrow's worry, now we will have to get you out. He's a fool, but not that much of a fool and he will submit a report, and those around him are not fools. So you must go."

"How?"

"I will think about it."

It was true my job was done; I had delivered such documents as had been entrusted to me, and I was in a position to clear Mahmoud as a source for the Resistance. No angel he, but he did not like the Germans.

Next day, he turned up with instructions: "Get your things

together. The minimum. What you can carry without looking obvious. Old clothes, please."

As if I had anything new.

"When are we off?" I couldn't help being both pleased and nervous at the same time.

"Now."

I was also worried. I had been given my exit formula: to ring a certain number at a certain time of the day, then await instructions.

"No time," said Mahmoud, "too slow. I want you out."

Chapter Seventeen

We took a country bus, there being no petrol for someone like Mahmoud, and anyway, he said he wouldn't risk buying it on the black market which, of course, flourished mightily. Nothing changed the French; laws were to be broken. On the other hand, no one wanted to make trouble with the Germans, now the occupying power of the whole country.

We did not leave the house together, nor did we sit on the bus side by side. In fact, we did not sit at all since the bus was so crowded, instead we stood. I kept my eyes on Mahmoud, and took note of the ticket he bought. I bought the same.

We were going out to the old Norman Vexin, shades of William the Conqueror and his grandson Richard I, and his Château Gaillard.

It was a bumpy ride through the suburbs of Paris and then out into the open countryside. I remember a farm with several horses that galloped along the edge of the fields keeping up with the bus, manes flying. Lovely creatures, so free and safe.

There was a big notice saying no horns were to be sounded in the bus on account of the horses. Naturally, the driver sounded his, loud and often as we passed. This was France, war or not, after all.

Listening to Mahmoud, I had bought a ticket to Briseux, which turned out to be a small country town. Here Mahmoud alighted, and so did most of the busload. Probably the route ended near here.

We were in a shabby, old-fashioned market square where the stalls were being cleared away, but there was the smell of vegetables still on the air.

We had started out in mid-afternoon, the bus had not hurried itself, and it was a dusky evening in early summer. Mahmoud nodded to me and we joined up. Ahead, round the corner of the market place, a narrow road made an exit. In this road was a shabby restaurant, and this was where we went.

I knew we were expected because I could see it in Madame's eyes, nervous and watchful, as she took our order for coffee. The table linen was none too clean, while the coffee when it came (and there was some delay here which made me nervous and Mahmoud too, I suspect, from his fidgeting) was ersatz. Acorns, I thought, but it was hot and strong.

Being thirsty, I drank mine readily. No food was offered. Mahmoud sipped his coffee – tiny, careful little mouthfuls. "We wait," he said. These were the first words we had exchanged.

It was getting very dark, but Madame turned on no lights. There were only two other customers, who soon went away. We were alone. Presently Madame herself listened, heard a noise, and went out through the door behind the counter.

We still sat on.

Then Madame came back; she walked across to the door which she locked and bolted. She nodded at Mahmoud who stood up, motioning to me to follow him.

We were led into the small sitting room behind the shop where some small signs of preparation had been made. An opened bottle of wine and some dry-looking biscuits were on a tray on the table. No one else was there, but I felt more souls were expected.

"Some wine, Mademoiselle?"

These were the first words she had spoken to me. I nodded. "Please."

Madame poured me a glass, then turned to Mahmoud. "For me, not," he said.

"To speed your journey," said Madame to me, which was the first intimation that she knew why I was here.

I sipped my wine, which was sweet and heavy, yet sour at the same time. I didn't blame Mahmoud for refusing. He'd been here before and knew the vintage, I thought. Perhaps Madame brewed it herself in the back yard; it was strange enough in flavour and a deep, dark red, almost black.

I finished it, then put my glass on the table. I wanted to get on with this departure. Madame was studying my face, but she

264

seemed to be wavering and nodding, an image that was changing. With difficulty, I turned to look at Mahmoud.

But he had gone.

When did he go? How? Why I had I not noticed. Then, as I sank back into unconsciousness, I guessed I had been betrayed.

In the deep, misty state into which I fell – yet in which I seemed to stir occasionally – I felt as if I was parcelled up, my face covered, my arms enclosed. There was a tightness all around me. I was here and yet not here, a person and not a person.

What was here? Who was I? The edges of life seemed to be changing and moving, with images swimming forward and then away before I could make out what they were. Forms came into my vision, then melted out out again.

Perhaps I was dead. Or dying? Possibly this was a dream of death.

I opened my eyes to see a man in uniform staring down at me. Even in my daze, I felt instant fear. The Gestapo?

My arms were still constricted, but I could move them free from what seemed to my confused eyes to be a sack.

I tried to take in the man. A German soldier . . . No, slowly I saw that the uniform was wrong. Not German.

The light was very dim; I struggled to sit up. He pushed me back.

"Don't."

I stared and let my mind start to work. "You spoke English."

He grinned. "Wake up, girl."

I lay back and assembled such thoughts as seemed to move into my mind: "RAF uniform."

He didn't answer but grinned again. I was becoming aware of movement, a throb of sound. An engine perhaps.

Now my eyes were working in conjunction with my mind; I saw where I was – the cabin of a small aeroplane. My gaze drifted around it. I was the only person in it except the man staring at me, but I could see the back of the pilot in the cockpit.

I looked at him silently: I was gradually realising that Mahmoud had not betrayed me, but had arranged my departure. A touch brutally, but this was war.

"I'm being flown out. You've rescued me."

My companion spoke, cheerily but without much emotion. "Oh we fly in fairly regularly, like a bus you know, only our timetable varies. We take in this and pick up that." He sounded casual.

"You didn't come just for me?"

"Oh it's business with us. Nothing special, we had this and that too."

"But what about the Germans?" I didn't mention the French, although one might suppose them to have an interest in this 'dropping in' too.

There was a shrug in his voice. "Perhaps they know, perhaps they don't. Occasionally one of us is for the chop."

I shivered.

"Sometimes I think they don't care all that much. This war is coming to an end. Perhaps the chap in charge wants to get in a good record with the Allies for after the war. Then there are the Resistance chappies. I don't suppose the German Gauleiter wants his throat slit one dark night. Or a bright one come to that – they're getting mighty bold."

I went back to what puzzled me. "How did you come to pick me up?"

"Oh." The vague look that I was already coming to know appeared on his face. "I heard of this Englishwoman who ought to get out. I delivered something, picked up something." He grinned at me, as if nothing mattered much. Just as well he wasn't the pilot, I thought.

"What's your name?"

"Call me Freddy." The smile again.

The plane began to swerve violently so that I rolled against Freddy.

"I suppose this is evasive action?" I said, my throat tight.

"And let's hope we evade."

From the way we bumped about, I guessed there was ack-ack fire as well as hostile aircraft.

For some time, we did not speak. I closed my eyes, but then opened them again. If I was going to die, I would die with my eyes open.

Freddy, I noticed, was wearing a parachute pack; I was not.

In some obscure way, I found that heartening. I would not die just yet.

After a while, the flight got steadier.

"It's all right," said Freddy, "we're well over the Channel now. Home in time for brekker."

We landed, bumpily but safely in an airfield, as the dawn was breaking. The pilot called cheerfully over his shoulder. "Home again, chaps. Hop. out please, in case the old crate decides to blow up."

I tried to stand up but my legs gave me no help, they were stiff and cold. "Sorry," I said, staggering forward.

Freddy caught me. "Take no notice of him, we won't blow up; his idea of a joke. Terrible sense of humour all pilots have."

Freddy helped me out, down the steps and gave me an arm to the building which stretched ahead in the rain. Of course it was raining. But I loved the smell of the damp English earth. I was home.

The building was one of those low prefabricated structures that the rest of Britain was beginning to get used to but which were still new to me after my time in prison.

I had almost wiped out that part of my life while in France, but it was back with me again now.

Freddy helped me through the door, gave me a gentle push, and then was gone.

I took a step into the room, which appeared to be a kind of general reception room with several tables and some comfortable chairs.

There was one person standing watching me.

His lordship, Johnny.

He came forward and took me in his arms.

"Oh my darling," he was saying. "You're back."

I raised my head to look at him. "I never thought I would be."

"Dodo . . ."

"Johnny."

Sparkling conversation. But it didn't matter. He kept his arms round me; we didn't kiss, there was no need, we were together. At last it was Johnny and Dodo.

We drove back together to his London flat. The airfield, although apparently nameless as all places were in wartime England, was in the Home Counties.

On that journey, my wits began to return and I had a question to put.

"Freddy told me that he just picked me up. Chance, nothing more. Yet there you were, waiting."

Johnny shook his head. "Picked you up! He was sent out for you. Emergency. Mahmoud got a message through.

"So you were in touch with Mahmoud all the way through?"

Johnny did not answer.

I was silent. Truth was hard to come by in this business. But one thing seemed clear.

"So Mahmoud is all right? Genuine."

Johnny shrugged. "Apparently. Anyway, it won't matter much longer."

"Why?"

He didn't answer.

We spent the night together. What a strange moment to realise that Johnny was my love.

Apart from those brief few hours before with Johnny, I did not remember how long it was since I had made love. I never forgot my husband Joe, but my body had forgotten him and turned to Johnny with surprised joy.

He said he felt the same but I took that for courtesy. Neither of us mentioned Val.

As I drifted off to sleep, I thought that lovemaking knew no age barriers and perhaps was enriched. You never know with hormones, do you? I had fought off the onslaughts of my fellow prisoners and their strange devices for a little sexual pleasure; I had ignored the tentative advances of Mahmoud, more a game he played by habit than design, but I had turned to Johnny with instant passion.

"Darling Dodo," he said in the morning. "I have loved you for a long while now. I hated sending you to France. Thank God, you are back."

"Val?" I questioned.

He laughed. "Val is in Washington still and in fine form." I had hardly had a thought for my own future, but now it came to

268

me: prison. I voiced my fears to Johnny. "No," he said, "that's done with. You have a pardon." He looked at me. "And you will even have some clothes coupons. I will take you to Hartnell myself to help you choose."

I could hardly take it all in.

A week later, on a windy day, the Allied forces landed in Normandy. Château Gaillard triumphed again.

And Mahmoud was proved genuine, because he was arrested and transported to a camp. Johnny said that the word was that he had been executed.

Every so often, sometimes at a point which one only recognises on looking back, one begins a new life. My new life began that wartime June.

Johnny had kissed me goodbye and gone off again to the war. I had one telephone call, fond and happy, and then silence. It was the way it went. He had left for war duties and was out of touch across the Channel. Too old to fight, I knew he was in some secret force.

Val was in New York now; she telephoned once, her voice unchanged, and promised letters and food parcels. Did I want some nylons? They made silk stockings look disgusting. She would send some; even in the USA they were hard to come by, but she had her contacts.

So she would, I thought, Val always did.

I even had a word with Sylvie who had a slight but charming American accent, bless her. Within a week of the invasion, London was under bombardment. The joke went round that the landing beaches were safer than the Strand. The city was crowded with soldiers and war workers, but as the bombs fell and people fled, it became easier to find somewhere to live. I took a small flat in Westminster. This was said to be a safe district and not on the route of any flying bomb. True enough, but better not relied upon as they fell short of their destinations frequently, or were knocked off course by our defending aircraft.

I worked some of the time on my own business affairs which had been well run in my absence, and part-time as an unpaid helper in a reception hostel for the bombed out. I did the cooking, and calmed the frightened and played with the children, and I began to make a few friends among the rest of the staff. No one asked questions about where I came from or who I was; in wartime London life was lived as it came. We might all be dead tomorrow.

There was no one I knew in the city. Honoria Madden was still alive, but she was immensely old and had withdrawn into her own mind.

But there was no secret about being back, and anyone who wanted to find me could get my address from the hostel.

No one did, as that violent June moved into an overcast and equally dangerous July. I heard nothing from Johnny either, and nor did Val's parcels arrive.

It was a strange time. I was always hungry, nearly always tired, and often very frightened; I found the flighted missiles very alarming. I felt sick, and occasionally I was, although I hid this shameful symptom of fear from those I worked with.

I had one day off a week when I usually put in a few hours at a canteen for ARP workers; I had been enrolled in WVS, a voluntary organisation of women helping in the war effort. Voluntary it was, but it was tightly run and there was no idling.

If I had a free evening, then I washed my hair and got some sleep. For amusement, I listened to the radio, and read all the books I had missed while in prison.

Once or twice I went to the cinema with a woman I had become friendly with at the reception centre. Elspeth Frend was older than me, with two sons in Normandy and one flying, so she was an anxious lady but willing to laugh at a film or show. She liked the theatre, so together we saw Noel Coward in *Blithe Spirit*, and several light revues.

We went together one evening in early August to see a show in Leicester Square. It was one of the revues so popular then with a series of sketches and a large and varied cast. One of the pieces, towards the end of the programme, was called *Old Friends*.

Elspeth was peering at the cast list. "Might as well be called *Dead Friends*," she said. "Some of these names my mother would have known; I suppose the young ones are called up."

Dougie Byng was one of the stars, not young himself.

Acting was not a reserved occupation, although if you were famous enough it seemed to be so.

It was a good sketch with plenty of laughs. In spite of what Elspeth said I thought I recognised one of the women myself, although she was so made-up and certainly wearing a wig, so it was hard to be sure.

I searched the cast list for a name I knew, but there was none. Silly to expect it really.

Soon after this, Elspeth heard that her son had been killed in Normandy so she took leave; I didn't see her again. The doodlebugs got worse so I ceased going to the theatre myself.

By degrees a lull came, and with it, a postcard from Johnny arrived, mudstained and battered, but with his writing on it. Goodness know where it came from, some field Post Office probably.

So he was alive and well.

To celebrate, I went by myself to see a revue at the Ambassadors: *Sweeter and Lower*, with Hermione Gingold.

That was the night the first of silent rockets hit London. We didn't know what it was, of course, it was just a bloody big explosion.

I was going to the tube station on my way home when it hit somewhere very close; I was still near the theatre, so I stood there for a while, getting my breath back. Everyone in the night-time crowd heard it but we decided not to comment except for the usual 'that was a big one', and 'near one,' – we all knew it was something different. But there are times in a war when it is better not to be specific.

Being in a position to know a little more than the ordinary Londoner, I guessed what it was: a first taste of Hitler's secret weapon.

The small woman standing near me drew in a breath with a shudder and I thought she would fall; she was very pale. I put my arm round her to hold her up. "Sorry," she breathed. "Old ticker not what it was."

Seen close to, she was older than I had thought, well made-up and smartly dressed. I stayed with her. There were other people close to where we were, still talking about the big explosion and wondering exactly where it had hit, but we were alone in the shadows of a shop doorway. You learnt to shelter where you could in those days, safe or not, you took your chance.

"I don't think there's going to be another bang," I said.

"Just a stray doodle Jerry got over, I suppose."

"Yes," I said, in a neutral tone, I didn't suppose it at all. Too painfully knowledgeable, I feared there was worse to come.

"I didn't hear a warning, did you?"

"There wasn't one."

By then I thought I knew her face, I had seen her in the revue that night with Elspeth, and I had seen her in the past; it was an old theatre face. I was trying for words but she got in first.

"Alice Morton, one of my names – you change 'em sometimes in my business. I'm in the revue down the road."

"Saw you in it."

"Did you?" She was searching my face too, as if she remembered me. "I'm surprised. Not top of the bill. Not any more."

There was a memory which I had not forgotten. How could I?

I could just see the faint remnants of the worldly, vibrant beauty she had been then. Not sensitive or subtle but full of energy and life. Not too much of that left now; I guessed she didn't get many parts and money might be short. The clothes were smart but not new, but then no one had new clothes now.

I didn't say anything, there was no point in reminding her of a ghostly world that neither of us would enter again.

"Are you all right now?" She was looking better, with real colour coming back under the rouge.

"Yes, passes off. Been overdoing it a bit . . . two shows a day, twice a week." She grinned – it took years off her. "Haven't got the go I had once."

She was still studying my face.

There was a taxi coming. They were not easily found in a war-time night, but they kept going as with the red omnibuses. You found them where you least expected after fire and bombs.

"You'd better take this." I said; I waved to the cabby.

"What about you?"

I could walk. Chillingham Place was not far away.

"I can manage."

Alice Morton held the cab door, as if she didn't want to go.

"Come on, ladies," said the cab driver. "I want to get home myself, there's a war on. you know."

We both got into the cab.

"Where to?"

"Waterloo Square, just over the bridge," said Alice.

"Chillingham Place," I said.

"Right oh," said the cabby. "You first, then. Waterloo Square is on my way home."

We sped off into the blackout. "You sure you're all right?" I said to my companion.

"Right as rain. I've got an audition tomorrow and they'll get a performance from me."

I tried to pay for both of us, as we stopped outside where I lived, but she beat my hand away. "Rubbish, dear." I could see her face, lined and haggard but full of amusement.

As the cab drew away, she leaned out of the window. "Goodbye, Mrs Jerningham. I wish you hadn't kept your gloves on."

I stood on the pavement, beneath the blue lamplight, and drew a deep breath. She knew me, and had my name off pat. But what did she mean about the gloves?

I drew off my soft suede, and looked down at my hands. Just hands.

There were more rockets as the autumn wore on, and to nerves already taut, they were hard to bear.

Three in one day, all close to where I was living. In the night, I heard a distant thud and then another. The only good thing about them was what soldiers used to say about being shelled: you don't hear the one that hits you.

So I turned over and went to sleep.

But I was up early, making coffee. Coffee you could always get. Unlike tea which was on ration.

The war news was half good, half alarming, with the Allied armies pushing eastward, while towards the Ardennes, the Germans were regrouping.

One bleak day just before Christmas, two rockets fell near to where I was working. It was a bad day, because it looked as though the German army would break through, possibly get to

Brussels and then cut the Allied armies into two. That way lay catastrophe. It didn't bear thinking about what might happen.

I was standing in front of a cracked, looking glass, cracked that morning in the latest blast. I was trying to brush the dust from the explosion from my hair when there was a knock on my office door.

A young lad stood there; he was wearing the dark blue uniform of the Heavy Rescue ARP. He only looked about fifteen but there were bandages on his hands and a bruise on his face; he had seen action all right.

"Mrs Jerningham?" He went on without waiting. "I pulled an old lady out of a house today . . . she gave me this address and asked if I could manage to get a message to you, to come and see her . . ."

"Who was she?" But I thought I knew.

"Alice, I think I heard her say." He looked exhausted beyond anything himself. "But I think she was taken to the Royal Victoria Hospital down Buckingham Palace Road . . . they're taking 'em there now."

"Thank you," I said. "I believe I know who it was." He was so young, so experienced in death. "Will you have a cup of tea or coffee?"

"No thanks." He managed a smile. "I got to get home . . . want to see if Mum's all right . . . they had a rocket on the Pimlico Road and we live there."

"Let's see if we can get you a taxi," I offered.

"I've got my bike," he said simply. "And you can get through with that when a car can't." He managed a grin. "I don't half pedal fast sometimes though, if I think something's coming over. At night you can see the streak of light."

Three rockets had fallen within the hour, but London carried on usual; I got a bus to near the hospital, with the bus driver cheerfully announcing to all passengers as they got on that he might have to go round the houses to avoid bomb damage. But in fact, he stuck to the normal route and I got to the hospital without trouble.

The Royal Victoria was busy but calm.

"I want to see a Miss Alice Morton . . . I think she was brought in this morning."

The woman at the reception desk, middle-aged, tired round the eyes but carefully groomed with hair curled and lipstick bright, nodded. "Casualty from this morning's present from Adolf? I'll check." She was not gone long. "Ward Four, top floor. The lift's not working so you'll have to walk."

I was surprised as I trudged up the stairs, at the ease with which I had been processed through; hospitals had their own ways of holding you back. Which must mean that Alice was dying, on the way out.

The nurse who met me at the door of the Lady Elisabeth Ward confirmed this fact. "I got the message you were on the way up. Mrs Jerningham? She's been asking for you."

The bed was surrounded by screens. Alice looked tiny, with bandages over her face.

"She's very weak, and I don't think she can see much . . . but when she's conscious, and she drifts in and out, she keeps talking about you."

Alice spoke at that moment. "I can hear," she said.

The nurse touched her wrist. "Your visitor is here . . . The one you wanted. Mrs Jerningham."

"I know. I knew you'd come."

The nurse gave me a warning look but said nothing. I knew what she meant: Alice isn't going to last for very long. "I'll leave you, not long mind."

"She thinks I am going to die," said Alice, not loudly but clearly. "But I'm not. They'll see."

I sat down by the bed. "Of course not."

"It was providence us meeting that time and me getting your address, I knew how it would be. Life had to join us up again . . . You don't know what I am talking about do you?"

"I remember meeting you years ago," I said cautiously. "I always have remembered."

"Well, you would, some things are there to be remembered. It's a pattern. I believe in a guiding hand . . ."

"So do I." I was not sure if I did but it seemed the thing to say.

"Hand . . . that's a joke – it's hands, fingers, I want to talk about."

She wasn't making sense.

"Years ago, a young woman had a baby, a girl, and in the same place, another young woman had a baby too, another girl. One mother died, and the other survived, but she ran away."

There was a pause while I heard her shallow, noisy breathing; she was struggling. "Leave it," I said. "Don't go on."

"Must. Important. No excuses, no excuses," she muttered. "Poor kids, lost, left behind like a bit of luggage."

Just for a second a pain shot through my guts, a remembered pain from the past. It had been how she said. Of course, she was talking about Val and me.

"Leave it," I repeated. "I know how it goes from then on." I had been there.

But she was not listening; what she had to say had to be said. "Later, when I had a bit of money, I tried to find you . . . too late . . . you'd gone, both of you to America."

Canada, I said inside myself.

"I got on you know, made money, made a name." She managed a smile. "Not always the same name, I have couple of stage names . . . called myself Lotty for a while – it's done, you know. Then I was quite famous, top of the bill . . . all gone now. Well, it was the drink." It seemed for a moment as if she might leave it there, but no. "Then one day I heard a bit of gossip about a rich lady who had tracked down her lost granddaughter and another girl with her and brought them home . . . one of her servants was telling it . . ."

Again silence, broken by rough breathing.

"I knew who it was, but I left you, you were well placed I thought, and it was before I made my mark, but I kept a watch out for you . . . I met you, you and the other one, that day in the old war, the other war. And the other girl was tall and had blue eyes and I knew she was Mrs Madden's all right, and you, you were mine. Oh how I looked at you."

I saw you once, I saw you twice, I wanted to say. But my throat closed up, I couldn't speak. I didn't know what I felt about her, whether it was anger or not.

276

The nurse crept back behind the screen; she stood there without speaking.

Alice was still talking, I had to lean forward to hear. "There is a way to show you are my daughter . . ." She managed to hold up her left hand where the little finger bent over on itself. "My baby had this . . . You have it too, haven't you? It's why you always wear gloves." She spoke up. "It is, isn't it? You have the bent finger, haven't you?"

Gently, I took her hand in mine. I had peeled off my glove; I knew she could no longer see – it is Val whose little finger is bent, not mine. "Oh yes," I said. "Don't worry, mother dear."

A little smile curved her lips. "Get away with you, dear," she said. "Not buttering me up . . . was a bit of a bad girl, you know, lots of men . . ."

Then she was quiet.

The nurse moved forward. I knew what she was going to say, and shook my head. I knew death when I saw it.

Lucky Alice, I thought, to die with a smile.

No, I had not lost a mother – I had lost her long ago at my birth, father too, but I had found a grandmother.

However, I had no desire to tell Honoria Madden, who was still alive but living in her own timeless, aged world. Let her be, I thought.

One day I would have to tell Val, and when I did so, she would laugh and say that she too had been a bit of bad girl, with lots of men.

Chapter Eighteen

The battle of the Ardennes was won, the Rhine was crossed, and very soon in early summer the war was over.

Johnny came back, and we were married. Darling Sylvie, Sally Jerrold's beautiful child, came back to live with us for a bit, but she had qualified as a doctor in America and soon left to take up her position there. I admired her greatly, she knew all about her mother now, and about me, but loved us all for what we were.

I am sure that many people, remembering the violent episodes of my life must have thought Johnny was mad to marry me, but society was wonderfully tolerant. I was a bit of a mystery but they decided to forgive me. And a few people probably said: Well, her first husband left her a great deal of money!

Quite speedily and to my surprise, I found I was pregnant. It was a quick and easy birth, and Johnny finally had the son he had always wanted. We were not young parents, far from it, but we were happy.

"L'enfant du miracle, isn't he?" said Charley when she visited me and the child. She was back in England, having been given great honour in the US where her works were being sold for thousands of dollars.

"Yes, I was astonished myself. But my obstetrician said that the ovaries did get a move on at times." He hadn't seemed sure if it was due to my age, with the hormones pushing for one more fling, or the war, which was apparently always stimulating.

Val had sent flowers, lots and lots almost every day and a box of delightful baby clothes. She was doing well so Charley said, and had set up her own firm handling publicity for all the nouveaux riches, of which there were many. It was so like Val to set up her stall in the right place at the right time.

"With the aid of her beautiful son," Charley added. "Whose father, judging by his looks, must have been a mighty good-looking Arab. Not the man in Paris as she told us that day, I am sure. Unless she has two sons? She can be a liar, darling Val if it suits her. She knows everyone, of course."

"She would."

"And how's Johnny?"

"You'll see him if you hang on. He didn't like the Labour government at first but now he's settled down to it. He says he doesn't mind being poor." And, of course, he was not, people like Johnny never are. Honoria Madden, on the other hand, had died impoverished. Swindled out of it all, Johnny said, by some of her hangers-on. In the end, Val and I had been supporting her. But that's another story.

"And you are happy?"

"We are."

"Your greatest love, sprung from your greatest hate?"

"Nothing like that. I never hated Johnny, although we didn't always like each other. But he's changed, and so have I." The violent one who had killed, killed twice, was dead, I hoped. She had better be. Charley was watching my face.

"Venus toute éntière a sa proie attaché?"

"What rubbish, Charley." I blushed. But she had something. I certainly had no intention of letting Johnny go.

"You are beautiful now, Dodo. Val isn't a touch on you." She studied me gravely. "From memory, I did a pretty oil of you as you once were, years ago. It's a good painting, better than that one that Joe never liked . . ." Charley never underestimated herself. "But now you are changed. I think you have the face for the new times. I think I will do a double portrait of you and Johnny."

"Please don't." I remembered some of her earlier efforts.

She looked wicked. "I am doing sculpture vivant now . . . they move."

"How?"

"Oh mechanics," she said vaguely.

"Well, leave us out, or if you must, leave the faces blank."

"It's not the faces, that interest people," she said with the hint of a giggle.

279

I knew what she meant. "Charley!"

She looked at me. "No, on second thoughts, I'll do you and the child."

And she did, a very simple charcoal drawing, all line and elegance and very beautiful. It is at present on loan to the Tate Gallery. The big oil she did from memory of me as a girl hangs in my bedroom.

It was one day after seeing Charley that I went to Fontenoy House which had been the Sunshine Home all those years ago; it seemed the right thing to do.

And that is really the end of our story. Except of course, that life always opens another chapter.

There is the story of Val's son and the story of my son, their meeting, and Charley's part in it all . . .

And, after all, 1952 was not the end of the world, although it sometimes felt like it.